T0165408

THE DEVIL
DOWN HOME

Also by Eve K. Sandstrom

DEATH DOWN HOME

THE DEVIL

A Sam and Nicky Titus Mystery

....

DOWN HOME

◆

Eve K. Sandstrom

CHARLES SCRIBNER'S SONS
NEW YORK

MAXWELL MACMILLAN CANADA
TORONTO

MAXWELL MACMILLAN INTERNATIONAL
NEW YORK OXFORD SINGAPORE SYDNEY

Copyright © 1991 by Eve K. Sandstrom

All rights reserved. No part of this book may be reproduced or transmitted in
any form or by any means, electronic or mechanical, including photocopying,
recording, or by any information storage and retrieval system, without permission in writing from the Publisher.

Charles Scribner's Sons   Maxwell Macmillan Canada, Inc.
Macmillan Publishing Company   200 Eglinton Avenue East, Suite 200
866 Third Avenue   Don Mills, Ontario M3C 3N1
New York, NY 10022

Macmillan Publishing Company is part of the Maxwell Communication Group
of Companies.

This is a work of fiction. Names, characters, places, and incidents either are
the product of the author's imagination or are used fictitiously. Any resemblance
to events or persons, living or dead, is entirely coincidental.

Library of Congress Cataloging-in-Publication Data
Sandstrom, Eve K.
    The devil down home : a Sam and Nicky Titus mystery / Eve K.
Sandstrom.
      p.   cm.
    ISBN 978-1-4516-1320-9
    I. Title.
PS3569.A51977D44   1991
813'.54—dc20   91-20161

10 9 8 7 6 5 4 3 2 1

Printed in the United States of America

For Nelda W. Kimbrell,
outstanding mother and discriminating mystery fan

Acknowledgments

In writing this book, I relied on technical advice from Inspector Jim Avance, Oklahoma State Bureau of Investigation; Joey Goodman, sports editor and cattleman; Floyd and Jeanine Kennedy, who count their cattle twice a day; Dr. Ralph Alexander, minister of Boulevard Congregational and Christian Church; Frieda Hudson, whose Kiowa name is Ahkontihaqui Kauahquo; and Mitch Meador, area editor for *The Lawton Constitution*.

I also drew on memories of the Halloween Haunted House operated once upon a time by the Lawton Junior Service League. That Haunted House gave me the only opportunity I've ever had to wear a long, glamorous blond wig—though I had to recline in a coffin to do it. My fellow League members and I had lots of problems with the Halloween Haunted House, but they did not include murder.

THE DEVIL
DOWN HOME

ONE

....

IT WAS A DARK AND STORMY NIGHT.

Well, it wasn't dark yet, but the sun had set somewhere beyond a bank of charcoal gray clouds hanging over the low, rocky line of mountains, and I could see the October night was definitely going to become stormy. A cool, damp wind was gusting out of the clouds, tearing across the prairie to tease my hair into tight black curls and to make my T-shirt alternately billow and cling. I could feel the wind rock the pipes of the stout farm gate I was holding open as Sam drove his official sheriff's car through the gap.

A new blast of wind left me in an eddy of dust, and I squinted my eyes as I closed the gate and ran for the car. Sam reached over and pushed the door open for me.

"Whew!" I said. "Are you sure this is a good time to check the old church? Between the dirt in the air and the rain in that cloud, we're due for one of those Oklahoma mud storms any minute."

"Probably we won't have to get out of the car," Sam said. His flat prairie accent turned the first word into "probly," but in almost six months of marriage I'd learned to translate Sam's version of Okie into standard English. I still had a little trouble with some of the other native accents of southwest Oklahoma.

Sam grinned at me. "But you're the one who's always wanting to stop and look at the old place."

"That's only because it's beautiful!"

Sam drove slowly down the gravel drive toward the deserted building, and I ogled the Titus Pecan Grove Church.

Five months earlier a family emergency had forced Sam to put his career as an army officer on hold, and he and I had come back to his home—the Titus Ranch, near Holton, Catlin County, southwest Oklahoma, Great Plains, U.S.A.

I was still a little frightened by the flat and open terrain. The prairies left me feeling vulnerable, unprotected. The arm of the Wichita Mountains hovering on the horizon, the lines of trees along the creeks and the fences, the solitary farmhouses and barns—they broke the skyline, but none of them seemed to give me anything to hide behind. So the old-fashioned church and its grove of truly tall trees had become a sanctuary to me.

It had become an inspiration, too. I'm a photographer by trade, and I'd taken roll after roll of the old building and the seventy-five-foot trees behind it.

"That church photographs like a dream," I said. Then I shut up. I hadn't developed all the pictures I'd taken of the church because I got tired of using a borrowed darkroom while my own enlarger sat in a crate in a corner of our apartment. I didn't want to talk to Sam about that, because I was determined not to become a nagging wife. Sam knew how I felt about not having a darkroom.

But the topic made me uncomfortable, so I might have rattled out my next words a little too fast. "I guess I like this spot because it reminds me of Michigan. There's an old brick church a lot like this one in the town where my father's brother lives. And these trees are tall and grow

2

thick like the ones up there, even if Michigan doesn't have pecans. Maybe the spot reminds me of the Yankee side of my family."

"It doesn't look very homey with this storm coming in."

I considered the weather and the church and the pecan trees. Then I decided to disagree. "Sure it looks homey! The evening may be spooky, with the wind and those threatening clouds and how suddenly the darkness came on. But the church is so solid. Its brick is so mellow—you can see that it's already weathered a lot of storms. It's like a castle. Inside that building you'd be perfectly safe in any kind of a gale."

"I'd have thought it would be a good place for that Halloween Haunted House you're working on."

"Certainly not! That's supposed to be scary! Only nice, comforting ghosts would hang out at the Titus Pecan Grove Church. If it were haunted, it would be by a pioneer grandmother serving cookies in the fellowship hall."

Sam drove on slowly, circling the church on its gravel drive. The building was located on his father's ranch, so now and then he checked the unused structure to see if it needed any maintenance. I knew my father-in-law, Big Sam Titus, would like to sell or rent it. He thought an empty building invited vandalism.

The church was a typical structure from before 1910. It was built of red brick that had been dulled to a deep rose by ninety years of prairie rain, snow, and sun. Its roof was steeply pitched, and a small square tower with a squatty steeple stood at one corner. I knew that a marvelous modified Gothic window dominated the interior, a clear-paned window that framed a glorious view of the mountains.

"Haunted House indeed," I said. "This place should be on some historical register, not chopped up to entertain kids."

Sam reached over and fondled my knee. Behind his glasses, his hazel eyes looked concerned. "How's your part of the Haunted House coming? Are you sick of the whole thing?"

"I wouldn't want the word to get around, but I think I'm enjoying it."

My comment seemed to surprise him. "I didn't know I was marrying a club woman."

"You knew you were getting an army brat. The Maids and Matrons are just the Holton version of the Officers' Wives Club. The Haunted House is giving me a chance to get acquainted. Katherine and I laughed all afternoon while we were lining Dracula's coffin." Katherine Dawkins was my partner—co-creator of Dracula's Tomb. "She brought us both some wax fangs."

Sam massaged my knee more firmly. "I may stop the car and bite your neck. Is Dracula going to be in the coffin?"

"Nope. Katherine and I will toss a coin for the honor of wearing the golden wig and lying there in satin splendor. Dracula will be standing behind it. When the kids come into the room, he'll lean over, and one of us dainty blondes—"

Sam chortled, and I slapped the hand that was creeping up my thigh. "This is serious, Sam! It won't work if you don't play it straight. I know neither of us is either dainty or blond, but that night we will be. The dainty blonde opens her eyes and sits up. Dracula turns around. His cape swings out. He shows his fangs, then moves toward the door."

Sam turned the car around the second corner of the church and headed back toward the road. "And then the screams start."

"We hope. But I think it would have been better for Dracula to be silhouetted against a scene of a dark forest,

4

maybe with a turret behind him. Then he could turn slowly, and the lights could hit him gradually."

Sam rounded the last corner of the church, turning toward the west. The wind shook the car, and a few big, oily drops of rain hit the windshield. Sam picked that moment to turn his headlights on, and the sudden brightness hit the entry to the church, the doorway leading into the square tower.

A figure was spotlighted against it.

I gasped, and Sam hit the brakes.

There, silhouetted against the wild and storm-whipped trees, with a turret standing out against the sky, stood a figure in a black cape. A high collar framed his face, which was dead white in the glare from the headlights. His black hair grew from a peak on his forehead and was plastered against his head. His cloak whipped in the wind.

"My God!" I said. "It really is Dracula!"

The black figure raised its hand, and my heart jumped. Did he have a weapon? A dueling pistol? A magic amulet capable of zapping us to hell?

Then the hand moved, and I recognized its esoteric signal.

Dracula was thumbing a ride.

Two

"WHAT'S A HITCHHIKER DOING AT THE CHURCH?" I said.

"Likely got caught by the storm. Or he could have car trouble." Sam eased the car forward. "I expect he's pretty desperate for a ride."

"You're not going to give him one!" I've driven all over Europe, alone in my antique Volkswagen. But I'm not dumb about it. Rule one is don't let a stranger into your car.

Sam stopped fifteen or twenty feet short of the ominous figure. He switched on the red and blue lights on the roof. Then he grinned.

"Nicky, this is part of the Titus Ranch. I've got to find out who's prowling around. And if he's just a hitchhiker—well, a sheriff's got to know who's on the road in his county. Besides, this storm's going to hit hard shortly, and I wouldn't be any kind of a public servant if I let the guy drown." He gestured over his shoulder at the wire mesh that caged off the backseat. "We'll put him back there."

He picked up the microphone that hung under the dashboard and spoke into it. "Holton, this is Catlin One. Nadine? I'm out by the Pecan Grove church, and I've stopped to check out a hitchhiker."

He touched the pistol he wore on his belt, put on the western hat he uses to protect his glasses from rain or sun, and got out. Then he leaned back in, grinning. "You can scope him out for the Holton grapevine."

As he stood up I heard him say, "Looks like you're about to get caught by this storm," in his flat accent. Then he slammed the door and blocked out the sound.

I considered being miffed by Sam's crack about the Holton grapevine, but I decided it was near enough the truth that I'd better let it go. During the past four months, since he had been appointed chief law enforcement officer of Catlin County, I'd discovered that a lot of the citizens expected the sheriff's wife to tell them the behind-the-scenes story on every case in the county. Sam coped with this expectation simply enough—he didn't tell me a lot of things he didn't want the public to know. This was the policy he had followed before we were married, back when he was a military police officer assigned to the army's Criminal Investigation Division in Germany.

The sensible half of me appreciated his policy; I didn't have to lie about anything or remember what I "knew" and what was off the record.

The madly curious half of me resented it.

Sometimes I managed to get around his policy. I'm a photographer by trade, so I took lots of pictures for evidence, even though I had to borrow a darkroom to print them. And now and then he let me take notes or witness an interrogation, if none of his three deputies was handy.

Now I studied Sam and the eerie hitchhiker as they talked. The hitchhiker was shrinking back, the way a guy in a shaky situation does when he's suddenly confronted with a cop. Sam was his usual self.

Sam's usual self is simply the epitome of understated, confident masculinity and the antithesis of childish machoism. Sam is good-looking, but his sandy hair, square jaw, and blunt nose add up to rugged, rather than classically handsome. He's intelligent and well read, but he values common sense more than education or IQ. He's healthy and keeps in great shape, but he never makes a big deal of those biceps and pecs. He's passionate about a lot of things, me included, but he controls his emotions carefully, rarely letting them cloud his judgment. And when he retires behind his glasses, it doesn't mean he isn't catching every nuance of what's happening around him.

Once again I wondered what he had seen in a short, peppery type who never hesitates to let him know what she thinks and whose one claim to beauty is naturally curly black hair—a mixed blessing in wet weather. Maybe he does have enough ego to enjoy being adored. I star in that category. Most of the time.

Sam made quite a contrast to the hitchhiker.

For starters, the man was several inches shorter than Sam's six feet, two inches. Thanks to the headlights, I could see that the Dracula effect was accidental. The man did have a deep widow's peak, but that was because his hairline was moving back over his temples. The slicked-down hair was simply wet, or maybe greasy. And the cape was a long, dark poncho that was being blown around by the wind.

The hitchhiker and Sam talked a moment, then Sam returned to the car with a name and a Social Security number written on his clipboard. He called Nadine for a check with the National Crime Information Center. The hitchhiker's name, I learned, was Damon Revels, and within a minute, Sam and I both knew there were no outstanding warrants against him in the United States.

In another two minutes, Sam led the pseudo-Dracula to the Chevy. I saw a bedroll swung on the guy's back. It was encased in a dark cover, and a star was painted or sewn on each end. Sam tossed it into the car's trunk; then the count slid into the backseat.

"Hiya," he said. He giggled, showing long eyeteeth that heightened the Dracula effect.

"Hello," I answered. "I hope you didn't get too wet."

"Not yet." The man ran his hands through his hair. It wasn't quite dripping. "I'm glad to get a ride." He gestured at the heavy wire that separated us. "Even in a chicken coop." Then he put his fists close to his shoulders and flapped his elbows like wings. "Cock-a-doodle-doo! Cluck! Cluck! Cluck!"

Weird.

I reminded myself that the cage was securely bolted into place.

Sam had gotten into the driver's seat, and now he laid his western-style hat between us. He turned his face slightly in my direction, and the side of his mouth that Revels couldn't see grinned. "Nicky, this is Mr. Revels. He's headed for Holton, so I said we'd give him a ride into town."

Revels leaned back in the seat, perhaps picturing himself as a chicken gone to roost. I decided it was time to start my scoping on behalf of the grapevine. "Are you from Holton, Mr. Revels?"

"Naw," he said. "How big a town is it?"

Sam answered. "Around twenty-five hundred. You headed someplace in particular, once you get to Holton?"

Revels shrugged and gave a cluck. "There's somebody I wanted to look up. Cluck. Cluck." He waggled his elbows again. "And I could use a job, if there's one available."

"I don't think of any right off," Sam answered. "I'm afraid Holton is like most small towns around here—barely staying even in jobs. A lot of people commute to Lawton or Wichita Falls."

Sam picked up the microphone and once again checked in with Nadine, who serves as secretary, dispatcher, and paperwork expert for the Catlin County Sheriff's Department. Then he drove on. The rain was coming down harder.

I turned around to look at our passenger. "Is this your first visit to Oklahoma?"

"Yep." Revels answered. He gave a roosterlike waggle of his elbows. "This is the flattest damn place—I mean darn place—I've ever seen."

"Catlin County's not nearly as flat as some parts of Oklahoma," I said. "Holton sits right up against an arm of the Wichita Mountains."

I was surprised to hear myself speaking defensively. Five months earlier I'd been a stranger in Catlin County, too, and I had thought it was the flattest damn place I'd ever seen.

"The mountains aren't too high, but they're rugged. I guess it's okay to be flat," I continued.

"Jeeze—I mean, sure." Revels smiled a rather secretive smile. "I guess the Good Lord had a reason for every kind of country He made."

I didn't know how to answer that one. "I guess so." Then I tried again. "Where are you from?"

"Oh, I spent last night in Dallas." He flapped his elbows and clucked once. What was this flapping and clucking business? Bizarre.

I started to ask if Dallas were his home, but courtesy intervened. A hitchhiker was unlikely simply to be traveling. Probably the guy didn't have a home. So I shut up, feeling as if I had let the Catlin County grapevine down. Revels began to cluck musically. The tune was "Jesus Loves Me."

The guy was a complete wacko, I decided as he hit

the chorus. "Cluuuck, cluck clu-clu-cluck. Cluuuck, cluck clu-clu-cluck. Cluuuck, cluck clu-clu-cluck. Cluck, cluck, cluck, cluck, cluck, cluck."

I kept my opinion to myself as we drove toward Holton. By now the rain was coming down hard. The wind was whacking us, first shoving the car toward the ditch, then easing up and letting the car swing back across the line that split the blacktop road. The old Chevy Caprice had deserved an honorable retirement after doing a hundred thousand miles on duty with the Highway Patrol, but Sam had grabbed it up at an auction because it fit the tiny budget of the Catlin County Sheriff's Department. So he refused to complain about its tendency to pull to the right.

When you approach Holton from the southwest, on the old state highway, the town nestles back, leaning against the mountain. By the time we reached the outskirts of town it was pretty dark, and the rain was still whipping against the car. I could see the few streetlights and the porch lights and the lights from windows where the citizens of Holton were eating dinner or watching television.

Right outside the city limits, the high school was a big dark block on the left. It's a two-story red brick building, built when several rural school systems consolidated with the Holton schools back in the 1940s. The school's stadium is next door, sharing a gravel parking lot. There was a light over the cement porch, with its two incongruous Corinthian pillars, and several more lights dotted the parking lot.

Across the road, the Holton Community Church spread its bland buff brick wings. It has to be the dullest building in southwestern Oklahoma. The best you can say is that it looks neat. Its parking lot is even less fancy than the school's; the soil had swallowed most of the gravel that once covered the area. This lot also had lights on high poles, and mud puddles glimmered here and there.

I'd almost forgotten our guest in the backseat when he leaned forward and tapped on the side window. "What in the name of all that's holy is that?"

"That" was the Halloween sign in the church parking lot. It was a twelve-foot-high plywood ghost that the church council had voted to allow the members of the Maids and Matrons Club to place in the parking lot, along with two spotlights powered by the church's electricity.

I'd helped design and paint the sign, and Sam had installed it on two stout metal fenceposts. It did look pretty scary, I thought smugly, especially with the rain lashing it. The ghost's sheet seemed to be blowing in the gale. It would look even better when we got the lettering on the bottom. Right now nothing identified it as a sign. It was just a big cutout of a ghost sitting in a parking lot.

"It's for the Haunted House," I said.

"Haunted house?"

"Yes. It's a fund-raiser for a Holton club."

Sam gestured toward the parking lot. "I see your chairman is still there."

Virginia Cramer's white Ford pickup sat on the far side of the old building that would house Dracula and other scary characters on Halloween. "I don't think she ever leaves," I said. "She comes over as soon as she gets out of class and stays until all hours." Virginia was an English teacher at Holton High School.

I turned back to Revels. "We're holding the Haunted House Halloween night in that old house just south of the church. It'll give the kids something wholesome to do."

Revels clucked and flapped his wings. "Turning over outhouses is discouraged in this town, huh?"

"If you can find one, you're welcome to turn it over,"

Sam answered. "Very few outhouses or even septic tanks in these parts since the EPA financed the new sewer system ten years back. Do you have any particular destination in mind, now that we're in Holton?"

"Is there a motel? Or a Salvation Army hostel?"

"Sorry. The closest motel is more than thirty miles—on I-44 in Lawton. And nearest Salvation Army is in Lawton, too. Do you know anybody here? Anybody who might put you up?"

Revels leaned forward and rested that deep widow's peak right against the wire grid. "I guess not," he said. "Way back—well, I came here to try to find somebody I knew fifteen years ago, but I'm not sure of my welcome. Is there a campground? Or a park? I've got my bedroll, praise the Lord."

I looked out the window at the rain. It was pouring. We could hardly drop the guy at the park when he didn't even seem to have a tent. That poncho wasn't going to do much good against the rain, even though the night was chilly rather than cold. I looked at Sam. Sam looked back at me and raised his eyebrows.

"I can offer you a cell," he said. "Unless something happened in the past few minutes, the jail's empty for once. It's not much, but it's dry."

Revels seemed to think about that one for a long moment. Then he gave a high, nervous cackling laugh, followed by three clucks. "Never thought I'd see the day when I'd go to jail voluntarily."

"I'll leave the door unlocked," Sam said. "It may be the best offer you get in Holton, at least for tonight."

Revels cackled again. "My Master said to visit the prisons. I'll take you up on it."

Sam reached down for his mike. "Holton, this is Catlin One. Nadine, we're at the edge of town, heading for the office."

Nadine's voice crackled as she answered. "Holton to Catlin One. I'm glad you're on the way in, Sam. Mr. Bullock is here, with Reverend Dawkins. They've got some secret stuff they want you to see."

Her tone barely missed sarcasm, and she stressed the word "you."

Sam grinned at me. "Sounds like somebody's failed to give Nadine her proper place on the pedestal. This Bullock may be in for trouble." Then he hit the mike's broadcast button. "Be there in a minute."

Nadine spoke again. "Bullock won't show this alleged evidence to me, but he keeps muttering to Reverend Dawkins about the forces of evil. Hurry home, boss."

C   h   a   p   t   e   r

THREE

....

EVERY OFFICE HAS SOME KEY PERSON—A SECRETARY, stenographer, or some other detail freak—who keeps it operating. Nadine Webster, a fiftyish widow, is the official office manager and unofficial dictator of the Catlin County Sheriff's Department. She keeps the deputies in line with a nod of her dyed black hair and seems to awe the trustees with a shake of her regal bosom. Even tough guys say "Yes, ma'am" when Nadine tells them to march into the jail or over to the courthouse.

Sam doesn't argue with her; he persuades her. Sometimes he introduces her as his "command sergeant major."

The Reverend Dawkins and this man Bullock had apparently tried the wrong tactics on Nadine.

Bullock's name seemed familiar, but I couldn't put a face with it. "Who's this Mr. Bullock?" I asked Sam.

"He's the new history teacher and assistant football coach at the high school," Sam said. "He was at that church meeting we got caught at."

"Oh." Now I remembered.

Sam spoke to the radio again. "Tell Tink and Mr. Bullock I'll be there in five minutes."

We knew the Rev. John Tinker—Tink—Dawkins well, of course. He had conducted the funeral for Sam's brother the previous June, and he'd been a big help to

15

Sam's mother and dad as they learned to cope with the problems life had handed them in the past five months. Sam's dad had suffered a vicious head wound at the same time his son had been murdered. He was now recovering—learning to talk, to walk, and to live with therapy, a wheelchair, and canes. And he was learning to live without Bill, the son who had shared his passion for ranching, and to rely on Sam, the son who had fled the farm.

Tink's wife was my partner in the Haunted House Dracula vignette, and we'd become close friends in the time I'd lived in Holton. Tink was a nice guy. Maybe a little holy, but never holier-than-thou.

I liked him.

I remembered Bullock, just as Sam did. A short, square guy, fortyish, with a white bald spot he tried to cover by parting his hair funny. Sam and I had both remembered him from the church business meeting two weeks earlier, where he talked a lot. Which was sort of odd behavior for a person who'd moved to Holton even more recently than I had.

I did not like him.

Sam hung his mike under the dash. "I wouldn't expect Tink to be hanging around with Bullock. Wonder what they want," he said.

We drove down the nondescript Main Street of Holton, past the five-block row of modest brick homes that dated from the fifties, the last time Holton's population had grown, and the white bungalows closer to the center of town. The IGA Supermarket was just closing, leaving open only the Fast Mart. Rhonda's Beauty Barn, in a remodeled detached garage, and the cement-block box that housed the offices of the town's two insurance men were locked up for the night. A row of cars and pickups marked one of the town's two restaurants, The Hangout, as the most popular business in town that evening. We swung around the mid-Depression-style courthouse and pulled into the sheriff's office parking lot.

The Catlin County Sheriff's Department is located in what was once a stately home by Holton standards—a 1915-era brick building now linked to the courthouse by a parking lot and a covered walkway. A carport has been added to the back of the building so that prisoners can be taken into the basement jail easily. The carport is just a metal shed, but at least it meant we would be able to get out of the car without getting soaked.

As Sam parked, I could see Bullock standing inside the back door, looking out and bouncing on his toes angrily, as if he were trying to stretch his height by a couple of inches. He was holding a black plastic garbage sack, a big one. It didn't seem to have much in it.

As Sam and I got out of the car, Bullock stepped into the carport. The bare bulb above him showed me that he was excited, but I thought that Tink Dawkins, who followed him out, looked pained. Bullock began to talk and to wave his arms around, but the rain beating on the metal roof of the carport kept me from hearing what he said. He was ignoring me, anyway. All his attention was focused on Sam.

As I walked around to the front of the car, I could see Sam give him a polite nod. Sam turned around to open the door to the back seat. There are no door handles on the inside back doors of lawmen's cars, of course, so Revels couldn't get out. When I got close enough to hear the conversation, Sam was speaking.

"Just a minute, Bullock. Let me get this fellow out of the car."

Bullock jumped back. "Sorry, Sheriff! I didn't know you were bringing in a prisoner."

"No prisoner. Just a hitchhiker."

Bullock's eyes bugged out. "A hitchhiker? You picked up a hitchhiker?"

Revel's sleek head poked out of the door, and he looked at Bullock and smiled a Dracula-type smile, flashing those long eyeteeth. He held his hands up and waggled them on either side of his head. Then he shouted, "Boo! Watch out! It's a wild and dangerous hitchhiker! Cock-a-doodle-doo!"

Bullock took another step back. He scowled. Then he reached up and patted the hair that almost covered his bald spot. He cleared his throat. "I'm simply surprised that you encourage hitchhiking, Sheriff."

"I don't," Sam said. I could see his mouth twitch, and I knew Revels's little act had amused him. "I don't encourage drowning either, and this rain seems to be a toad strangler." Then he went toward the back of the car.

Bullock "ahem-ed" again. "Reverend Dawkins and I have something important to show you, Sheriff."

"Sure." Sam tossed the word over his shoulder. "I'll just get Mr. Revels's bedroll out of the trunk. Then we'll go in the office and see what you have there."

While Sam opened the trunk and handed Revels his star-spangled bedroll, Bullock danced from foot to foot, looking like a balloon tugging at its tether in a stiff breeze. I was inclined to laugh at the pompous little man until I glanced at Tink Dawkins. He looked miserable.

Around ten years ago—as Sam's mother had explained it—Holton's Methodists, Presbyterians, United Church of Christ members, and other mainline Protestant church types had faced up to the fact their congregations were shrinking at the same rate Holton's population was. They were trying to run five or six churches and complete with Oklahoma's powerful Southern Baptists with only enough members to populate one fair-sized congregation. So they combined, dropped their denominational affiliations, and agreed to let each member do his own thing theologically. The result was the Holton Community Church, and Tink Dawkins was its pastor—or preacher or minister, depending on what title each member liked.

Since I'd been raised in army chapels, which were usually simply labeled "Protestant," I liked the church fine. And I liked Tink. He was in his mid-twenties, like me. He was tall and thin, a former basketball player, with brown hair and gray eyes. This was his first church, and two days a week he was still a student at a seminary in Texas.

He'd been a friend of Sam's brother, Bill, and when Bill was murdered, the open way he shared the family's grief had been strangely comforting.

Now he looked as if he needed comforting himself. His thin face was solemn, and his eyes seemed pinched together. But as Sam and Damon Revels headed into the office, Tink fell into step beside Revels.

"Do you have a place to stay tonight?" he asked.

"The sheriff said I could stay in the jail. Who are you?"

Tink smiled. "Oh. Holton's such a small town most people know me, even if I don't know them. I'm Tink Dawkins. I'm the minister of the Holton Community Church." He held out his hand to Revels.

Bullock cleared his throat, staring at Revels and Tink Dawkins shaking hands.

Revels glanced toward Bullock. "I usually camp out," he told Tink, "but this rain has persuaded me to take the sheriff up on his offer. I thank the Eternal Father that he made it."

Tink cleared his throat. "Er—yes," he said. "Well, if you need dinner, the church has a little fund for emergencies."

Revels smiled. "Spoken like a true Christian, Brother

Dawkins. But I think I have enough money for dinner, and I saw a restaurant open down the street." He turned around and surveyed the office. "You show me where to put my stuff, Sheriff."

Bullock bounced into action again. "Put your stuff! Put your stuff?" He swung to face Sam, who was hanging his hat on the oak hat tree. "You're really letting this vagrant stay here?"

"Well, if Mr. Revels has money for dinner, I guess he's not a vagrant, Bullock," Sam said.

Sam nodded at Nadine, who was sitting at her desk glaring at Bullock from under her unnaturally black hair.

"As far as letting him stay here, I'd rather do that than drive him thirty miles over to Lawton to the nearest motel. And I can't think of any other place he could stay in Holton. Unless you have a better idea?"

Bullock's face swelled into a red balloon. "Holton has a wholesome atmosphere, Sheriff. That's the main reason I moved here from Dallas. I oppose any action that will draw undesirables to the area."

"Oh, I don't think Holton has any particular attraction for the homeless," Sam said. "I think Mr. Revels has business here. I'll show him where to put his gear, then I'll be right back to attend to you and Reverend Dawkins."

"I'm tired of being put off," Bullock said. "First the city police—now you. I want action on this."

With that, he swung his plastic garbage bag in front of him and held it over Nadine's desk. He grabbed it by the bottom and dumped out a mishmash of junk.

A rattlesnake seemed to slither across the blotter.

Nadine screamed, jumping to her feet.

The snake didn't move. It had no obvious wound, but it was dead.

Nadine backed against the wall. "Good Lord!"

Bullock grinned in triumph. "Well may you say so. 'Good Lord' indeed."

Sam glared. "Just what is all this stuff, Bullock?"

"Evidence," the short man answered. "It's evidence! Evidence that we've got devil worshipers! Witches! Satanists! Right here in Holton!"

FOUR

....

THERE WAS A LONG PAUSE—AFTER ALL, WHAT DO YOU answer to a remark like that one?

Then a fearful cackle broke the silence.

It came from Revels. "That's rich! Sheriff, I'm not sure I want to stay around here. Ghosts on the edge of town and devil worshipers in the sheriff's office!"

"Revels. Shut up." Sam used his military officer voice.

He acts so mild mannered most of the time that few people know he has a military voice. But when it's necessary, he can throw his weight around like a colonel or even a command sergeant major—and he can do it without yelling.

So he took command of the situation calmly. "Revels, put your stuff there in the hall, by the basement door. Nadine, you go on home. I can't afford any more overtime." He looked at her. "You know the drill, right?"

"Sure, Sam. I won't say anything." Nadine gestured at her desk, then glared at Bullock. "What about this mess?"

"I'll put a new blotter down—after I get Mr. Bullock's 'evidence' properly taken care of. Bullock, you and Tink sit down while I get out the tape recorder."

In a few minutes he had Bullock deflated into an oak office chair. Tink was in the chair beside him, staring miserably either at his sneakers or at the green tile floor. Nadine had left by the back door. Revels was slipping his poncho back over his head and heading for the front door. He hadn't quit "he-he-he-ing," but he was doing it quietly.

"Revels." Sam still wasn't raising his voice, but the hitchhiker turned obediently. "I don't want to hear about this from any source that can be traced back to you or that cafe where you're headed for dinner. I could arrange for that cell door to be locked. Get it?"

Revels grinned. "I get it, Sheriff. You don't like gossip. Shhh!" He pressed his forefinger to his mouth. When he spoke again, the cadence of his speech parodied television evangelists. "Mum's the word. Or is it mummy? I'll just go about my business, praising the Lord, who in the book of Matthew overcame the Gerasene demons and who has a great sense of humor. The creatures He created must have Him rolling in the aisles that lead up to those Pearly Gates. Cock-a-doodle-doo!" He flapped his elbows, threw his shoulders back, and strutted.

That was too much for Bullock. He bounced to his feet. "Now, listen here! Devil worship is a well-known phenomenon of our times! It's—"

Sam shut him up with a gesture. "Sit down, Bullock. Revels, get out of here—and you'd better not say anything down at that cafe but 'pass the ketchup, please.' "

Revels gave a mock salute. "*Oui, oui, mon capitaine.* To hear is to obey. Loose lips sink ships. And all that shi—cra—stuff."

He flapped his elbows, cackled, and went out the door.

Sam glanced back at me, and we exchanged firm looks. He was thinking about ordering me out, too, but I didn't want to miss this. I folded my arms. He hid a grin, and I knew I had won.

"Nicky, please operate the tape recorder," Sam

said. He turned back to Bullock. "I tape all important interviews."

Actually, he taped two types of interviews—those he expected to need for evidence and those he thought might cause trouble later. I didn't offer to clarify his comment. I guess both types are important.

"Very wise," Bullock said. The little man was back in his pontifical mode. He sat down, leaned back, and tapped his fingers together over his paunch, then patted his bald spot, making sure the strands of hair were in place. Tink looked at Sam with the eyes of a whipped puppy.

I nodded to tell Sam the tape recorder was set up, and Sam began by listing the time and the people present for the benefit of the recording. His businesslike approach seemed to annoy Bullock. "Yes! yes!" he said when Sam asked him to state for the record that he knew the tape recorder was running.

Sam nodded. "What is this material you've brought in here, Bullock?"

"I told you, Sheriff. It's evidence of devil worship. Right here in Holton."

"Where did you find it?"

"At that picnic spot on the outskirts of town—Lattimore's Park."

"How did you happen across it?"

"One of my students told me strange things had been seen out there." He stopped and cleared his throat. "I assured him I'd keep his identity confidential, of course."

"Did you now?" Sam looked intently at Bullock and waited until he started fidgeting before he went on.

"When did you find the things?"

"This afternoon. About three o'clock. I went out there before football practice. I gathered them up, but then I had to go to practice before I could come to the authorities."

24

"Three o'clock was quite a while back, Mr. Bullock. It's now past seven."

Bullock cleared his throat. "Well, I first took the items to the police chief."

"Lattimore's Park is not in his jurisdiction."

"So he told me—rather rudely. He said he was leaving for the weekend, and he simply brushed off my information. He seemed to consider it only a case of youngsters holding a beer party. He missed the point entirely. So I asked Reverend Dawkins to accompany me here."

Sam looked at Tink. Tink seemed to be shrinking back, away from Bullock. "I didn't feel that I could refuse," he said quietly.

"You couldn't," Sam said. He turned back to Bullock. "Where were these things? What part of the park?"

"Well, it's hard to describe. Way back at the back— as far as you can get from the highway."

"Was it on the road, the road that circles the grove?"

"Oh, no! Way back—there was just a path to the area."

"Sounds as if your student gave you a pretty detailed description of how to get there."

"He drew me a map."

Sam held his hand out.

Bullock reached in his shirt pocket and pulled out a piece of notebook paper, folded several times.

"Sheriff, I want to repeat that I gave my word to this student. I promised that he would not be harassed by the authorities and would not be identified as an informant to his fellow students."

"I try not to cause problems for good citizens of any age, Mr. Bullock."

Sam spread the map on the corner of his desk. I looked over at it. It was drawn on ordinary wide-ruled notebook paper. It had been ripped out of the notebook, to judge by the tears in the three holes on the left-hand side. The map was crude—it merely showed a line marked Highway 201, a circle for the dirt road that looped through Lattimore's Park, then some hen scratches in what would have been the northwest corner. A narrow line trickled off toward the hen scratches—I guess that signified the path.

A star was scrawled on the edge, with an arrow pointing to a spot near the hen scratches.

Bullock leaned over and tapped his finger on the star. "See! A pentagram." His voice gloated.

Sam's voice was flat and matter-of-fact. "Looks like a star from a flag to me."

"Well, what was it doing out there, Sheriff?"

"Did you see it?"

"I certainly did. It was right there where N—where the student said it would be. A pentagram outlined in the dirt. It looked like it had been drawn with a stick. All sorts of crazy symbols were scrawled in the dirt. I can show you the spot."

"I'm sure you can, Mr. Bullock. But we won't find anything. This rain will have destroyed any lines in the dirt." He turned toward me. "Nicky, hand me a couple of sheets of paper. Maybe Mr. Bullock can draw us a sketch of the scene and of the individual designs."

Bullock was beginning to see that Sam was unhappy with him. "Sheriff, I can swear to what I saw."

"Mr. Bullock, you can swear until the earth is level, and your statements will not have as much impact as one photograph would have had. If you had called this office immediately, we could have had someone out there to check the scene before the rain hit. The next time you find something you consider suspicious, I recommend that you take your garbage bag and cover the suspicious items up, rather than putting them into the bag and bringing them away."

I handed Sam three sheets of typing paper, fastened to a clipboard, and Sam passed it on to Bullock. "Please draw us a sketch of the site," he said.

Bullock grimaced, but he complied. Then he and Sam went to Nadine's desk. I took the tape recorder along and looked over Sam's shoulder while they sorted through the junk Bullock had dumped out of the bag.

The dead snake, Bullock said, had been found in the center of the star. It had been coiled, with the head propped on a rock. It had been surrounded by symbols drawn in the dirt, symbols Bullock considered diabolical. One was a stick with a sort of whip at the end. One looked to me like a mouth with jagged teeth. Arrows, skulls, and swastikas had been drawn here and there. From Bullock's description, it didn't sound as if there'd been any real pattern. Someone had built a fire in the area, but it had been off to one side.

Bullock had gathered up one or two other artifacts. One was a piece of metal an inch in diameter, cut into a five-sided shape.

Bullock tapped it triumphantly. "See! I suppose you know what that is?"

"Yes, Mr. Bullock, anybody who's served in the U.S. Army recognizes a pentagon when he sees one."

"Well, you know its significance to Satanists, don't you?"

"I'm aware that Satanists supposedly use a pentagram—an inverted five-pointed star—in their ceremonies, but I never heard of the pentagon having any significance. When I was on active duty, of course, I used to think that directives from there came straight from the devil, but I don't think there was anything supernatural about it."

Bullock took a deep breath. "Sheriff—" he began, but Sam cut him off.

"Mr. Bullock, you may not be aware that the practice

of Satanism is protected by the First Amendment of the United States Constitution."

I could almost see the air whiz as Bullock deflated. He began to stammer. "Wha—what? You mean this sort of thing is legal?"

Sam shrugged. "We don't know what went on out there," he answered. "This evidence doesn't tell us if it was a bunch of kids drinking beer and kidding around or if it was a serious event. So I think Chief Evans over at City Hall was probably right in his assessment. What we have here may be a case of underage drinking, or maybe cruelty to animals, though it's pretty hard to get anybody excited about killing a rattlesnake. But I'll certainly look into it."

Bullock seemed to puff up again.

"I guess I should have known that you would only be interested in covering the whole thing up."

"Oh, really?" Sam sat on the edge of Nadine's desk and folded his arms. "Why is that?" I could have told Bullock that the mild tone Sam used was a warning signal.

"Because most of the leaders of this community seem to have links—knowing or unknowing—to a type of Satanism."

"Is that so? What are you basing that charge on, Mr. Bullock?"

Bullock waved his arm wildly. "Even the church is involved!"

"What are you talking about?" Sam asked.

Bullock's face grew as red as a prize-winning tomato in the Catlin County Free Fair.

"That Haunted House!"

There was a moment of silence. His accusation seemed totally idiotic. I'd been hanging around at that Haunted House since August, and I hadn't witnessed anything more diabolical than a bit of creative swearing from a husband who whanged his hammer on his thumb instead of a nail.

I began to laugh.

This caused Bullock to turn on me, of course, and the glance I got from Sam was on the baleful side as well, so I tried to tone my reaction down to a gentle chuckle.

"Excuse me, Mr. Bullock," I said sweetly. "Our Haunted House is just for fun—for children. You're joking, aren't you?"

"Certainly not!"

"But—"

"Wait a minute, Nicky," Sam said. "Mr. Bullock, are you basing this charge on the connection of the Haunted House with the celebration of Halloween?"

"Halloween is a major holiday for witches and Satanists," Bullock said.

Sam sighed. "I know very little about Satanism," he said, "but I believe that outbreaks often are linked to that holiday, as well as to solstices and equinoxes."

I'd never heard the plural of either of those terms referring to the movements of the earth around the sun, so I hoped Sam was pronouncing them right. At any rate, the terms made Bullock look a bit more impressed.

But Sam went on before Bullock could say anything. "Yes, you may be right about the importance of the holiday to Satanists, Mr. Bullock. But what makes you think it has a similar importance to the Holton, Oklahoma, Maids and Matrons Club?"

Bullock was puffing up again. "I used the word 'unknowing,' Sheriff." He gestured toward Tink. "I'd like to feel sure, for example, that Reverend Dawkins's wife is ignorant of the link."

Tink sat forward. "Katherine would certainly not be involved in anything that peculiar, Mr. Bullock—and neither would the church itself! As you're surely aware, the church council gave the Maids and Matrons permission to use that old house on church property. And they're providing electricity for the project. The council certainly would not have okayed that if they had thought it was promoting a non-Christian religion!"

"Not knowingly," Bullock said. "Not everyone on the council, of course."

"What!"

That one had really gotten to Tink. He took a step toward the teacher. "Now see here, Mr. Bullock—"

I could see that Bullock was growing happier by the minute, and I knew that Sam disliked that attitude. He hates it when people take pleasure from crimes or from their neighbors' wrongdoing. So I wasn't surprised when Sam intervened.

"Tink, just a minute," he said. "Sit down, please, and let me finish questioning Mr. Bullock. The tape's still running."

Tink swallowed a couple of times, but he sat down.

Sam turned to Bullock. "I'll investigate this, of course, Bullock, but I'll need to ask your help."

Then Bullock did puff up. "Certainly, Sheriff. I'll take you to that spot any time."

"Oh, I grew up right outside Holton, and that spot you described is familiar to me. It's the traditional spot for high school beer busts. I expect three generations of Holton folks have had their first drink at that spot. The Lattimores have complained about it for years, but it has the advantage of being quite secluded, so it's hard for the sheriff's department to do much about it. And at least we know where the kids are after the homecoming game."

Bullock interrupted. "Sheriff—"

Sam kept talking. "No, the help I need from you may be quite difficult for you to perform."

"I know my duty as a citizen," Bullock said stiffly. "I'll certainly cooperate. Just what do you want me to do?"

"Nothing."

The word sort of hung there a minute. Then Bullock caught it and threw it back.

"Nothing! You mean nothing will be done about this—this outrage?"

"No. I mean *you* won't do anything about it."

"But, Sheriff—"

"Bullock." Sam was using that military voice again. "I'm a native of Catlin County, and I know how this place works. The worst enemy we have in investigating this is gossip."

"Gossip! But I'm not a gossip, Sheriff."

"Of course not, Mr. Bullock. But you're from a big city. You may not be aware that it'll take only one mention of this in the teachers' lounge to start a real, actual, honest-to-God outbreak of Satanism."

He leaned toward Bullock and dropped his voice. "Copycat crimes."

"Oh!"

Sam nodded seriously. "It could cloud the case until we never find out what happened. So I have to rely on you to do absolutely nothing—particularly not talk."

Bullock frowned. "But, Sheriff—"

"Oh. I gather from your reaction that you've already spread the word."

"No, no!" Bullock's denial was vehement. "But how about the student who told me?"

"I suggest that you tell him the matter is being investigated by the proper authorities. Frankly, his reaction will be a valuable clue."

"A clue?"

"Right. If he keeps it quiet, that will indicate he takes

it seriously and is actually fearful. If he spreads it around, it will mean he considers the whole thing a joke. And if that happens, I'll pull him in for questioning."

"But, Sheriff, I promised him I wouldn't reveal his identity!"

"You won't need to. If he starts talking, I'll know who he is within twenty-four hours."

"Oh." The thought deflated Bullock.

"And you might want to check with your doctor."

Bullock stared. "My doctor?"

Sam nodded. "Of course, I'm sure you handled the snake carefully. There's probably not much chance of infection."

Bullock didn't quite panic. His eyes got real big, and he laughed weakly. Then he smoothed his hair over his bald spot. His hand shook slightly.

I hid a laugh. I thought Sam was extremely smart to use the fear of disease to keep Bullock in line. It seemed to work. The coach was more subdued as Sam made a list of the items he'd brought along and gave him a receipt.

Bullock was frowning as he headed for the front door of the office, but before he could touch it, that door swung open in his face.

Bullock jumped back about a foot. "Nolan! Nolan!" He blustered. He seemed completely bumfuzzled, as Sam's dad would have said. He turned toward Sam, then back to the door, and I thought he was going to wring his hands.

I craned my neck to see what had startled him.

A fresh-faced and handsome farm boy–type teenager stood on the porch. A matching blond girl was with him. And between them was a clean-cut young Indian. They looked extremely wholesome, like a poster for the Boy Scouts or the YMCA. I couldn't imagine what they had done to scare Bullock.

"Hello, Coach Bullock," the farm boy said. "Hello, Sheriff Titus."

"Hi, Nolan," Sam said. "I'd forgotten y'all were coming over tonight."

Bullock regained his calm. "Hello, Nolan," he said. He nodded to the girl and the young Indian. Then he pushed by them and went out onto the wide porch that shields the front of the Catlin County Sheriff's Department. He picked up an open umbrella that was sitting out there and went down the steps, looking like a squatty mushroom.

Tink followed him, muttering "I'm sorry about all this" as he passed Sam.

Sam gave him one of those male-bonding shoulder punches. "You only did your job, Tink," he said. "We'll try to see you Sunday." Sam and I aren't terribly good about church attendance.

"No big deal," Tink answered. "Sometimes I feel that members of the congregation would get more good out of a little reading or meditation than they do out of anything I say." He pulled on a plastic raincoat that had been draped over the porch rail and went off, ducking his head. I couldn't tell if he was depressed or simply trying to keep his glasses out of the rain.

The teenagers wiped their feet on the mat on the porch, then wiped them again on the throw rug Nadine puts down inside the door when it rains.

Sam turned to me. "Nicky, this is Nolan Porter." The farm boy grinned.

"Starr Engelman." The girl smiled.

"And Tom Blacksaddle." The young Indian nodded.

I looked at the third kid. "Are you . . . ?"

He spread his hands wide and gave a grimace that was half smile and half frown. "I confess! I'm Sonny's little brother, and I guess I always will be.

FIVE

....

SONNY BLACKSADDLE WAS ONE OF SAM'S THREE DEPU-
ties, so I knew him very well. Tom was shorter than
Sonny, as well as six or seven years younger, but they
both had square, bony faces.

The girl was also vaguely familiar, though I couldn't
place her right off.

The farm boy, Nolan, was one of a group of Holton
kids I teased Sam about. I called them his "reliable infor-
mants" or "usual suspects" or sometimes his "running
buddies." I was careful to joke this way only in privacy,
because they seemed to be nice kids who had no apparent
connection with crime.

I had discovered their existence a month earlier. Since
July Sam had been running three miles every morning.
He left our apartment—four furnished rooms on the third
floor of the sheriff's building—before seven o'clock. He
told me he jogged out to the high school track, did a
couple of miles there, and jogged back.

Then around the middle of September, I weighed
myself. I discovered I'd added a pound for every month
of married life. Four pounds goes a long way on a five-
foot, three-inch frame, so I decided I'd better take steps.
Literally. I resolved to get more exercise.

I mentioned my plan to Sam in bed that night. "How

about my joining you at the track?" I asked. "I could walk over there, then run a few laps with you."

Sam hadn't jumped at my suggestion. He'd looked dismayed.

I'd fixed him with a stony eye. "All you have to do is say no, buster," I said. "You don't have to act as if I'm poaching in macho waters."

He'd laughed then. "Well, in a way you might be," he said. "I'm not sure I want to admit it, but I do have an ulterior motive when I head for the track every morning. See, a lot of the high school athletes do the same thing."

"Oh?"

"Yeah. Conditioning is the head coach's big emphasis for both boys and girls. They do some weight training, chin-ups—stuff like that."

"Hang out."

"You got it. I don't try to join them, but I do a few chin-ups myself, then sit around and look sweaty and approachable for ten or fifteen minutes."

"Just one of the guys."

"No, I don't want to be that. But as long as I'm sheriff, I've got to look like a person a kid or a teacher or just anybody can talk to casually for a few minutes."

"I see. You're insinuating yourself into the fabric of the community. They might run into something you want to know."

"Got it. I want to look approachable. And I want them to have an unobtrusive way to approach. Besides, I want those high school jocks to know that even an old guy nearly thirty can be in good enough shape that if I say 'jump,' they'd better ask 'how high' on the way up."

"Showing off your muscles, huh?"

"Yeah." He nuzzled my collarbone. "Wanta see 'em?"

The conversation deteriorated after that. Anyway, I

told Nadine about my plan to start running, and I was greeted with surprise.

"Are you sure? Isn't running harmful to young women?" she asked.

I had never heard that, but after one of my mother-in-law's friends had much the same reaction, I mentioned it to Sam's mom, Marty.

She laughed. "That's some idea they've gotten from reading about women who exercise until their body fat ratio drops so low they stop ovulating. You've got better sense than that, Nicky. Run if you want. Just watch the heat. It really is dangerous to run in the middle of the day this time of the year in Oklahoma."

So I thought it over. I'd realized by then that although Holton people were friendly, they were still a bit wary of me. I was a general's daughter. I'd lived in Europe and in New York. One old farmer patted my hand and told Sam, "I jes luv to hear yore little bride tawk thet Yankee lingo."

Yes, I was a stranger to Holton. But if there's one lesson an army brat learns, it's how to acclimate to a new community. I was careful. I never mentioned Paris, Frankfurt, New York, or Ann Arbor, Michigan. I never referred to my father by any rank higher than "Daddy." I saved all my remarks about Okie accents until Sam and I were alone. And I got my exercise by walking instead of running.

After I found Katherine Dawkins as a walking companion, I didn't mind a bit. It's hard to talk while you're running, and Katherine's conversation was well worth the slower pace. We set a route that covered two miles, and we tried to do it in less than thirty minutes.

Our walk took us by the high school, but I'm a lawperson's wife, not a lawperson. I try not to get in Sam's way, so I stayed off the track itself, even though I teased Sam about his "reliable sources."

This was the first time one of the "usual suspects" had showed up at the office.

Nolan was a handsome young man. He had hazel eyes and dark hair that curled over his collar, and he was as tall as Sam is. His jeans and blue Future Farmers of America jacket seemed to stretch across his muscles. He had an open farm-boy face, and in any of the three high schools I attended he would have been known as "a hunk." His accent was broadly Okie, but he used good grammar.

Tom Blacksaddle's cheerful, alert expression seemed to display friendliness and intelligence, which were also traits of his lawman brother. The difference between Tom and Sonny that was easiest to see was their hair; Sonny kept his in long braids, and Tom's was short—ultra short and spiky looking. He wore a Holton High School letter jacket over a solid red T-shirt and blue jeans.

I'd never known any Indians before I came to Holton with Sam, although my father said he had served with several as he made his way through the U.S. Army ranks from second lieutenant to brigadier general. But southwest Oklahoma has plenty of Indians: Comanches and Kiowas along with a sprinkling of Apaches, Wichitas, and others. They live on farms or in town, just like other Americans, because there are no reservations in Oklahoma.

There is an "Indian" accent, a quiet way of speaking that sounds rather tentative and questioning. But Tom's speech didn't show this as much as Sonny's did. I wondered what that meant.

Starr was a tall blonde with smooth, shining hair. Her accent was less broadly Okie than Nolan's, and she didn't have that small town look, a look that can veer either toward I-buy-my-makeup-by-the-feedsack or toward

I-can-shovel-manure-good. No, Starr could have modeled for L. L. Bean or Land's End. In fact, I wondered if I hadn't seen the outfit she was wearing in a catalog. Her only concession to Holton High School fads was her shoes; all three kids wore the "in" sneakers.

Starr's corduroy slacks and cotton sweater exactly matched her blue eyes. She wasn't as naturally good looking as Nolan and Tom, I decided. She was more the type who makes the best of what she's got. Her nose was a bit crooked, for example, and the office light showed me that she'd used shading to hide the hump. That's a fairly sophisticated technique for a high school girl. Then she blinked, and I realized her eyes were contact lens blue. I wondered if she had lenses to match all her sweaters.

"Nolan, Tom, and Starr are all applying for appointments to one of the military academies, Nicky," Sam said. "I said I'd tell them a little about the military life. But there's no reason we can't do it upstairs."

He turned to the three teenagers. "Nicky and I haven't had dinner yet. If you don't mind, we'll eat while we talk. I'll just forward the calls."

The Catlin County Sheriff's Department doesn't run to a night dispatcher, so the jailer does double duty after Nadine goes home. But since the jail was empty—except for Revels—the jailer had taken a night off, and Sam had agreed to forward the calls through to our phone.

I locked the tape recorder in a filing cabinet, and when I turned back around, Sam was holding out a big manila envelope. "I guess this had better go in the freezer, Nicky."

I hope I didn't shrink back. I knew that envelope held the dead rattlesnake, which Sam had earlier placed in a paper evidence bag. It was the last thing I wanted in with the ice cream and frozen peas.

"Oh?"

Sam nodded. "I'd like to hang on to it for a few days."

I took the envelope, trying to hold it casually, and Sam got the key to the evidence closet from Nadine's desk and put the bag holding the rest of the so-called Satanic items away. He locked the outside doors, while I led the three kids up the interior staircase to our third-floor apartment.

Sam was simply born to be a lawman, just the way his father was born to be a rancher. I hadn't realized this until after Sam and I were married. He'd been a captain assigned to the Criminal Investigation Division in Frankfurt, Germany, when we met. He'd worked hard at it, but he hadn't seemed compulsive.

Then his father, Big Sam Titus, was injured in a murderous attack, and Sam's brother, Bill, who had been a partner in the Titus Ranch, disappeared. The twin disasters forced Sam to take a compassionate leave from the army and come back to run the ranch—at least temporarily.

He didn't complain. But for the first two weeks we were back, he didn't sleep much either.

One night I'd awakened at three o'clock, once again alone in Sam's mother's guest room. I found Sam on the upstairs deck, sitting in a director's chair, staring into the summer night and listening to the frogs that inhabited the nearest stock pond. I unfolded a second chair and sat down beside him.

"Shhh," he said. "We're right over Mom's head."

"I know." I touched his wrist, and he responded by gripping my hand firmly. "Sam, I know we haven't been living together very long, but I don't recall that you had this much trouble sleeping before we got back to Oklahoma. Is it Bill? Your dad?"

A long moment passed before Sam answered. "It's all

pretty hard to accept," he said. "But I guess I'm mainly kicking against my fate. I'll get used to the situation pretty soon."

"Your dad's getting better, Sam. Maybe we won't have to stay too long."

"I'm trying not to think too far ahead."

"Or maybe Big Sam will decide to sell out."

"The chance of a snowball where?"

We sat there holding hands a few moments; then I moved over and sat in his lap. When he put his arms around me, I could feel the tight muscles in his back. The twenty-hour-old stubble of his beard prickled my collarbone.

His voice was a whisper. "I've got to stay, Nicky. It's not really going to kill me."

Just make you wish you were dead, I thought. But I didn't say it out loud. What good would that do?

The next day the Catlin County Commissioners offered to appoint Sam sheriff. That night Sam slept ten hours straight.

The job probably saved his sanity, and I know for sure it saved his relationship with his father. Because Big Sam Titus didn't even question Sam's decision to leave the army or thank him for the family loyalty he was showing. He'd never understood why Sam left Catlin County in the first place. Coming back to take care of the Titus Ranch was perfectly logical to him.

And Sam never explained it to his dad. Sam was incapable of using his own sacrifice to make his dad feel guilty. I was proud to be his wife. I wanted to do everything I could to help him.

I put the snake in the freezer, nestling it next to a package of hamburger. Sam made salad and Texas toast, his specialties, and I did steaks—the Tituses feed their own beef—on an indoor broiler we'd gotten as a wedding gift. I resigned myself to talking about military life when I really wanted to talk about Bullock and Satanism.

They seemed to be nice kids. Starr told me she was the granddaughter of Lucretia Engelman, and I realized that I knew her grandmother. Lucretia Engelman was a stern gray-haired woman who ran the preschool and day care center that rented space from the Community Church.

"I've dropped Sam's niece and nephew off there once or twice," I told Starr. "The school seems to be really good, and the kids just love to go there."

Starr smiled. "Billy and Lee Anna are special," she said. "And Brenda's always great." Brenda is Sam's sister-in-law.

"Then you work there, too?"

Starr nodded. "Just in the kitchen. I go in every morning before school. Grandmother says she'd have to pay somebody, and it might as well be me. But I'm not trained the way she wants her teachers trained. For a career I'm interested in science."

"Starr and Tom worked on a project that won the biggest prize at the three-state science fair," Nolan said. "They studied prairie animals, even mounted half a dozen species."

Tom shrugged. "Starr did the mounting," he said. "I just caught the specimens."

Starr looked properly modest. "My parents were both scientists. My mother went to Vassar, you know."

"No, I'm afraid I don't know anything about your parents, Starr."

"My father was a doctor, and my mother was a chemist. She met my dad in college. He came from one of those old families where everyone went to Harvard. They were both killed in an accident when I was five, so I came here to stay with Grandmother. She was my mother's mother, but I use her name, just to keep things simple."

I turned to Nolan. "Are you a Holton native?"

"Yes, ma'am." He flashed me that cheek-of-tan smile again. "It's a wonderful place, but I'd like to get out and see the world. Like your husband did, ma'am."

"How about you, Tom? Do you want to see the world, too?"

Tom tapped his right fist into his left palm with a nervous rhythm. "Sure. My mom wants me to stay home—go to Southern Oklahoma State and be an ecologist. So if I can get in a good school and not have to be financially dependent on my folks and the Kiowa Tribe's scholarships, I'll feel a lot better about not doing what she wants me to."

Sam quizzed the kids a bit—about their grades and school activities and such. All three were athletes. Nolan and Tom were out for football, and Starr was a center on the girls' basketball team. They'd all taken college level courses at the closest state university. They seemed to be in a three-way tie to be Holton High School valedictorian, but both boys said that Starr had the highest ACT and SAT scores.

"Ninety-eighth percentile," Tom said, wagging his thumb at Starr. Starr looked modest again.

Then Sam told them about the alternatives to the service academies, such as ROTC scholarships—which is how he got through school and into the army. And he talked about some of the bad things about the military, such as having to move a lot. They thought that would be wonderful.

"With all these budget cutbacks," Sam said, "promotion may be slower in all branches of the military." That didn't bother them either.

"And if you go to a service academy, you can't get married until you graduate," I pointed out.

This made all three of them laugh uneasily. Nolan's ears got red, and Tom stared at the floor.

Starr patted Tom on the arm. "We're just friends, Mrs. Titus," she said. "It seems as if Nolan and Tom are the only guys at Holton High who are really interested in making something of themselves. And I feel the same way. None of us wants to get married for a long time—to anybody."

After forty-five minutes or so of this—they joined us for apple pie that Nora Rich, a friend of Sam's mom, had dropped by—Sam cleared his throat a couple of times and said, "Let me ask y'all about something else."

Nolan looked more open than ever, Tom grinned broadly and made an expansive gesture, and Starr nodded.

"What do the students think of Mr. Bullock?" Sam did his innocent act. It makes him look like a nerd, but it doesn't mean he is one.

They all looked at each other.

"This is confidential," Sam said.

Starr shrugged. She still appeared impassive. "You know him better," she said to Nolan. "Since he helps coach football."

So Nolan frowned, then spoke. "It's kind of hard to tell. He's sort of out of touch, you know."

"Out of touch?"

"Yeah! I mean, I guess he knows a bunch about living in a city, but he doesn't know from up about a small town. I mean, he was surprised that the Future Farmers got out of class to go to the fair. He thought a fair was like a carnival! He didn't know what a barrow was. Or even a cross. You know, simple stuff like that."

Ah ha. I knew that "simple stuff." Or I knew something about it. A barrow is a pig of some sort. And a

43

cross means a crossbred sheep or cow or whatever. Hereford-Angus cross, maybe. They have competitions for crossbreds at fairs.

"Well, if he's asking, I guess he's trying to learn," Sam said.

"Yeah. I guess so." Nolan's ears turned red again.

Starr stirred, then took a deep breath, then shut her mouth. Sam turned and looked at her steadily. Hardly anyone can resist saying something—anything—after Sam has looked at them mildly for about forty-five seconds.

"He seems—well, as if he's up to something," she said.

"What?"

Starr used her fork to draw a design in apple pie goo on her empty plate. "I work in the office fourth hour," she said. "He's in there a lot, looking through the records. Sometimes it's not just the student records." She leaned forward and looked at Sam directly. "The principal—well, Mr. Kelleher is my uncle, you know. He doesn't say anything, but I can see he doesn't like him. And I can see why. Mr. Bullock is always telling the secretaries or the teachers or the students how something or other should be done—and it's usually different from what Uncle Ramsey wants."

That was as specific as any of them got. The party broke up at nine-thirty, and Sam walked the kids downstairs to let them out through the office.

"I'll stay down there a few minutes," he told me as he started down the steps.

I must have looked surprised, because he went on. "I've got some paperwork, and I'll just sort it out until our houseguest shows up."

Someone gasped, and I guess it was me. It seemed to echo in the stairwell.

"I'd forgotten Damon Revels," I said. "He's certainly

taking his time with dinner. He's been gone two hours. You could eat your way through the whole menu at The Hangout in that time."

"I didn't realize you had company," Nolan said.

"He's not company," Sam said. "Just a stray hitch-hiker. It's easier to let him stay in the jail than get him to Lawton or Wichita Falls or someplace where there's a motel."

He gestured toward the bedroll at the bottom of the steps. I could see the star shining in the dim hallway. "He left his gear. He'll be back."

I followed them down. I was dying to ask Sam what he thought of Bullock and his devil worship plot. So I was really glad to see the kids leave. I heard a burst of laughter from Nolan as soon as the door closed, then Starr squelched him. I couldn't understand her words, but her tone clearly said, "Shut up."

They walked on down the steps and spoke again at the end of the walk. By some fluke those words did sound through the office window. "I'm staying out of it. Let's go down to The Hangout," Starr said. "But I've got to be home by eleven."

Sam went back into his own office and sat down at the desk. He looked at me. "Out with it," he said. "What do you want to know?"

I plunked myself down in an oak chair. "Bullock's crazy, isn't he? There can't be Satanists in Holton, U.S.A."

Sam shrugged. "I don't want to slough off Bullock's suspicions. Satanism can be a serious problem. But it's usually associated with a youth drug culture, not the kind of problems I've run into in Holton. I don't know a lot about it."

"Sam, nobody could seriously worship the devil!"

"Anything's possible."

"But just about everybody around here is a Southern Baptist!"

"Not everybody. I'm not. You're not. Starr's not. The Blacksaddles go to the Indian Baptist. I don't know if that's Southern Baptist or not. Nolan's Assembly of God."

"How'd you know that?"

"I know his parents. They farm east of town."

"But Sam, people around here don't even lock their doors!"

"You wouldn't think this would be a big area for drug labs, either. But they sure busted a major one over in Jefferson County a while back."

I didn't answer. I knew that Sam had been trying to trace a rumor that a drug lab was operating in Catlin County. So far he hadn't had any luck.

He spoke again. "Satanists aren't required to live in cities."

"Well, if it's just an offbeat religion, the way you're talking, what's the big deal?"

"Maybe nothing. The way I told Bullock, if people want to worship the devil in outdoor ceremonies, the Constitution says they can. The problem is what they do during their ceremonies."

"What do they do?"

"Well, one rumor is that they sacrifice cats. That's why this rattlesnake surprises me. It doesn't fit the pattern."

"Is there an expert on Satanism anywhere?"

"Oh, sure. I can get a source from the OSBI." The Oklahoma State Bureau of Investigation acts as a backup unit for local law enforcement, providing technical assistance and investigators for small counties and towns.

Sam was still frowning. "You can believe anything you want in the U.S. of A.," he said. "What you think can't get you in trouble. But you can't perform actions that break the law. You can't keep your kids out of school. You can't refuse medical treatment to kids too young to decide for themselves. And you can't be cruel to animals. But a rattlesnake's not going to get a lot of sympathy."

"Cruelty's not Bullock's objection, is it?"

"I don't think so. But I don't really know the man."

I sat there a minute, remembering the church's annual meeting, when Mr. Bullock had first made his presence known. Sam and I weren't active members of the Community Church; we had blundered into the meeting because it followed a service featuring a song by the four-year-old Sunday school class. Sam's nephew Billy was one of the performers.

Sam never said anything out loud, but I knew he felt some guilt over his brother's death. They'd argued, and Bill had gone off on his own to confront a person he hadn't realized was dangerous. Sam will always feel, probably falsely, that if he'd handled Bill more tactfully, he might have waited until Sam could go with him—and lived. As a result, maybe Sam feels an extra responsibility toward Bill's children. And I'm glad he does. If Billy doesn't have a father, at least he has an Uncle Sam to take him to father-son banquets and teach him how to handle cattle and how to make a slingshot. And to show up at church to tell him he sings great.

Protestant congregational meetings are usually routine. The board chairman presents the budget chairman, who presents the budget. Moved, seconded, all in favor. The nominations chairman presents a list. Anybody who'll agree to do a job can have it. Moved, seconded, all in favor. Old business, new business, move to adjourn. Twenty minutes, tops.

But Bullock had gotten up on his hind legs when they called for new business. He proposed that a committee be formed to write a creed for the church. He thought we needed some doctrinal unity.

There had been maybe ninety people there, and one hundred and eighty eyes had looked at him askance. I mean, here were ninety people who had agreed to merge five different theologies into one nondenominational church. And he wanted a creed. The potential for disaster was enormous, and his suggestion was voted down with very little discussion. Bullock hadn't been pleased, but he hadn't left the church over it.

Now I leaned forward again. "What's Bullock up to?" I asked.

Sam shook his head. "I don't know. But I thought Starr's information about him going through the files was sort of suggestive. I wonder how he got his job."

"What do you mean? Don't schools just advertise for teachers?"

Sam grinned at me. "This is a small town, Nicky. The school board politics can be unbelievable. Especially if you get a board member who doesn't always recall that the superintendent—not the board—is in charge of hiring and firing the faculty."

He reached for his "in" basket. "I'll ask around about Mr. Bullock—after I check out that site at Lattimore's Park. But now I really am going to do some paperwork. Nadine'll get after me if she shows up tomorrow and this stuff isn't done. I'll come up as soon as I get Revels settled."

I went on up, did the dishes, then got in bed with a book. It was eleven o'clock when Sam came up the stairs.

"I didn't hear Revels come in," I said.

"He never showed up. I'm not going to sit up all night over some transient. If he bangs loud enough, I'll go down and let him in when he does show."

But the night was undisturbed. The rain stopped

sometime after midnight, and when I went out to walk at six-forty-five, Revels's bedroll was still stashed in the hall, next to the door to the basement cells.

Count Dracula had been caught by the daylight.

Well, Revels had seemed to be only slightly cracked. He could take care of himself. I did wonder where he'd spent the night. I didn't think he was likely to pick up a romantic partner at The Holton Hangout, the restaurant around the corner. Holton's two taverns were out at the edge of town. Maybe he'd gotten a ride out there and was sleeping it off under a table.

I shrugged and put on my sweatshirt. He'd show up.

I always jogged the two blocks to the parsonage.

Katherine Dawkins liked the early morning because Tink was there in case their toddler woke up, and I liked it because I enjoy seeing the sun rise and because it can get hot in southwestern Oklahoma by nine o'clock—even in October. Everybody kept telling me that we were due for a hard freeze any day and assuring me that we'd have real snow and blizzards before the winter was over, but so far I'd seen no evidence that winter ever came to this part of Oklahoma. After the baking heat of summer, the October weather had been ideal—lows in the fifties and highs in the seventies. The only hint of winter's approach were halos of golden leaves on the cottonwoods and pecans.

Katherine and I had laid out a course that almost circled the town, if it's possible to say a route made up entirely of straight lines and right angles "circled." Because there's nothing curved in Holton. The town is a checker-board laid out on a pattern the government surveyors picked back in 1901, a pattern that has no relationship to the terrain. Holton is flat, but it's not that flat. It undulates.

So Katherine and I had selected a path that took us

through the town by way of the most interesting houses and most colorful yards. Our route zigzagged past entertaining lawn statuary and multicolored roofs, sidewalks that had been uprooted by ancient cottonwood trees, an abandoned geodesic dome constructed of weathered redwood, and a barn on which some folk artist had painted an Alpine scene, complete with black-and-white cows.

After about a mile and a half of this, our route reached the church and high school, just outside the city limits. We turned around there and headed back "downtown," where we both lived.

Katherine was also fighting the battle of the bulge, though she had a bit more to go than I did. In fact, she'd told me she wanted to lose twenty pounds. She's even shorter than I am—no more than five-foot-one. She has extremely straight brown hair, which hangs in bangs over her forehead and a ponytail down her back, and she usually wears either sweatpants or flowered dresses.

Her face always reminded me of a fried pie, somehow. It was round, pretty, and neatly closed in, the edges crimped with a fork. But sometimes a little of the filling leaked out, letting you see what's inside—apple, cherry, peach, or apricot. And the glimpses I'd gotten of what was behind Katherine Dawkins's facade indicated that there was something yummy in there, hidden away.

The Community Church congregation is mixed in its feelings about Katherine. Her secretive exterior puts people off, but it also makes them curious. People wonder why she doesn't work, for example, when Tink doesn't make much money. She's taught English in the past, but when the high school principal, Starr's uncle Ramsey Kelleher, asked her to apply for an opening, she declined. This annoyed Leona Kephart, editor of the local weekly, the *Courier*, and president of both the school board and the church board. Leona had asked Ramsey to ask Katherine.

Of course, Katherine has a small child, but few other young Holton mothers can afford to stay home. How does she manage it? Tink and Katherine don't seem to be that hard up. They have two cars—small cars, but two of them. Neither of them wears clothes from K mart. Their son has an expensive tricycle—and a pedal car. What does she do with her time, and where do they get their money? Holton's inquiring minds want to know.

But even the IGA crowd admits that Katherine has many good qualities. She's a wonderful mother, with a beautiful and well-behaved two-year-old son. Tink always looks neat and clean, and he seems to dote on Katherine. She sponsors the senior high youth group. Her house is straight whenever members of the congregation drop by, and she takes her turn at circle. In fact, the devotional she gave in August still has people talking. They suspect Tink wrote it for her. She was the person who suggested the Haunted House project to the Maids and Matrons. And she's a very creative cook. She even raises her own herbs.

Katherine has another good quality, too. However the gossip goes about her, she rarely gossips back. So I was surprised when she asked me what I thought about Bullock's Satanism report.

"I think it's pretty silly," I said. "Let's face it, Katherine, people today have enough trouble believing in God. If they claim to worship Satan, they're just showing off."

"Well, I feel the same way, but he sure did upset Tink. Especially that part about the Haunted House."

"Surely Tink didn't take that seriously."

She smiled. "Well, this is Tink's first church, you know. He wants to do well."

"He's doing fine. He'd better not listen to an idiot like Bullock. He ought to tell him to get lost."

"Did Sam just tell Bullock to get lost?"

"Oh no! He wouldn't do that. Every citizen's report—"
I looked at Katherine. She was smiling.

"Okay," I said. "I get it. I know Tink can't tell Bullock to get lost, any more than Sam can. But I don't think Tink should take it too seriously. The congregation's definitely behind the Haunted House. Look at the support it's gotten."

"Not from Leona Kephart."

I thought about that. "She didn't vote against it, did she?"

"She can't. She's chairman of the board, so she only gets to vote in case of a tie. But she talked against it in the church and in the club."

"Do you think Bullock is fronting for Leona?"

She shook her head. "I don't know, Nicky. I know they're friends, but surely he wouldn't try to sabotage the Haunted House now. Halloween's less than a week away!"

We walked on silently until we reached the next corner and turned toward the church and the high school.

Then Katherine sort of burst out: "I've enjoyed the Haunted House! I just joined Maids and Matrons because I felt obligated—probably the same reason they asked me to become a member. But somehow, when you spend a whole afternoon painting or—or—"

"Or lining a coffin," I interjected.

Katherine laughed. "Right! For the first time I don't feel like an outsider in this town. I feel as if I have friends. Does that make sense?"

"It sure does," I answered. "I just joined because Brenda had to drop out, and I said I'd fill in the gap. But when this is over, I think I'll even look at the slavedriver as a friend. See, she's already there."

I pointed down the street toward the church. We

could see the old ramshackle house next door to it clearly. That was the site of our Haunted House, and it was a perfect setting—tumbledown and spooky even in the fresh sunlight of a fall morning, with the Oklahoma atmosphere rinsed dust-free by rain. And outside the Haunted House was the pickup we knew so well. The white one driven by the chairman of the Haunted House, Virginia Cramer.

Katherine laughed. "Does she work there even before she goes to school?"

"I guess so. She makes me feel bad. I must be the laziest woman in Holton, I guess. I don't work. I don't have children to take care of. I don't—"

A scream shattered our conversation.

Katherine grabbed my arm.

The scream came again. Now it became a siren, a European siren rising and falling.

"Where's it coming from?" I yelled.

Then I saw a woman rush out from behind the church. She wore gray slacks and jacket, and she was waving her arms in the air as she ran. It was Virginia Cramer.

Across the street, at the high school, the athletes were turning around and moving tentatively toward Virginia. I could see Sam on the far end of the track. He broke his jogging stride and began to run across the middle of the football field, toward the sound.

Then Virginia slipped in a patch of mud and sat down hard in the gravel of the parking lot. She stayed there, giving keening sobs, not trying to get up.

"Come on!" Katherine yelled. She and I began to run. We were closest to Virginia, so we reached her first. Katherine dropped on her knees beside her.

"Virginia! What's happened?"

Virginia's sobbing dropped to a moan. She didn't

speak, but she waved her arm behind her. I realized she was pointing at the church's storage shed. What could have given Virginia such a fright?

I looked at the shed. It was simply a miniature tin barn, probably ordered from Sears. Some of the Haunted House props had been stored in it, and we'd been using it as a workroom. Katherine and I had spent two hours in there the previous Saturday, lining a packing case that was to serve as Dracula's coffin.

I walked toward the building. The double doors stood open, but the interior was dim. Then I realized that someone had been fooling around there. The plastic sheet that had protected the coffin was gone. The burned-out stub of a white candle stood on the rim of the coffin, in a puddle of candle wax.

But Virginia hadn't been frightened by a candle. Something was inside the coffin.

I dreaded looking, but I stepped closer.

The figure inside looked completely unintelligent, blank, peaceful, and not at all human. Damon Revels's hair was still sleeked back, and his deep widow's peak still marked his pale face, now paler than ever. His lack of expression was in strong contrast to the bright orange star drawn on his bare chest. It also contrasted with the knife protruding from the center of that star.

Dracula had flitted for the final time.

Six

....

I DIDN'T SCREAM, I GUESS BECAUSE VIRGINIA'S HYSTE-
ria had prepared me for the worst. And Revels didn't look
scary, exactly. He didn't look real.

Besides, I didn't have time to scream. I could hear voices
in the parking lot, and the part of me that's a lawman's wife
woke up. That church is just outside the Holton city limits,
so Sam would be handling this. I knew he wouldn't want
a bunch of people contaminating his crime scene.

I blocked the door to the shed, holding my arms
across the opening. I found myself facing Nolan Porter,
his dark hair blowing, and his hazel eyes intent.

"What's happened?" he said. "What made Mrs.
Cramer so crazy?"

I tried to sound brisk and official, the way Sam would
have. "Nolan, you and the other football players circle the
parking lot and keep everybody out of this mud," I said.
I tried to make my voice a bark. "Sam might want to look
at the tracks."

"But what's happened?"

"There's been a crime." I know I barked that time.
"Get back! Keep everybody away until Sam gets here!"

I was almost surprised when he obeyed. "Come on,
y'all!" he yelled, turning around. "We're supposed to keep
everybody out of the parking lot."

By then, Sam had trotted into the area. He looked at Virginia, who had stopped moaning, then looked at me, and I motioned for him to come on.

"What's happened?" he asked.

"It's Damon Revels." I stood aside and watched as Sam went into the storage shed.

He stepped lightly. I knew he was trying not to leave tracks. He looked down at Revels's body, touched Revels's arm.

"Not much doubt he's dead." He nodded. "Already cold."

Then I did jump with fear. Because at that moment someone laid a hand on my shoulder. I hadn't realized anyone else had approached, and the touch startled me.

I whirled around to find myself facing George Bullock.

"What are you doing here?" I yelled at him. "I told Nolan to keep everybody out."

Bullock ignored me. He shoved me aside, took two strides, leaving giant muddy footprints on the storage shed's floor, and stood beside Sam. He leaned over Revels's body. Then he looked up, smiling.

"A pentagram! A candle! A ritual knife! Now you'll believe me, Sheriff!"

He strode back to the door, pushed me aside again, then stood in the doorway and orated to the high school athletes outside.

"The Satanists have turned to human sacrifice!"

I was so mad at Bullock that I could have joyfully sacrificed him—and I wouldn't have needed a ritual knife. I could easily have lashed him to death with my tongue. But before I could even open my mouth, Sam took charge.

"Bullock!" His M.P. voice boomed. "Stand right where you are!"

Bullock looked startled, but he obeyed.

"I won't have any further disruption of the scene of

this crime," Sam said. His voice carried better than Bullock's, but Sam didn't need to yell. "Nicky, you go over to the church, and walk right next to this building. Look where you're stepping and if there's a footprint there, be careful not to step in it. Call Nadine and have her send every deputy out here to keep all additional unauthorized persons out of this area. And tell her to ask the Holton police to help. Then call the OSBI and get the technical team over here. Get Tink or someone to take you back to the office to get your camera. Then come back and wait until I need you."

He turned to Bullock. "You follow Nicky over to the church, Bullock, and you don't step an inch out of her tracks. You go in that church, and you sit in one spot, and you don't move until I come in and talk to you."

"But Sheriff—I have to go to class."

"No. You're not going anywhere until I find out why you claim to know so damn much about what's happening on the Catlin County crime front."

"But—"

"Move!"

It was a crestfallen Bullock who followed me into the church.

I was on the phone before the whole situation sank in, and then my heart began to race. But an image more striking than the sight of Revels in his satin-lined coffin came to mind. I kept remembering the athletes, as well as Virginia and Katherine, all staring at Bullock as he made his oration on human sacrifice.

Had anyone but me seen the look on Nolan Porter's face?

But right that moment, as Sam's string of instructions had indicated, there was too much to do for me to worry about Nolan.

We were lucky and found the Oklahoma State Bureau

of Investigation's mobile lab still at its base thirty-five miles away, so that unit got there within forty-five minutes. The Catlin County deputies were more effective at keeping people out of the area than the high school football players had been, and investigative routine took over. Sam was in his element. This was his law enforcement specialty, the part he loves as much as he hates crowd control and traffic. He'd received special training in investigation at the National FBI Academy while he was in the army, and he can deduce worlds from an atom of evidence and see the gaps in witnesses' stories a mile away.

I stayed out of the way, going into the church office, where Bullock was sitting, to set up my camera equipment. I wanted to be ready when Sam called me to do my photography thing.

Bullock seemed amazed when I came in with my padded bag loaded with lenses and film.

"You mean your husband would force you to visit the scene of a murder!"

"He wouldn't force me to do anything," I answered. "I'm officially enrolled as a member of the Catlin County Sheriff's Reserve, and I do it as a volunteer."

"But he'd ask you to take pictures of a corpse?"

"I already saw the corpse," I said. I deliberately turned my back on Bullock and checked my strobe unit by flashing it at the wall. "He didn't look so bad. Car wrecks—that's what I hate."

"But to ask a woman—"

I wasn't going to talk to Bullock anymore, but another voice spoke up.

"Women have always handled the ugly parts of life, Mr. Bullock."

I turned to see Lucretia Engelman standing in the office door. She was a woman of at least sixty, heavily built and as tall as her granddaughter, Starr. Her hair was iron gray. She was holding a Styrofoam cup in each hand.

"I brought you two some coffee," she said.

"How's Virginia Cramer?" I asked. I had seen Katherine taking her into the church earlier.

"I think she's more embarrassed than anything," Mrs. Engelman said. "She kept apologizing for making a spectacle of herself."

"That was a terrible sight for a woman," Bullock said.

"Women are used to terrible sights," Mrs. Engelman said briskly. "It's women who have traditionally nursed the sick and wounded—and who have laid out the dead. Through every generation up to and including my mother's, women sewed pads, of newspaper or straw, to soak up the blood when they gave birth—that was a more important part of the preparation than knitting little booties. And primitive tribes turn their prisoners over to the women to torture.

"Men won't even change a diaper, and then they have the nerve to bawl around about women being the weaker sex. You all make me sick. If Mrs. Titus can help the process of justice along by taking a few pictures, she'd better do it."

She pulled a tiny plastic straw out of her pocket and thrust it at Bullock, seeming to aim it at his midsection like a shiv.

"Here's a stirrer," she said. "I've got to help keep the day care kids calm." She gave him a final glare and left.

I wasn't sure I'd needed her protection, but she had shut Bullock up. I turned to face the wall and flashed the strobe a few more times until the corners of my mouth stopped twitching. When I looked around, Bullock was staring at the floor like a sulky child. He didn't say any more until Sam came in.

Then he jumped to his feet. "Sheriff! I—"

But Sam ignored him. He motioned to me. "Ready?"

"Sure." I gulped a couple of times, but I followed Sam out.

Despite my brave words to Bullock, I'm not that wild about taking pictures of corpses. In the four months Sam had been sheriff, he hadn't investigated a murder. But both the sheriff of the next county over and the district OSBI man had discovered I could take close-ups that showed a lot of detail—after all, I'm a professional photographer, though I'd always specialized in artistic photography until I married a lawman. Now I just pretend that the weapons, wounds, and bashed-in back doors are fruit and flowers posing for still lifes and use the same camera settings.

Once the OSBI man had asked me to fill in when his usual lab man was tied up and he wanted some can't-wait photos of a beaten child. Now that's a hard assignment. A corpse is easy to photograph compared to a three-year-old whose father had blacked both her eyes and cracked her ribs.

But routine lets you cope. I believe that's how lots of people—combat nurses and suicide prevention teams and police and the others we hire to do society's dirty work—get through. You do one part of the job at a time and keep reminding yourself that each little piece adds up to a whole that makes the system better.

Or that's how I do it.

And I keep reminding myself that Sam could use the OSBI's photos for evidence, but he says he likes mine better. So I take all he wants. Color and black and white.

The first thing he wanted photographed was Revels's poncho. It was in a heap inside the back door of the shed. After I'd gotten a view that showed the poncho's position, he picked it up. Underneath was a big puddle of dried blood. Sam and Sonny Blacksaddle stood by while I photographed that.

Sonny Blacksaddle is the nearest to a professionally trained deputy that Sam has. He has an associate degree in criminal justice and also finished the state's training course in Oklahoma City. Sam says Sonny is more thorough than brilliant, and Sam says thorough is better than brilliant.

Sonny is a member of the Kiowa tribe, and he's tall and lean, though lots of Plains Indians are on the heavy side. He's really very conservative, but he wears his hair in braids that hang to his waist. He says the braids are part of his hobby, which is competitive war dancing. Sonny is an impressive sight in his feathers, moccasins, warpaint, and breech cloth. He just looks businesslike in a deputy's tan shirt.

Of course, five months ago I'd never met a real Indian, so Sonny had fascinated me at first. Then I found out he was a regular guy, just with a little different accent—sort of singsong. Sam says it's the common Plains Indian accent. They pronounce English words perfectly, but they use a different rhythm in their sentences. I can't put my finger on it exactly, and it's less pronounced in Sonny's generation than in older Indians like Sonny's grandmother, and it had barely been noticeable in Sonny's younger brother.

But when Sonny pointed at the poncho and said, "Looks like he was wearing it," I couldn't tell if he was asking Sam's opinion or if the tentative note in his voice was simply his accent.

"Certainly he was wearing it," I said. "We saw him in it."

"He was wearing it when he was killed," Sam explained. "Or at least someone with black hair was wearing it when he got hit in the head. I think we can assume it was Revels."

Sam turned the inside of the poncho's hood toward

the light. I could see that hair was stuck inside, glued there with a brown substance.

"Then someone hit him before they stabbed him?"

Sonny looked at me and waved his hands again. "The knife was just window dressing, Nicky. He was dead before he was stabbed."

"Oh." I should have realized that. "No blood on his chest."

Sam nodded. "Right. The stab wound did not bleed. He was dead from a blow to the back of the head before he was placed in the coffin. Or at least I think that's what the postmortem will show. If somebody clubbed him and stabbed him, surely they didn't poison him or smother him as well."

The knife, Sam said, appeared to be an ordinary steak knife with a wooden handle, despite Bullock's calling it "a ritual dagger."

"It's been through a dishwasher a bunch of times." Sonny's fingers rubbed together, seeming to avoid touching a distasteful object. "Handle's all white and funny."

The white shirt Revels had been wearing was thrown into a different corner. It also had blood on the collar and down the back. And water spots dotted the inside of the coffin—a cardboard packing case Katherine and I had carefully painted black outside and lined with cheap red satin. The satin under Revels's worn boots was covered with the brown clay mud from the parking lot.

It appeared, Sam and Sonny agreed, that Revels had walked into the shed. There someone had whacked him in the back of the head, probably with a short piece of lumber that had been left propped against the end of the coffin. The unknown person had hoisted Revels into the casket, then stripped off his poncho and shirt. Sam said the orange pentagon appeared to be drawn on in lipstick.

That, the knife, and probably the candle were added after Revels had been laid out.

"Sam," I asked, "could Bullock be right? Is this a case of Satanism?"

Sam shrugged. "Anything's possible, Nicky."

Sonny nodded seriously and waved his hands. "You hear about all kind of crazy things. Do you think this guy came to Holton to make contact with some sort of Satanists?"

"He came here to see somebody," Sam answered. "He told us as much. But I don't expect he came here with the idea of being a sacrifice—certainly not to Satan."

"Oh, no," I said. "Remember? He kept saying 'Praise the Lord' and such. I had the impression he was some sort of religious fanatic—and I don't mean the Satanic religion. But he mentioned that there was somebody in Holton he'd known way back."

"Fifteen years," Sam said firmly. "I guess the first thing to do is try to find out if he found them. I suspect that he did."

Sonny was dispatched to the office to run the name Damon Revels through the Los Angeles and State of California records. Revels's billfold had disappeared, but when we picked him up he had shown Sam a license with an L.A. address. Sam stood by while I took the rest of the pictures he wanted and the OSBI man took the ones he wanted. Then the ambulance took Revels away, and the OSBI lab crew began to load up the physical evidence—such as the makeshift coffin.

It was a shock to see it carried out and hoisted into a van.

"My God!" I said, clutching Sam's arm. "Katherine and I have lost our room for the Haunted House!"

Damn. We'd worked hard on that coffin, not to mention spending hours on the fake pillars that went with it.

Now I certainly didn't want to use those props to entertain kids. Would Revels's murder force the Maids and Matrons to drop the whole Haunted House project? After weeks of work? All of a sudden I found myself taking Revels's murder quite personally.

Sam gestured toward the church. "Speaking of the Haunted House, I guess I'd better take Virginia Cramer's statement." He sighed. "Then I ought to let Bullock off the hook."

He looked around. The high school kids had been herded inside the school. Only one patrol car, a single deputy, and a line of "crime scene" tape remained to keep people away from the shed.

"Looks like you're going to have to be my witness," he said. He started for the church, and I trailed along.

"By the way," I said, "I put your clothes in Tink's office."

Sam looked down at himself. He seemed amazed to see that he was still wearing gym shorts, running shoes, and a T-shirt with "University of Oklahoma Sooners" across the front in red script.

"Thanks," he said. "I'll try to look more professional when I talk to Virginia. She could be a key witness, since she was probably the last person here last night and the first here this morning."

After Sam had put on his khaki pants and matching shirt with the Catlin County Sheriff's Department patches on the sleeves, he came into the church parlor, where Virginia had been lying down on the couch.

Virginia was around thirty-five, an English teacher for Holton High School and Junior High. She organized her looks as efficiently as she did the Haunted House, with briskly professional brown hair, disciplined makeup, and pants and jackets from the "coordinates" rack. I saw now that she'd taken off her muddy slacks, replacing them with a pair of jeans. I knew she usually changed clothes after school and before she took on her Haunted House duties, so I deduced that she'd had extra clothes in her truck.

I'd already set up the tape recorder for Sam, so he got through the formalities quickly.

"I'm relying on you to help me with a time line on this Revels," he told Virginia. "How late did you stay at the Haunted House last night?"

She stared at her hands before she answered. "I'm not really sure. I guess it was sometime after nine when I left. Maybe even—after ten."

"Were you in the storage shed?"

"Yes. I was fixing up a shelf of equipment for Dr. Frankenstein's lab. I glued everything in place, so it would be hard for it to get broken. The rain didn't help."

"Were you in the shed until ten? Or in the house itself?"

Again she looked at her hands before she answered. "I worked in the shed early in the evening. I spent most of the time last night in the house. But I locked that shed up before I left!"

"Did you look inside?"

"Well, yes and no. I opened the door and looked in to make sure I'd switched off that battery lamp we use out there."

"Was it off?"

"I think so. I honestly don't remember. I could have reached in and switched off the lamp from the door. But there certainly wasn't a dead man in there!"

I wondered how she would have known there wasn't— if the lights were out. I didn't say anything. She would have noticed a candle.

"When did you come back this morning?"

"Not long before I—a few minutes before seven, I guess."

"Did you notice anything different before you went into the shed?"

"No. In fact, I didn't notice anything different when I first opened the door. I'd brought some costumes, and I went in and laid them on that old chair. Then I saw that candle. It scared me."

"Why?"

"Because of the fire danger. I know that building's metal, but we're using paint and turpentine and all sorts of flammable things in there. I've been real nervous about fire. So I went right over to look at that candle. That's when I saw something in the coffin."

She turned to me. "I thought for a minute that you and Katherine had come over and fixed up a dummy of some sort. I guess that was why I got so crazy when I realized that it was a real body."

I smiled. "Katherine and I aren't that gung ho. I assure you we'll never show up at the Haunted House before seven o'clock."

"Oh, I didn't expect you to do that. I thought you'd been there the night before."

Sam nodded and told Virginia she could go. "Do you want a deputy to drive you home?"

"Oh, no. I'll go on to school," she said. "Mr. Kelleher is probably having to fill in for my classes. It leaves him up a creek if a teacher is absent without warning."

Sam raised his eyebrows. Two teachers, I thought. I knew he was remembering Bullock, stewing in the church office, and sure enough, as soon as Virginia left Sam gestured in that direction.

"I guess I'd better go ahead and talk to Bullock," he said. "I sure do hate to lecture adults."

"You'd think a forty-year-old man, a teacher, would have some sense," I said. "You'd think he wouldn't go shooting his mouth off."

Sam laughed. "Yeah. I do think so."

"What do you mean?"

"I mean he's up to something, Nicky. He thinks that this stupid public proclamation will help him in some way." He jerked a thumb over his shoulder. "You put in a new tape, and I'll go get him. I might as well ask him straight out what's going on."

Sam swung out the door, sighing sadly. Poor guy. He just hates showoffs and hot dogs like Bullock was proving to be. I set up the tape and stood there, feeling sorry for him. And he wasn't even mad at Bullock anymore. Even anger would have made it easier to handle the jerk.

At that moment the door to the church parlor swung back and crashed against the wall. Sam stood in the opening. His face was grim.

"In here, mister."

He turned around and swung his arm into the parlor, fingers held as stiff as a military salute.

"Get in here and sit down," he ordered.

Bullock appeared behind him. He cleared his throat and smoothed the hair over his bald spot. "Sheriff," he said in a subdued voice. "I'm as surprised—"

"Sit down, Bullock. Don't say anything until the tape is running."

"Sheriff?" Bullock made a timid effort, then sat down in an easy chair and kept quiet while Sam handled the routine of the tape recording in a frosty voice.

"Bullock, will you state for the record that you are aware that the tape is running?"

"Yes, Sheriff Titus. But let me say I'm eager to help—"

"Just answer my questions, please, Mr. Bullock. And the first question is—Why did you think it would help solve this case if you called a Dallas television station and told them that devil worshipers were openly holding human sacrifices in Holton, Oklahoma?"

SEVEN

···

BULLOCK TOOK TWO DEEP BREATHS. "SHERIFF, YOU cannot possibly hope to keep a death linked to Satanism away from the press."

"True, Mr. Bullock. But I had hoped to know a few facts before I got the first phone call."

"Even in this remote spot, the power of the press—"

"Yes, Mr. Bullock, even in this remote, backwoods county, we are aware of the power of the press to present an image of our town, our neighbors, to the outside world. Do you think this remote, backwoodsy community will appreciate being presented to the world as a haven for devil worshipers?"

Bullock pouted and smoothed his hair. "People need to know the truth."

"I agree. Do you know it? Do you know the truth of a situation we have not yet investigated properly?"

"But the knife, Sheriff. The candle. The pentagram! They've got to be linked to Satanism!" Bullock squirmed. "Not to mention the evidence I brought you yesterday!"

"Unfortunately, I can't depend only on that sort of evidence, Bullock. I need other types of facts—like fingerprints, bloodstains, time schedules. I need to know who Revels talked to after he left my office. And who was at the church last night."

"Well, I wasn't!"

It hadn't occurred to me that he might have been around the church the night before. But now it did.

Sam gave one of those blinks that hint that he's surprised, at least to those few of us lucky enough to know him well. The blink told me that he hadn't suspected that Bullock had been around the church either. But his expression didn't change.

"Oh, you weren't there?" Sam looked at Bullock steadily.

"No!" Bullock gulped.

Sam paused a full forty-five seconds before he spoke again.

"Just what did you do yesterday evening, Mr. Bullock, after you left my office?"

"Well, I went home and ate dinner."

Another long silence.

Bullock twitched. "Then I finished grading my second hour's quiz." He looked up and stared at Sam. "Then I watched the news and went to bed."

Sam gave him another long silence before he spoke again. "Mr. Bullock, when did you give the second hour quiz?"

"Yesterday."

"And after school you went out to Lattimore's Park, looking for evidence of Satanism?"

"Well, yes. But that wasn't really after school. It was during fifth hour. I'm free then, but I had to be back for football practice."

"Did you take the test papers to Lattimore's Park with you?"

"Oh, no. I knew I was coming right back."

"So you picked them up before football practice?"

"Well, no. I—I was a little late."

"And after football practice, you went to see Chief Evans over at City Hall."

Bullock nodded.

"Then you picked up Tink and came to see me. So when did you pick up the test papers?"

Bullock sighed. "Well, after dinner."

"So after you left my office you went home and had dinner. Then you went back to the school?"

Bullock spoke rapidly. "I just sat down in my classroom and graded them. Then I posted the marks in my grade book. I wasn't there long!"

"So you weren't at the church yesterday evening, but you were at the high school. Seventy-five yards away."

"A lot of people were at the high school last night, Sheriff. There was a meeting of the band boosters. Nearly all the band parents were there. That meeting was breaking up as I got there." He gave a nervous laugh. "And Mr. Kelleher was there. He'll know I didn't go near the church." Bullock sat back in his easy chair and patted his hair again.

"Did you know Revels?"

"Who?"

"The victim, Mr. Bullock. The man you saw in my office yesterday evening."

Bullock stared. "Was that the man! I didn't remember— I didn't recognize him! Sheriff Titus, I tried to tell you not to encourage riffraff—"

"Did you know him?" Sam spoke a little more loudly, and the question sent Bullock back into his pompous mode.

"Certainly not!"

"Where did you live fifteen years ago?"

Bullock looked surprised. "Fifteen years ago? Why do you want to know that?"

"Just answer the question, please."

"I was teaching in the Richardson, Texas, school system at that time."

"So you were living in the Dallas area?"

"That is correct."

"What made you decide to give up big city life?"

The coach went through his throat-clearing routine before he replied. "Well, I was ready for a change. My life—well, my wife and I got a divorce, and I felt that a clean break would make it easier for both of us."

"What attracted you to Holton?"

"The job, Sheriff. I wanted to get back into coaching."

"How did you hear about the job?"

More throat clearing. "Well. There was an ad in a professional journal."

"You didn't know anybody here in town?"

"Well, yes. Years ago I taught with Leona Kephart. She left teaching. Now she's the publisher of the *Courier*."

Sam nodded solemnly. "Yes. And she's president of the Holton Board of Education, isn't she?"

"Sheriff, I assure you—there was nothing improper in my employment! I am fully qualified as a teacher and coach. Mr. Kelleher himself told me that my experience was far wider than any other applicant's."

"I'm sure it was, Mr. Bullock. A town the size of Holton attracts two kinds of teachers—young ones looking for experience and older ones who have family ties in the area. I guess I'm just trying to fit you into the pattern."

Bullock laughed nervously again.

"And you don't fit," Sam said. "So why are you here?"

"I told you, Sheriff. I wanted to make a clean break— get back into coaching—take up life in a new community!"

"How will it benefit you if Satanism is being practiced in Holton?"

"Benefit me! Benefit me? It won't benefit me in any way! I find the whole idea shocking. I'm appalled at the prospect!"

"Then why do you keep telling people about it? People like Dallas television reporters?"

"You can't hide the truth! I won't be a party to any sort of cover-up!"

Sam leaned forward. "Neither will I," he said. The very quietness of his voice emphasized his statement. "But I won't be stampeded into making statements to the press when I don't know anything yet." He gestured in the direction of the door. "You can go, Bullock, but I'd appreciate your not speculating to reporters about what's happened here—at least until we get a few facts."

Bullock bounced to his feet, but Sam spoke again as the coach put his hand out to open the door. "Nolan Porter was the student who told you about the stuff you picked up over at Lattimore's Park, wasn't he?"

"I didn't tell you that!"

"Yes, you did, Mr. Bullock. You told me that last night by the way you acted when you met Nolan on the porch of the sheriff's office."

"Sheriff!"

"Good-bye, Mr. Bullock."

"But what should I tell Nolan?"

"Nothing. Good-bye."

After the door closed behind him, I grinned at Sam. "Good job," I said.

Sam grinned back. "He's a cream puff."

"Why did he come to Holton, Sam? Why does he keep butting in? What is he up to?"

"I'll check with his previous employer, but I'm willing to bet he was either bounced or allowed to resign. He probably turned to his old girlfriend Leona Kephart and pressured her for help getting a job in a small town school system."

"Oh. Then he's just trying to hide lack of professional success?"

Sam shook his head. "No, that wouldn't explain his delight over this Satanism stuff. There's more to it. He takes entirely too much pleasure in that."

"Then what is he after?"

"Who knows? Kelleher's job, maybe? Remember what Starr said about his poking around in the office all the time?"

Then the door opened, and Sonny Blacksaddle came back in. He and Sam sorted out a few details while I rewound the tapes and repacked my camera bag. Sonny went to the school to get a list of everyone who had been there the night before.

Sam turned to me. "I'm starving," he said. "We missed breakfast, and it's after eleven. Think you could stand a hamburger at The Hangout? Maybe Ollie will know something about Revels."

The Hangout is the social and information exchange center of Holton, U.S.A. Ollie is The Hangout's absolute monarch, and her husband, Lou, makes the best hamburgers in the United States. It had been the only restaurant open in Holton the night before, and it was the place Revels had been bound for when he left the sheriff's office. If Ollie had cross-examined the guy, she'd know his whole life history.

The Hangout is on Main Street, in a block that was once the core of the three-block business district of a prosperous little farming community. But today about half the buildings on Main Street are deserted. The bank hangs on, and a hardware store and one clothing store keep going despite the competition from discount stores in neighboring towns. Holton doesn't rate a Wal-Mart.

But The Hangout does a good business, because the smell of grease from its exhaust fan lures hamburger freaks for fifty miles around. As Sam angled the patrol car into a parking place across the street from the courthouse, in front of the restaurant, I saw that the late-morning lull was on. The ten o'clock coffee drinkers had headed back to work, and the lunch bunch hadn't hit.

Ollie was a tall, gaunt woman who wore her hair teased eight inches high. As usual, she wore a white uniform covered with a flowered apron. Today's apron featured pink, orange, and yellow flowers, and its edges were bound with pink bias tape that didn't quite match the pink in the print. Her huge pink plastic earrings didn't match either tape or print, but they drew the eye directly to her elephantine ears.

"Howdy, Young Sam!" she croaked. "Hi there, Nicky! I was hopin' y'all would drop in. What's goin' on out there at the church?"

"I don't know yet, Ollie," Sam said. "All I know is it made me miss my breakfast. I'll have two cheeseburgers, with pickles and mustard. Skip the onions today. And a Coke."

He slid onto one of the stools at the Formica-topped counter, and I sat beside him. "One cheeseburger for me, Ollie. The usual. With french fries. Sam'll help me eat them."

"Lou, you ol' fool! Get them burgers on!"

Ollie hollered our orders back to Lou, her husband. In four months of patronizing The Hangout several times a week, I'd never heard Ollie say anything pleasant to the poor guy. He was a meek, hairless man, very clean looking, who seemed to spend his whole life in the tiny kitchen visible behind The Hangout's counter. But Ollie's rough talk didn't seem to bother him; I had never seen him when he wasn't smiling.

"I'm glad you mentioned this deal at the church, Ollie," Sam went on. "I'm going to have to ask you and Lou to make statements about the guy who's been killed. He did eat supper in here last night, didn't he?"

Ollie squinted at us. "That stranger? Then it was him?"

"Yeah. That's the one. We gave him a lift into town, then he said he was coming down here for dinner."

"Liver and onions." The words came from the kitchen, and the voice that said them was loud and deep. I stared through the pass-through window. Lou had spoken. I had begun to think the man was a mute. Now he looked at us through the opening, grinning and nodding.

Ollie nodded, too. "Yes, that was what he had. Liver and onions, mashed potatoes, and corn. Coleslaw. Black coffee. Lemon pie." She leaned across the counter and lowered her voice. "He was a strange one."

"Why?"

"Well, all that giggling. When I ask a feller if he wants a piece of pie, and the question makes him laugh— well, he made me nervous. I thought he was drunk—or something. Then I decided he was just sort of silly. He kept sayin' things, religious things. 'Praise the Lord!' for cole slaw and 'Thank you, Jesus!' over a piece of liver. Just makin' a spectacle of himself."

"Did you have any conversation with him?"

"Not to speak of. A'course, I asked him what brought him to Holton. He said he was lookin' for a job. And I told him he was probably wastin' his time here."

"Did he say what kind of a job? Or where he was from? Or give you any other sort of personal information?"

Ollie shook her head.

"He was a teacher." Lou's deep voice boomed out the information.

"Lou, you ol' fool! Where'd you get that idea?"

"He was asking you about the schools hereabouts." Lou made the pronouncement, then disappeared from sight, moving into the deeper recesses of the kitchen.

Ollie turned back to us and lifted her eyebrows. "Well, I guess Lou is right. He did ask about schools. But he acted so pee-culiar that I never thought of him as a teacher. I wouldn't even want to see him take on a job around kids—even as a janitor!"

"He didn't tell you where he was from?"

Ollie shook her head, sending the pink earrings swinging.

"Did you ever see him before?"

"Nope. And I'da remembered that feller, too."

"Well, who all was in here last night?" Sam asked.

"Lordy! Who all wasn't? They had that band boosters meeting, you know. Of course, a lot of the band parents are mad, as usual, so there was a big gang there. A bunch of people came by here at the end of it. They were arguing about the letter jackets."

"Was Revels still here when they came?"

"No, he'd left by then, I reckon. Let's see. Who was in here earlier?" Ollie took a pencil from her uniform pocket and delicately inserted its point into her teased hair. She scratched a spot on her scalp, frowning.

"That bunch of football players was by. Then that Engelman girl came in with a couple more of them later. Nolan Porter and that Blacksaddle boy. I hope her grandmother don't hear about that."

"Mrs. Engelman doesn't approve of Starr being out with Nolan?" Sam sounded puzzled.

"It ain't Nolan she was out with, Young Sam, it was Tom. And 'Cretia Engelman's an old-timer. She don't want her granddaughter hangin' around with Indians, though that Tom acts nicer than the white boys. And I hear tell that Mary Blacksaddle feels the same way. She's real active in tribal affairs, you know. She'd be happier if Tom dated Indian girls—long as they's Kiowas."

Sam nodded, and Ollie went on.

"The kids was all laughin' and carryin' on. Some of the other girls came a little later—Doreen Lyons and Karen Schultz. Maybe one or two others. Leona Kephart came in. Hamburger steak and french fries and lots of ketchup. Said she'd been workin' late. Brock Blevins and Jack Rich. They sat in the back booth and had some kind of big confab. Didn't order nothin' but coffee and pie. Ramsey Kelleher ate dinner in here like he does most nights. Chicken fried steak and cream gravy. And Virginia Cramer came by and got a hamburger to go. Said she was on her way out to that Haunted House to work."

Sam had pulled out his notebook and scribbled the names down in his illegible scrawl. "I was afraid you'd had a crowd," he said. "I'll have to ask every one of them if they noticed Revels."

"All of 'em noticed him, Young Sam. Like I said, he was weird. The high school kids got to mimickin' him. I thought we'd have a fight on our hands, but it didn't seem to bother this fellow—Revels? Was that his name? But those boys was cuttin' up something fierce, and the girls was tellin' them to shut up, then gigglin' and eggin' them on. All except that Engelman girl. She's real serious, you know. She got kinda mad and finally walked out with Tom. But the kids did quiet down after that—without me havin' to tell 'em to. I was ready to go back there. Then the kids all left—'cept Nolan. He hung around a while, lookin' out the window. Then he run out, too."

"So Revels didn't seem to know anybody?"

"Not that I noticed. But they might not have admitted it—he was actin' that peculiar. A'course, he wasn't the only peculiar-actin' person in last night." Ollie turned to me and nodded wisely. "You Maids and Matrons better keep an eye on your chairman—she might haunt that house personal."

"Virginia?" I was surprised. "She's been working awfully hard, but she seems to be her usual efficient self."

"Well, she was actin' strange last night. I think that husband of hers has finally drove her right round the bend. She hardly spoke to her own boss."

"To Mr. Kelleher?"

"Snubbed him. Sez he, 'Hello, Ginny.' Sez she, 'Good evenin', Mr. Kelleher.' 'I see you've got another busy evenin' comin' up,' sez he. And she don't even answer. Just nods and moves clear down on the other side of that stranger to wait for her hamburger." Ollie nodded like a dowager who didn't want her tiara to wobble. "It's that husband of hers. He's got her so spooked she's afraid to even act normal."

Virginia Cramer's husband was an alcoholic, and his problem was no secret around Holton. Apparently he was one of these morose drunks. Since he owned a restaurant and bar, he had plenty of evenings to sit around out there drinking—all alone, according to the gossip about how poor his business was. It must have made for a nerve-racking situation for Virginia. I had wondered if her unsatisfactory home life was one reason that she took on jobs such as Haunted House chief, volunteer jobs that kept her busy after work.

"She's got her problems," I said.

Ollie and I both nodded wisely, then we jumped in unison as an electronic voice broke the silence. "Sam. Where are you?"

"Sorry, ladies. It's the boss." Sam reached for his belt and moved his mobile radio close to his mouth.

"Nadine, this is Sam."

"Where are you?"

"At The Hangout. Sorry I forgot to check in."

"Well, you get over here. I want to report a crime."

Sam blinked. "Well, you've got the forms, Nadine. Is it a serious crime?"

"I'd say that a burglary of the Catlin County Sheriff's Office is pretty serious! You get over here!"

Sam almost lost his imperturbable facade as he jumped to his feet, but Ollie never turned a hair.

"Lou!" she yelled. "Make them cheeseburgers to go!"

EIGHT

. . . .

I WOUND UP PAYING FOR THE CHEESEBURGERS, SO Sam beat me in the one-block race to the office. But I was hard on his heels as I ran across the porch and burst into the main door.

Nadine was near the tantrum stage.

"Came right in here! Right in the front door!"

"You're okay?" Sam asked. "You didn't get hurt?"

"Hurt! I didn't even see the guy! And I wouldn't have been the one to get hurt! I could kill him! Breaking and entering! First-degree burglary! Right in the sheriff's own office!"

Sam blinked. "Second-degree burglary," he said. "First degree has to occur during hours of darkness."

"Whatever!" Nadine threw herself into her swivel chair with such vigor that the chair rolled backward and hit the wall. She sat glaring at Sam. Her skinny ankles were sticking out of neat brown slacks, and her right foot tapped out a nervous rhythm with a loafer heel.

Sam pulled up a chair and sat down. "Hand me a cheeseburger, Nicky. And let's get Nadine to give us a statement."

The statement boiled down to this. Nadine had been in the office, using the radio to do her businesslike best to keep an eye on what was going on out at the church, when the phone rang. A husky voice said, "I don't want to get involved, but someone's trying to break in your back door."

Nadine, once she had made sure they meant the sheriff's back door, not the caller's back door, had dropped the phone and headed for the back of the building, to the door that led to the carport. She hadn't found anyone there, but there had been scratches around the lock and the metal doorframe was bent. Someone had tried to pry the door open.

As she had stood in the carport, looking at the scratches and being careful not to touch anything, she had heard a noise inside the office. She had opened the door and called out. No one answered, but she heard a door shut. She crept cautiously through the back hall and into the office. No one was there, and for a minute Nadine had been relieved. Then she realized that one of her desk drawers was open.

Her purse was out on top of the desk. The implication was that somebody had lured her out the back door so they could sneak in the front and rifle her desk.

"Did they take anything?" Sam asked.

"I haven't looked," Nadine answered. "I want everything in the office fingerprinted! I haven't touched a thing but that radio, and I'm not touching a thing until either you or Sonny has gone over this office! And y'all better not smear hamburger grease on any evidence!"

Sam didn't try to explain the unlikelihood of finding fingerprints. Nadine had worked for the city police and the sheriff's office for ten years; she knew that fingerprints are hardly ever usable. She was just mad, and there'd be no satisfying her with less than a full investigation.

So Sam called the mobile lab man to come by and look at the scratches around the back door's lock, and he got me to photograph them. The lab man checked

Nadine's purse, which was a shiny vinyl, but there were no fingerprints on it except her own. He and Sam concluded that the intruder had worn some sort of gloves.

And when they looked inside the purse, nothing was missing.

"Looks like you scared him off," Sam said.

By then Nadine had calmed down. "Well, it seems like a lot of trouble for a petty thief to go to," she said. "Surely no one would have tried to break in that back door just to steal my lunch money. Anybody would know a county employee wouldn't be carrying a bunch of cash, and I don't make a habit of keeping the family fortune in my desk drawer." The phone rang, and she picked it up. "Catlin County Sheriff's Office."

Sam and I moved into the back hall. "That back door is the puzzling part," he said. "I don't believe that happened while Nadine was in the office, because she would have heard something. And I think I would have noticed those scratches when I went out to run this morning. I'd have noticed those dents in the doorframe."

The sheriff's office had been deserted after I left for my morning walk. Usually the jailer is there to answer the phone, but last night's dearth of prisoners had left a gap filled by a little deal Sam has with the Holton Police Department and his call-forwarding gadget.

The back door is usually kept locked. Sam, the deputies, the jailers, Nadine, and I all have keys, though Nadine often uses the front door, as she had that morning. I'd gone in the front, too, when I came back for my camera bag, and I'd dashed back out without looking at the door. If the deputies are bringing in a prisoner, they radio ahead and someone meets them to open the back door. The door opens into a square entry hall that has more doors than wall space. There's the outside door, the door to the basement cells, the door to the front office, the door to the office restroom, and the door to the stairs. The stairs lead up to the second floor—storage and a deputies' lounge—and the third-floor apartment Sam and I were living in.

Like Sam, I hadn't noticed any scratches around the lock when I went out the back door to meet Katherine. So we concluded that the attempted break-in had come between six-forty-five and the time Nadine had arrived, seven-thirty.

"But what were they after?" I asked. "It couldn't have been Nadine's billfold if she wasn't even in the office yet."

I stared around the back entry. Sam insisted that the area be kept clear, with all doors shut. There wasn't a throw rug on the tile floor or a wastebasket in the corner. The floor was completely bare.

Suddenly I realized what was missing.

"Revels's bedroll!"

Sam and I yelled it out at the same moment. The canvas cover with a star on each end had been sitting in the back hall, just beside the door to the jail. It was gone.

Had the intruder taken it? It could be crucial evidence. It might reveal where Revels came from or even who he knew in Holton.

Sam whirled and strode into the office. "Nadine!"

She was just hanging up the telephone. "Some idiot wanting to gossip about your corpse out there. Said she heard he had horns and a tail."

"Nadine! Did you see that bedroll?"

Nadine stared blankly. "Bedroll? You mean that bag out there in the back hall?"

"Yes. Could the burglar have taken it?"

My heart was down around my knees. Why hadn't I put the bedroll in a safe place when I came back to get my camera gear?

But Nadine just shrugged. "I put it in the closet."

"Thank God!" Sam grabbed the key from Nadine's

desk, crossed the office in two jumps, and opened the storage closet. There on the floor was the navy blue canvas bag.

"Nadine, I may kiss you!" Sam said.

"Humph." Nadine snorted firmly. "All I did was follow the routine you set up yourself. You said you didn't want anything left in that back entry to trip over. What is that bag, anyway?"

I did kiss Nadine. Then I explained that the bag was evidence, that it might even hold all the earthly belongings of a murder victim. We speculated that the murderer had tried to break in the back door to get it, but had been unsuccessful. Luckily Nadine had hidden it away in the closet, so he still hadn't found it—if that's what the break-in was all about.

We all looked the bag over. It was a yard or so long and maybe a foot or a little more in diameter. A shiny vinyl star glittered on each end.

But as Sam lifted the case onto a table, it rolled over on its side. And suddenly the star took on a subtly different shape. With two points at the top, rather than at the bottom, it became a pentagram.

I shivered. Would the Satanism motif continue to haunt this case?

I saw Sam eyeing the star, too, but he said nothing. Then he unzipped the bag. "We'd better inventory this, Nadine. And Nicky, we might need pictures."

Revels's belongings had been rolled into a thin orange nylon sleeping bag, then stuffed into the canvas holder. Sam pulled the sleeping bag out and laid it on the office work table.

He looked into the canvas holder. "The rest seems to be cooking stuff." He laid the bag on the floor, then began to unroll the sleeping bag. Each turn revealed Revels's pitiful life.

There were three pairs of clean underpants and two pairs of dirty ones, with the dirty ones wrapped in plastic. The plastic also held two pairs of dirty socks. A toothbrush and a small tube of toothpaste in a color that matched the dried stuff stuck in the bristles. A plastic bag holding three throwaway razors. Small can of shaving cream. Soap dish holding three motel-sized bars. One clean shirt, plaid flannel. It was a printed plaid, not a woven one, and Nadine and I explained to Sam that this indicated a cheap brand.

Two T-shirts, one white and one black. Neither had a message. An extra pair of jeans and three pairs of white cotton socks. A towel and a washcloth. A sweatshirt.

Each of the larger items—jeans, flannel shirts, towel— was laid out flat inside the sleeping bag, and the smaller items—toothbrush, soap, socks—were spaced along it so that the whole thing would roll up into the smallest possible bundle.

After Nadine had made a list of the items rolled into the sleeping bag, Sam picked up the canvas container. "Let's see about this."

The rest of Revels's belongings seemed just as ordinary. A battered Boy Scout camping set—plate, cup, and skillet that all fit together. A paring knife and a bent fork and spoon. A chunk of cheese in a deli sack and crackers in a flat plastic container. An apple. A small package of Kleenex. Matches. A flashlight. And a Bible.

The Bible was a King James Version, on onionskin paper, featuring tiny type. Sam thumbed through it.

"It's all underlined," he said. "I guess he used it for study."

"He talked about God so much, I guess that's only logical," I said.

"Ah ha!" Sam pointed to the flyleaf. "Someone's written in it."

The inscription was brief. "To a new brother in the faith. May your life be richly blessed." It was signed in the same handwriting. "Pastor Sydney Jenkins Jones." A date about a year back was written below.

"I'm afraid that doesn't tell us much," Sam said. "Whoops!"

A piece of cloth had fallen out of the back of the Bible and fluttered to the floor. Sam picked it up.

"What's this?" He held it out and the three of us examined it.

"It's almost like a sampler," Nadine said.

It was a scrap of white fabric, linen or cotton, around eighteen inches square. It was covered with tiny designs and centered with a large blue star. Or was it a pentagram? The overall design was really circular, and that made it impossible to tell which way was right side up.

The figures surrounding the star were Greek columns, dainty red flowers, and—I looked closely to be sure—yes, they were tiny bulls. Cute little critters in various poses. And some of the red flowers grew on vines that were climbing up some of the Greek columns.

These were the main elements of the design, but the entire cloth was covered with esoteric patterns—small stars, lunettes, tiny suns with extended rays, and rainbows. Each of them was an individual design and each used different embroidery stitches. I decided Nadine had identified it correctly. It was a sampler.

And it was beautifully done. The work was exquisite, with tiny stitches in exact lines. The overall design was a bit naive, maybe, but samplers are supposed to be naive. It was a lovely piece of work. And it had been washed, if not ironed, recently. Revels had tried to take care of it.

What was it doing in a tramp's bedroll? Tucked inside a Bible? And what did it mean? Were the symbols Satanic? Or was it just a design?

"Stranger and stranger," Sam said. "I hope there's something about Revels on the California records."

"The teletype came in. I put it on your desk," Nadine answered. "He did have a record."

Sam laid the sampler across the pile of items from the bedroll and picked up the carrying case. "I think that's all." He opened the case wide and shook it. Something rattled. "One last item."

Sam pulled out a tangled silver chain with something silver wrapped in it. He painstakingly unwound the chain until the pointed object was clear of its tangles, then laid it across Revels's flannel shirt.

There was no question about this star. It was definitely upside down. A pentagram.

Sam turned it over. It had once had a loop that held it right side up, making it a star. That loop had been pried off and a second one soldered on to make it a pentagram.

"Damn." Sam said. "Don't let Bullock see this."

I told Nadine about Bullock's announcement to the high school athletes and to the Dallas television station.

"That Bullock's an odd one," she said. "My son's in his second hour. He says the kids all make fun of him."

We had the items listed, photographed, and all packed away in the bedroll before Sonny came into the office. Sonny looked worried.

"Here's that list of names for you, Sam," he said. "Do you think I can go out on my regular patrol now?"

Sam blinked, and I expect I did, too. Cops are like anybody else. They like excitement. When there's a big case on—and any kind of a killing was a big case in Catlin County—they all want to be involved. The problem is in continuing to handle the routine business. Officers rarely want to leave the murder investigation to go back to their regular patrols.

Sam pulled out his little notebook and looked over

the scrawls it contained. "I think you and I need to split up the band booster list and the list I got from Ollie, and we need to start questioning all these people about what they saw over at the church last night. Did you have something on your regular patrol that was particularly pressing?"

Sonny shook his head slowly. "No. I guess not."

"I know you've been trying to track down that drug lab rumor, but surely that can wait."

"It could tie in," Nadine said. "I told you the teletype came in from California. Revels had a drug record."

Sam and Sonny read the teletype, and Nadine filled me in. "Revels did five years hard time in California for manufacturing amphetamines," she said. "He was paroled five years ago and received his final release last year."

Sonny was staring at the floor. For once he wasn't gesturing. "I didn't want drugs to get mixed up in this," he said.

"Does his record show any link with this part of the country?" I asked.

"No," Nadine said. "He was born in California. He did a shorter stint in prison in Massachusetts, getting out nine years ago. That was for possession with intent to distribute, but he got a light sentence since it was a first conviction. His last known residence is in Los Angeles."

Sam looked up. "That address was a year ago. Maybe that's where he knew this Pastor Sydney Jenkins Jones. What's the area code for L.A.?"

The phone rang then, with another call from a citizen who had heard that devil worshipers had invaded Holton. It was obvious Nadine was going to be tied up, so I volunteered to try to track down Pastor Jones.

Sam and Sonny began to coordinate the list of people who had been at the school with the list of those who had been at The Hangout. The people who were on both lists would be the first people quizzed, Sam said. But every band booster would have to be asked if he'd seen anything at the church the evening before. They both sighed deeply. It was going to be a big job, and Sam had only a few people to do it.

I went to the telephone and called Los Angeles information. It took me only a minute to discover there was no "Jones, Sydney Jenkins" in the Los Angeles area. Since we had no idea of Jones's denomination, it looked as if the next step was a call to the L.A. police or sheriff's department.

Then I had a hunch—the first one I'd ever had. I called Tink and asked him which denominations used the title "pastor."

"Lutheran," he said. "But any of them can. Catholic priests who are in charge of a parish church, for example, are officially titled 'Pastor,' though most people would call them 'Father.' How come you need to know?"

I explained.

Tink thought about it. "Well, that leaves the field wide open, Nicky. If Revels was a kind of down-and-outer, he may have been at some mission—the Salvation Army or some sort of independent shelter. I don't know what to tell you."

I thought about that a minute, with Nadine's conversations soaking into my subconscious ("No, the sheriff's not sure it was witchcraft, ma'am. No, no one has reported any sacrifices of cattle.") Then I thanked Tink and asked the L.A. information operator for the *Los Angeles Times*. In minutes I was talking to a reporter in the religion section.

"Pastor Sydney Jenkins Jones? Just a minute." There was the click, click of a computer keyboard. "I thought I remembered the name. We have a Pastor Sydney Jenkins Jones listed at the New Eden Mission."

"Do you know anything about the mission?"

"Not really. We used them in a roundup story on agencies that offer aid to the homeless and such. Now you say this is a sheriff's office? In Oklahoma? Is the pastor in trouble?"

I told her it was an attempt to identify a drifter found dead in Catlin County, and she lost interest. I hung up with the telephone number of the New Eden Mission and a better understanding of just why reporters can be so suspicious of lawmen. After all, I'd just deliberately misled one. I hadn't mentioned Revels was dead as in murdered.

But the person who answered the phone at the New Eden Mission wasn't surprised to hear a request for Pastor Sydney Jenkins Jones, and in a couple of minutes a pleasant and very feminine contralto said, "Hello."

"I'm trying to reach Pastor Sydney Jenkins Jones."

"This is Syd."

"Oh?" I cursed the surprise I'd let creep into my voice. "Sheriff Sam Titus of Catlin County, Oklahoma, has a few questions for you. Please hold while I get him on the line."

I touched the hold button and yelled, "Sam! Pastor Jones is on the line. She's a woman!"

Then I looked down and realized the hold button hadn't caught. I had yelled right in the pastor's ear.

"Oh, my God!" I was doing worse and worse. "Sorry, Pastor Jones. I didn't mean to deafen you."

I heard a throaty laugh. "Don't let it bother you. First my parents gave me a name of ambiguous gender, then I went into a profession associated with masculinity, so I confuse everybody. I think I heard a click. Is the sheriff on the line?"

"Yes, ma'am," Sam said. "Nicky, will you please take notes."

"Well, Sheriff, if you're in Oklahoma, you must be calling about Damon Revels. That's the only one of my parishioners that I know was headed in that direction. Is Damon in trouble?"

"I'm afraid so, Pastor Jones. Pretty bad trouble. He's dead."

"Oh, no! Not Damon! I thought we had him pretty well straightened out. It wasn't an overdose?"

"No, ma'am. Mr. Revels apparently was killed by a blow to the back of the head. I'm afraid it's murder."

Quickly Sam sketched the situation in which Revels's body was discovered and told the pastor how little information he had available. "We discovered your name on a Bible he carried in his swag," he concluded.

"Poor Damon."

"I agree, Pastor Jones. We don't like people getting killed this way around here, and I assure you we'll do everything we can to catch the person who did this. I'm hoping you can help us. Revels indicated he'd come to Holton to see someone, someone he'd known in the past. Would you know who that was?"

"No, but it makes sense."

"Why is that?"

"Well, Damon—as I'm sure you gathered from his prison record—was a former drug user, abuser, seller, manufacturer. About a year ago he had a sort of epiphany, and he did a complete switch and became actively antidrug."

"Sort of like a reformed drunk who smashes bottles?"

"Exactly! But Damon—well, I suspect the years of drug abuse had left him with some brain damage."

"I suspect that myself. One of the women who met him said he acted 'real silly,' and that was my impression, too."

"So you see what I'm talking about." The contralto

sounded relieved. "Damon didn't always have real good judgment. A couple of months ago, for example, he went to one of the hottest corners in town—hottest for the drug trade, I mean—and began preaching against drugs right there on the street."

"Not real smart."

"Naturally he got beaten up. When I scolded him for doing such a foolish thing, he smiled and told me it was the Lord's will. And I think he took a notion it was the Lord's will for him to go to Oklahoma."

"Well, I don't know that our drug dealers are any less likely to beat a guy up—"

"No, it was some other reason, Sheriff. Something I didn't fully understand. I was away at a meeting last week, before he left, or I would have quizzed him."

"Then you don't know why he came?"

"No, but I can take a guess." Pastor Jones took a couple of deep breaths before she went on. "Damon had become fixated on atonement, on making things up to people he had wronged in the past. He would seek out people—his brother, for example—to ask for their forgiveness.

"Of course, I tried to explain to Damon that forgiveness comes from God and that we can only accept His grace, not worry too much about other people's forgiveness. But he was sort of cracked on the concept. Part of his brain damage, I guess."

"I can see that as a potentially dangerous habit."

"I'm afraid you're right, Sheriff. His brother wasn't glad to see him. Most of us would rather simply let the past stay buried. And most of us are not very strong on forgiveness. But he kept on, trying to tell people he was sorry."

"But you don't know which resident of Holton he thought he had wronged?"

"No, Sheriff. I'm no help to you there."

"Could Revels have been involved in Satanism? Demonology?"

"Absolutely not!" Pastor Jones's voice was strong and firm. "He considered all that sort of thing as linked to the drug culture. He was very much against it."

Sam thanked her and promised to tell her when Revels's body was released for burial so that she could make arrangements. "We can't afford to bring the body back," she said. "Besides, what happens to the earthly shell—that's not important. We'll hold a memorial service here at the mission. I don't know if his brother will want to be involved or not."

Sam collected the name of Revels's brother and the town he lived in. "I don't think he'll be able to tell you anything," Pastor Jones said as she hung up.

"And she's probably right," Sam was saying as I went into his office. "I think that when Revels entered the drug culture, his family dropped him. When he turned his back on the drug culture, his friends dropped him. He'd become a real loner."

"If he was going around trying to atone for past misdeeds—" I started. Then I quit talking.

Sam put my thought into words. "What citizen of Holton, U.S.A., is going to admit being mixed up with some sort of crazy druggie—even fifteen years ago?"

The phone was still getting a workout from concerned citizens who had heard that demons were loose in Catlin County, so I didn't react when it rang again. But this time Nadine called my name.

"Nicky! It's for you! Brenda! Line one!"

Brenda. Sam's sister-in-law. The very person who had convinced me I should join the Maids and Matrons Club and who had talked me into taking over as chairman of the Dracula's Tomb vignette. She'd been the original chairman, but she wanted to drop it when she enrolled in college. We'd become friends, in a way, though we didn't have a lot in common. I didn't want to talk to her right now, but I couldn't see how to avoid it.

I picked up the phone on Sam's desk and punched the right button.

"Hi. What's up?"

"I'm sorry to call you there, but I couldn't raise you at the apartment."

"That's okay. I'm just trying to help out down here."

"Can you get loose for a meeting at four o'clock?"

"A meeting? What sort of meeting?"

"Haunted House. Virginia asked me to call everyone I can reach. She says we've got to decide whether we should drop the whole project or not."

NINE

....

SAM HAD LEFT ONLY ONE CORNER OF THE CHURCH parking lot off limits, but the murder scene drew a lot of attention as the Maids and Matrons arrived at the church for the called meeting. Everyone was pointing in that direction.

I admit that I stared at the little metal barn and its outline of yellow tape as I parked my tomato red Volkswagen as far away as I could get, and Katherine Dawkins was staring at it so hard she nearly bumped into me as she got out of her Fiesta.

"Hi," I said. She jumped all over and whirled around, ponytail flying.

"Oh, hi, Nicky." Katherine pushed back her straight brown bangs. "Some excitement we walked into this morning."

"Yeah. And this meeting may turn out to be pretty exciting, too. What do you think they'll do about the Haunted House?"

"I don't know. I sure hate to waste all that work. But on the other hand, there's such a thing as good taste. A real murder seems a bit too authentic for a fund-raising project."

We walked into the church together and followed the sound of women's voices to the senior high Sunday school classroom, where a group of fifteen or so was already gathered. Virginia Cramer had taken the head of the table and was looking through a ledger. She was back in control, every hair in place, and wearing a coordinated outfit. Brenda was seated halfway down one side.

Katherine and I, as befits new members, took seats at the back of the classroom, with our backs against the chalkboard. The room wasn't going to hold many more. All the folding chairs were full, and the plastic-topped table was surrounded. So when Leona Kephart came in a minute later, she simply stood beside me at the back of the room and greeted us in her usual nasal whine. "Hi, y'all."

"I'll get you a chair," Katherine told her, rising.

"Oh, no, don't bother for me," Leona said. She hugged her thin body with her toothpick arms. "I've been bent over in that darkroom for an hour, printing a picture for the next issue, and I'm ready to stand up straight a minute. 'Sides, Virginia's 'bout to start."

Virginia rapped for order—she was a great one for following Robert's Rules to the last semicolon—and started passing around a stack of photocopies. As the stack headed down the side of the table, I could see that she was handing out a financial report.

"I'm sure we're all shocked by the dreadful occurrence discovered this morning in the storage shed," Virginia said briskly. "My first thought was that this crime would mean we should drop the entire Haunted House project."

A few groans went up, and some I-told-you-sos.

Virginia raised her voice just enough to still the murmurs. "Then I asked for a financial report, which I'm passing out to you now. And that puts a different face on the matter."

By now the sheets had reached our end of the table, and I took one from Katherine for myself and handed the last one to Leona Kephart. A glance at the big fat figure in the debit column identified Virginia's concern.

"We owe that much?" Brenda said plaintively.

Virginia nodded. "You all voted to borrow the money. Sorry about that."

"I don't suppose there's any act-of-God insurance," I said.

"I don't think you can call a murder an act of God, anyway," Katherine murmured.

We all stared glumly at the financial sheet. We'd blithely borrowed money to finance the Haunted House from the First State Bank of Holton, confident we'd make it back on soft-drink sales alone. We'd spent the loan money and the club treasury, too. If we called off the project, we'd be deeply in debt.

Virginia cleared her throat. "Do I hear a motion?"

"Well." Leona Kephart's voice was whinier than ever. "Well. I see the problem, but I just don't see how we can go on with the Haunted House."

"Do you have an alternate plan for raising the money?"

"No." Leona sighed and waved a skinny hand. "But maybe we ought to drop it. You all know that I opposed this project from the first."

She looked around at the other members. Their faces looked pretty stony to me. But Leona went on. "As Geor—well, as someone told me this morning, maybe this is an omen. Or something."

"Personally, I don't believe in omen-seeking," Virginia said firmly. "Does anybody have another suggestion on how we could raise this money?"

Silence.

"Is any member willing to pick up the loan out of the family budget?"

More silence. There are few wealthy people in Holton. I suppose the Tituses are as well off as anyone—or at least they own a lot of land. But big chunks of that land were mortgaged, and Big Sam's injury and his rehabilitation expenses had left cash tight. Sam often drew only part of the salary he was allotted for running the ranch, and he and I lived on his earnings as sheriff. In a personal emergency Sam and I could borrow money from my dad, since generals take home pretty good salaries, but my dad was looking at retirement within a couple of years, and he needed to conserve his assets to be ready to make a change in life-style. He'd inherited zilch from his family.

Besides, who wants to start their married life in debt to their families? So Sam and I had no more resources to help out the Maids and Matrons than any of the other members of the club did. And none of them seemed to be on the well-to-do list.

Finally I held up my hand. "I move we continue the Haunted House project."

"Second." That was Brenda.

Virginia seemed relieved. "Any discussion?"

"Well," Leona whined, "well, are you sure this is okay with the sheriff, Nicky?"

"I don't think he'd like us to use the shed, and I certainly don't want to go near it, for that matter. But he can hardly keep people away from the church, and the Haunted House building was not involved in the crime in any way. So why would he object?"

"Because of the Satanism link."

"What Satanism link?" Virginia's voice was incredulous.

"Well, George Bullock—" Leona paused and put a hand to her stringy neck. She gulped before she went on. "George is an old friend of mine, and he says Halloween is a major holiday for Satanists. And we all know that this terrible crime has some link with Satanism."

Virginia's eyes bugged. "Do we know that? I didn't know it."

Leona gave a whiny titter. "Well, there was the evidence George found over at Lattimore's Park. There was the pentagram, the candle—"

Her voice trailed off, but I could see Virginia getting pinched around the mouth. Virginia knew more about the pentagram and the candle than Leona did. She was bearing up, but she hadn't enjoyed starting her day by getting up close and personal with a murder victim.

"I hadn't heard about any of this," Virginia said.

That surprised me, since the phone at the sheriff's office was still bringing in new gossip and rumors with every ring. And Virginia had been there when George Bullock made his first announcement after Revels's body was discovered. How had she missed it?

But maybe people didn't want to talk to Virginia about it—since she'd found the body. Or maybe she'd refused to talk or to listen to them. She was getting as white in the face as one of Big Sam's Hereford cows.

So I spoke up fast. "Sam doesn't want me to comment on his investigations, of course, but there are a lot more possibilities to this case than Satanism."

"Well, George says—"

"When I left the office, Leona, you hadn't been by to talk to Sam about the case. And, of course, Sam will want to talk to you, to ask the newspaper's help in scotching these ridiculous rumors that are flying around. Somebody called and asked if the victim had horns and a tail!"

There were some titters at that, and the atmosphere lightened. Virginia called for a vote. When Leona saw that hers would be the only nay, she abstained.

"Okay, y'all, back to work!" Virginia said. "Nicky and Katherine, you two stay a minute."

Leona sat down as the chair next to me was vacated. "Nicky, does Sam think there's a coven in Holton?"

"He doesn't tell me everything he thinks, but a coven is associated with witchcraft, isn't it?"

"Well, yes. With that pentagram and that candle—"

"Those things are associated with Satanism. That's different from witchcraft."

"Oh. Well, George says—"

I interrupted. "You're a newspaper editor, Leona. You need to get your information straight from Sam, not from me or from George Bullock. Okay?"

"But Sam is looking at Satanism, isn't he?"

"Among other things. He likes hard evidence, the way most cops do. You know, footprints, fingerprints, hair, proximity—stuff like that."

"Proximity?"

"Finding out who was at the church yesterday evening."

Leona blinked, and I once again wondered if her IQ was in the normal range.

"Oh," she said. "You mean, like Katherine was up here?"

"Katherine?" My voice probably sounded as vacant as Leona's. I turned to Katherine.

What I saw shocked me. Katherine's face had flushed bright red. She didn't gasp, clutch her bosom, or faint, but she sure looked guilty. Her voice sounded calm enough when she spoke, though. "I came up to use the copier last night. I'll be glad to talk to Sam about it, but I didn't see anything."

Then what was eating her? I tried not to react as I turned back to Leona. "He'll want to talk to everybody who was at the church and to everybody who was at the school."

She nodded vacantly and stood up as Virginia walked toward us.

"Okay, you two are next," Virginia said. "We're keeping the Haunted House, but I think we're going to have to drop Dracula's Tomb. Got any ideas for a quick replacement?"

Leona left, and we discussed it. I was totally blank, but Katherine had an idea.

"Cannibal stew," she said.

"Great," Virginia said. "You can wear grass skirts."

"We'd have to wear them over long underwear," Katherine said. "It's cold in that basement. How about furry tunics instead? I'll contribute the old fake leopard bedspread Tink and I started housekeeping with."

"That would work. You can stick some leaves on the top of those pillars you were making into ruined columns for Dracula's tomb. Then wrap them with burlap and you'll have palm trees. Now, how about a kettle?"

I thought there was an old galvanized metal washtub out at the Titus ranch and an unused garbage can rack at the sheriff's department. We could build a papier-mâché kettle around the tub and put it on the rack, we decided. I was assigned to find some giant bones, not too hard a chore in cattle country, to dress the set, and Katherine said she'd make a fake fire out of colored paper and a yellow light bulb. As we started debating the relative effectiveness of masks versus makeup, Virginia left us.

"I haven't even been inside the Haunted House today," she said. "I was going to sort costumes before I went to school. So I'm way behind."

Katherine and I decided the cannibals could wear bright face paint, which would save us from having to make masks, as well as a kettle, out of papier-mâché.

"The church has a bunch of face paint," Katherine said. "They used it at the Bible school last summer. We can take that and replace it. I'll tell Tink what we're doing. Virginia's Sunday school superintendent, so she won't mind."

We trotted down to the Sunday school storage closet, which opened off the hall next to the day care center. I could hear the voices of Holton's children through the door. Most of them sounded happy. Lucretia Engelman was apparently succeeding in keeping the day care regimen undisturbed.

The storage closet was neatly organized, with every cardboard box on the shelves labeled and every plastic sack tagged. So the dried mud on the floor was out of place.

"Whoops!" Katherine said, pointing to the bits of dirt. "Someone's tracked in. Virginia will have a fit."

"Virginia?"

"Uh-huh. As Sunday school superintendent she's in charge of this, and she's real picky about neatness."

Katherine reached for a shoebox. "Face paint," she read. "She's also picky about labeling."

She carried the box back into the senior high classroom and opened it. It was a mishmash of half-used tubes of acrylic paint, brushes, lipsticks, containers of blush, and packs of eyeshadow in strange shades of purple and blue.

"Where'd the makeup come from?" I asked.

"Oh, the kids had a choice at the Bible school picnic. They could have their faces painted with a design, or they could have a 'glamour makeup.' A lot of the girls went for that. You should have seen Leona Kephart's face when her ten-year-old came out looking like a tart."

I laughed.

"She was wearing this Apricot Surprise lipstick that might be perfect for cannibals," Katherine said. "We could put it in stripes across the cheekbones. It might be easier to apply than this acrylic, and I don't see how it could be harder to get off."

She dug through the box, picking up lipsticks, reading their labels, and discarding them. "Purple Passion,

Plum Pink, Riotous Red—what's happened to the Apricot Surprise?"

She looked up at me, frowning. "Well, I guess we can use this purple. But that Apricot Surprise would have been great. It was the most marvelous bright orange."

Her words set off a bright orange flash in my mind. The last time I had seen something that color it had been drawn on the chest of Damon Revels.

"Bright orange lipstick?" My voice sounded weak, even to me.

"Right. I guess it didn't get back in the box," Katherine said.

Could the Bible school lipstick have been used to draw a pentagram on Damon Revels's chest?

No, I told myself. It was ridiculous.

Then I heard a quiet voice behind me. "Katherine? Where is the worship committee keeping the candles these days?"

It was Tink. He was standing in the doorway, frowning slightly.

"Oh, they're in a box in the storage closet," Katherine said. "They're labeled. But there were new ones out on the altar Sunday."

"I broke one of the new ones." Tink's voice sounded meek. "I moved the candlestick, and it fell right out. It hit the floor and snapped in two. A brand-new candle."

"It's not a big deal," Katherine said. "And it wasn't a really brand-new candle, because I know they'd been used last Sunday." She led the way to the storage closet. "I'll get you a new one."

She reached confidently for a box near the closet door, pulled it out, and opened it. "I'll give you two new candles. They ought to match." Then her eyes widened.

"Oh. There's only one candle in the box. Here, take it, and we'll burn it down to match the other one. But that's funny. The box holds a dozen, and we always use them in pairs. It's odd to find only one left over."

Tink frowned. "Maybe another got broken." He shrugged and turned toward the sanctuary.

I stared at him. Then I stared at the box of face paint and makeup. Candles. Orange lipstick.

"Wait a minute here," I said. "I think Sam ought to know about this."

Sam was there in a few minutes, and he agreed that the missing objects could be significant. Maybe. He had brought my camera bag, and the first thing he wanted photographed was the dirt on the closet floor. I resisted the temptation to ask why, at least until I got Sam alone. Then Sam gently scooped the dirt up, put it into a small cardboard box, and slid the box into an evidence sack.

"What does that mean?" Tink asked. "Can scientists find out where the dirt came from?"

"I can tell you that without consulting the scientists," Sam answered. "It came from that flower bed outside the south door of the church."

"Does that tell you anything?"

"No. I just thought that one hunk of dirt was an interesting shape. It reminded me of a worm."

Tink looked at Sam strangely. "Oh."

Sam nodded. "Now I want you to do me a favor, Tink. Go in to Mrs. Engelman and ask her if she noticed that something had been spilled in that closet when she got her supplies out of it this morning."

"But she doesn't use that closet, Sam."

Sam nodded again. "I didn't think she did."

"And it didn't have anything spilled in it."

"I know, Tink. Now will you ask her?"

Tink took off his glasses and rubbed his right eye. He frowned.

Katherine sighed. "Tink, Sam wants to find out if

Mrs. Engelman or some of her helpers could have tracked that mud in, but he doesn't want to alert her to the possibility that the killer got into the church and took something out of that closet. Okay? He's not trying to trap her, he just wants an impartial answer."

Sam grinned. "And I'm putting Katherine on the payroll. She sees right through me, and I want her on my side."

While Tink talked to Mrs. Engelman, Sam went into the church kitchen and went through the silverware drawers. The Community Church's kitchen was largely stocked with old silverware members had donated when the family knives and forks were replaced. Sam put five wooden-handled steak knives into an evidence bag and labeled them.

"Do they match the one that stabbed Revels?" I asked.

Sam shrugged. "Hard to say. They've been through the dishwasher a bunch, the way that one had. And there are only five of them. The folks' old set came in a group of six, as I recall."

Tink came back to report that Mrs. Engelman said neither she nor any of her staff members had been near the Sunday school closet that morning. So Sam nodded and checked the south door, the one nearest the shed. There was no sign of a break-in.

He and Tink made a complete circuit of the church, looking at all the doors and windows. There was no sign of a break-in at any of the other doors or windows, either. Any footmarks in the flower beds were just indistinct smears.

They were back at the south door, cleaning their shoes, when George Bullock pulled up in his Toyota.

"Well, Sheriff, I see you're still investigating," he said, shoving his elbow out the window. "Have you found out anything yet?"

"Most of what we've learned so far is negative. Of course, that's still helpful."

"How can negative information be helpful?"

"Well, Reverend Dawkins and I just ascertained that there are no signs that anyone broke into the church last night. That's pretty interesting."

Bullock stared at Sam. "Well, if you say so, Sheriff. I'd hope you're thoroughly checking the Satanism aspect."

"I've run into a problem with that, Mr. Bullock. I haven't been able to find Nolan. Did you tell him I was looking for him?"

"I haven't talked to him, Sheriff."

Sam nodded. "I understand."

Bullock colored and cleared his throat, and I realized that Sam had caught him in a lie. Bullock might not have talked to Nolan, but I was willing to bet he had passed the word through another student. Katherine's not the only one around here who can make a few deductions.

Bullock shifted gears. "I have to get over there to meet the football team," he said. "They're playing the Baldwin Badgers tonight." He pulled away. "Nolan had better show up for that. Do you want me to tell him you need to see him?"

"No. Let him play his game. I'll talk to him later."

Bullock drove off.

Sam turned to Tink. "Next question. Who has keys to the church?"

Tink looked stricken. "Then you think someone did get into the church last night?"

"I can't say for sure, Tink. The mud, the lipstick, the knife, the candles—well, that makes it look as if they did. But if—I repeat, if—they were Satanists, it makes the whole thing kind of odd."

"Why?"

"Well, Revels was laid out as if he'd been killed as

part of a ceremony, right? But if they had access to the church, why perform the ceremony in that shed?"

Tink's eyes widened. "You mean—a Black Mass?"

"Right. Supposedly, Satanists would be thrilled to turn a Christian ceremony upside down. So why go out to that shed to do it, when they could have used the church?"

We kicked it around a few minutes. Could they have been afraid they'd be seen? The sanctuary lights might have attracted attention, true, but they might not have attracted any more notice than activity at the shed would have.

Tink's idea was probably as good as any. He said the Holton Community Church might not be "holy" enough.

"I mean, to a nondenominational group like ours," he said, "a church building is just a meeting place. It's not regarded as sanctified ground in the sense a Catholic church or a religious shrine of some sort would be."

We all nodded, and Sam and Tink went back to the question of keys. Tink looked pained as he listed the number out, and Sam looked a bit pained himself by the time Tink totaled up the list. One key opened all the church's outside doors. Tink had one. So did the church secretary, the treasurer, Mrs. Engelman, the Sunday school superintendent, the organist, the part-time janitor, and the chairman of the maintenance committee.

I knew that some of these names were already on the lists Sam and Sonny had compiled, the lists of people who had been at the band meeting and at The Hangout. Holton's biggest banker, Brock Blevins, was serving a term as church treasurer, for example, and he'd been in The Hangout having coffee with Jack Rich, who was chairman of the maintenance committee. Virginia Cramer was Sunday school superintendent, another of the volunteer jobs I suspected she used as excuses to keep away from her husband. They'd all have keys.

"Can y'all keep this quiet?" Sam asked Tink and Katherine. "I'd like to know something about this case that George Bullock doesn't."

They nodded. Then Katherine spoke. "Sam, Nicky says you're taking statements from everybody who was at the church or the school last night."

"That's right."

"Well, as Leona Kephart was careful to tell Nicky, I was here. I came up to use the church copier. But I didn't see anything." She brushed her bangs back nervously, but she didn't seem as guilt stricken as she had when Leona first brought up her presence at the church.

"Oh? When was this?"

"About nine-thirty. I got John Peter in bed before I came. I guess I was here about forty-five minutes."

"Were there any other cars in the parking lot?"

"Just Virginia's truck. It was here when I came and still here when I left. There was nobody else around."

Sam nodded again, and we left. He loaded the camera bag into the Volkswagen for me and stood by to slam the door after I got in.

"I'll go over to the high school and use the darkroom," I said. "I checked with Mr. Kelleher. He said Leona Kephart was coming by earlier, but I know she's nearly through now."

Sam seemed to think seriously about that. "Well, maybe I'll come along if Mrs. Kephart's over there," he said.

"Why?"

"She wasn't on the list of people who attended the band boosters meeting. It would be interesting to know just how she came to find out that Katherine was up at the church last night."

TEN

....

LEONA KEPHART PUBLISHED THE *CATLIN COUNTY Weekly Courier*. A divorcee, she worked with her father, a morose old printer who stuck strictly to his typesetting computer and printing press. The newspaper was, I'd gathered, a sideline for the print shop and copy business, and it wasn't much as far as news went, relying mainly on rural correspondents and handouts from the county agent. If you gave them something typed, they'd put it straight into the paper with no changes, or at least that was the report I heard from the publicity chairman of Maids and Matrons. The county commissioners and Holton City Council received perfunctory coverage.

But the *Courier* looked fairly good typographically, maybe because its owners were printers, rather than news professionals. And Leona took lots of pictures for it. Her composition stank, from a photographer's point of view, but her father made good engravings, and Leona understood the importance of beginning with a clear print. I'd had only one class in photojournalism, so I didn't know much more about it than she did.

Leona and I were the major users of the high school darkroom. Holton High had once had a newspaper, but now it had only a yearbook, and the staff sent its film to a Dallas lab for developing and printing. But the primitive darkroom was still there, and Sam had arranged for the sheriff's department to rent it when I needed to print my black-and-whites for evidence, and for me to rent it when I wanted to do a little of my own work. Lots of photo-artists never go into the darkroom, but I've always liked fooling around in there, working on special effects, montages, heightening contrast, and taking clear negatives and printing them out of focus. Sometimes the results surprise me.

This kind of work was really difficult using a temporary setup, and I'd almost stopped taking pictures out of discouragement. Sam kept telling me the high school darkroom was a temporary expedient, the same thing he kept saying about our apartment in the sheriff's building.

There's nothing particularly wrong with the apartment. In fact, it had been great when we needed to get out of Sam's parents' house, and our furniture was still on its way from Sam's last army duty station in Germany. But Sam doesn't want to do anything to the county's plumbing, and that eliminates any sort of permanent darkroom.

So in the meantime, my enlarger sat in a crate in the corner of our bedroom, waiting for a decision on where we were actually going to live—a decision Sam might not be able to make for a year.

The high school darkroom was off a classroom. Its door opened as Sam and I approached, and Leona Kephart stepped out, all five feet, four inches of her. Each of her thin hands was pinched up into a claw, and each claw held a photo by a corner.

"Hi!" she said enthusiastically. "Glad to see you two. I'm just about through here. These are nearly dry."

She seemed so pleased about something that her voice had almost lost its whiny twang and her shoulders their downtrodden set. It was quite a transformation from the

Leona of an hour earlier, and it made me wonder what she was up to. In Leona, enthusiasm always seemed phony. She hadn't had an opponent when she'd run for the school board. She probably couldn't have been elected if voters had had any other choice.

Other people's foibles rarely bother Sam, and he gave Leona his usual calm greeting. "Hi, Leona. I wanted to catch you."

Leona wriggled her thin body uneasily. "Oh, hi, Sheriff. Anything I can do to further the cause of justice in Catlin County?"

"Well, I need you to run an appeal, an appeal asking anybody who was at the school or at the Community Church last night to come by and give me a statement."

Leona widened her eyes. "That's going to take in a bunch of people, Sheriff."

"Yeah. All the band boosters, for starters. But I need to know if anybody saw anything over by that shed. I guess there's nothing for it but a public appeal. Anybody driving by might have noticed something."

"Sure, sure. Get Nadine to type it up, and I'll put it in. But this is Friday, and the *Courier* won't be out until next Wednesday." Leona tipped her head sideways. "You sure planned this murder for the wrong time for my deadline."

"Sorry, Leona. I'll try to do better on the next murder."

Leona laughed. "Of course, a hotshot detective like you, Sam—you'll probably have made an arrest by Wednesday. That can be my scoop."

"Well, I'm questioning a bunch of people already. I've identified a lot of the folks who were around the school or the church." Sam looked at Leona calmly and said no more. As usual, his silent treatment worked. Leona cleared her throat and nervously waved the photos she was holding. "Well, as a matter of fact—" She ahem-ed again. "I was over at the church myself. Just out in the parking lot."

"Oh?" Sam let the pause grow.

"Yes. I went by to get a time exposure on that ghost sign."

"When was that?"

"About ten o'clock." Leona waved the photos more vigorously. "Katherine Dawkins's car was over by the church."

"How about Virginia Cramer's truck?"

"She usually parks behind the Haunted House. I couldn't see that part of the property while I was photographing the sign. And I didn't look as I left. She probably was there—she usually is."

"How about the school? Were there still people over here?"

"The crowd had cleared out by ten. The parking lot was empty, anyway. Is that what you needed to know?"

"That helps. Had you ever seen or heard of this Damon Revels before?"

"Sure hadn't."

"One more question. I'm asking everybody this. Where were you fifteen years ago?"

Leona's eyes did bug at that. "Fifteen years ago! Why do you need to know that?"

"I'd rather not reveal my reason at this time, Leona. But I'm asking everybody. Where were you?"

Leona waved her photos. "That was the year I got married," she said. "The stupidest year of my life. We were living in a small town in California then—up near Sacramento. I'd sure like to know the reason for that question."

"I hope I can explain later. For now you can just put it down to idle curiosity."

I was curious about one thing myself. "How come you were over at the church last night, taking pictures in the rain?"

Leona beamed and waved the photos enthusiastically. "I wanted to get a time exposure of that sign being lashed by rain. I thought it would look real spooky. But I'm using the picture for a different plan. Wait'll you see these, Nicky. I think even an artist like you will be impressed. I'm real proud of them."

She went over to the window and spread her photos out on top of a built-in bookshelf.

"Just look at these," she said proudly. "Pretty wild, huh?"

I stared at the pictures. "They're wild, all right," I said.

The pictures were montages—two images combined. One shot showed the shed, surrounded by its crime scene tape. Superimposed on it was the night shot of the big ghost sign from the parking lot.

Leona had printed a long shot of the shed, then added a ghost in a dark sky—a specter looming over the scene of the murder. It was the ghost from the sign I had painted to advertise the Maids and Matrons Haunted House.

I was horrified, and Sam's silence told me he was as dismayed as I was.

Leona was beaming. "I can just see the headline— 'Occult Murder Shocks Catlin County.' "

"Well," Sam said. "Well, that picture's going to shock Catlin County, if the murder hasn't already."

"Leona!" I said. "You can't print that."

"Why not?"

"It implies that the Haunted House has some connection with the murder. And it doesn't!"

"Well, it happened right there!"

113

"Not in the Haunted House itself, Leona! It happened in a storage shed. You might as well say the crime was connected to the church—or to Mrs. Engelman's day care center!"

"Well—" she said. "There were those cases in California."

I took a deep breath, and I guess Leona and I would have gone at it, but Sam ended the argument before it started.

He laughed. "Leona, if you think any hanky-panky could go on at the Holton Day Care Center and Preschool, you never talked to my nephew. He repeats every event of every day to my mother as soon as she picks him up. We all know about the field trip to see the puppies, and the time Jason Keating threw a tantrum, and the time his little sister wet her pants. There are no secrets in Holton—even at the preschool level."

Sam laughed again. "Not one parent kept their child away from the preschool today—I know, because I got Tink to ask Mrs. Engelman. But the Maids and Matrons will be damn mad if you tried to link them with this killing. So you might want to check with a good lawyer before you decide to print that picture."

He turned to me. "Nicky, let's leave Leona to finish up. You can do your film tomorrow. I'm going to see if Mr. Kelleher's still around."

We left Leona frowning at her montage, and I followed Sam down the hall to Ramsey Kelleher's office.

It was easy to see that Ramsey was related to Lucretia Engelman and to Starr. Mother, son, and granddaughter—their features weren't too much alike, but they had all dipped into a gene pool that laid out specifications for tall, heavy-boned, handsome people.

As he stood up behind his desk, Ramsey towered over Sam's six-feet plus. His neck was thick, and an enormous hand shook mine, yet there seemed to be no fat on his giant frame.

"I thought you might be by, Sam," he said. "Even though I told Sonny Blacksaddle all I knew about people who were at the school last night."

"Did you stay until the end of the band boosters' meeting?"

"Oh, yes. Better me than the custodian." Ramsey sat down behind a metal desk that could qualify as an antique and motioned us into metal-framed office chairs. "Somebody has to lock up, and the custodian gets overtime."

"I wanted to ask you about Nolan Porter," Sam said. "He seems like a nice kid."

"Nolan's as good a kid as you'll find in Holton—or anywhere. He's not in trouble?"

"No. He just came by and talked to me about the army last night. Along with Tom Blacksaddle and your niece."

"Yeah. I know all three of them applied for West Point appointments. Starr's not really interested. She's such a whiz at science—I tried to get her to look at MIT."

Ramsey smiled at us ruefully. "Do y'all know how rare it is for a student from an Oklahoma public high school the size of Holton to get a crack at a big-name school?"

"I know it's unusual," Sam said. "OU or OSU were as ambitious as anybody in my class got. Most of us wound up at smaller colleges."

"Right. We're happy if we can get our kids to go as far away as Cameron, over at Lawton, or as far as Midwestern, down at Wichita Falls. Heck, we're happy if they'll go to vo-tech." He leaned forward. "My sister Maryrose was the last Holton graduate—I think she was the only one ever—to go to a fancy eastern school. And now Starr—well, she's been working with a professor over at

SOSU, her test scores are amazing, and I really think she has a good chance at just about any school. And she's picked on Vassar."

"You don't think it's the best choice for her?"

"Oh, it'll be quite a feather in my mother's cap. Somehow Vassar has that 'halls of ivy' mystique to Mother, and she's managed to drill it into two generations now. But for Starr, well, the West Point application is a sort of backup plan.

"But Nolan—well, West Point could do a lot worse than Nolan. He's smart, real athletic—and a natural leader."

"Oh?"

"Yes, sirree." Ramsey laughed, and I thought I detected a nervous twist in his left eyebrow.

Sam may have detected it, too, because he nodded, blinked, and gave the principal the silent treatment.

It took only thirty seconds for Ramsey to break. "Yes, sirree," he repeated. Then he gave that nervous laugh again and clinched one giant hand. "Maybe that's Nolan's problem—leadership. Sometimes he stirs things up."

"Oh?"

"Well, he was the one who organized the big Mystery Meat Mutiny."

Sam laughed. "Mystery meat? That was the least popular dish back when I ate at the Holton High cafeteria on a regular basis. Are y'all still serving that?"

"Well, actually, we're not anymore. Thanks to Nolan we have a hamburger bar—fix 'em to suit yourself—and a salad bar. He organized a picket line, complete with signs, slogans, and a brown-bag-in. There was one week when the cafeteria completely shut down. Not one student ate there all week."

"Nolan organized this? Quite a leader, I'd say."

"Yeah. And that was last year, when he was only a

junior." Ramsey nodded. "But Nolan's just a kid. He didn't anticipate all the ramifications of the protest."

Sam merely raised his eyebrows and waited for Ramsey to go on.

"The board revamped the cafeteria setup, true. But the cafeteria director quit her job over it. Somehow that came as a total shock to Nolan."

Ramsey looked at Sam steadily. "He came in my office with tears in his eyes over it. He couldn't believe he could cause trouble and hurt feelings with signs that said things such as 'Massacre Mystery Meat,' 'Meet the Mystery Meat Menace,' and 'Mystery Meat Mustn't Meet My Muzzle.' "

I laughed. "Mystery Meat Mustn't Meet My Muzzle?"

Ramsey grinned. "It was pretty funny. I kept having to go hide in the faculty lounge. I wasn't going to let Nolan see me laugh! But the cafeteria director didn't have much of a sense of humor."

"And Nolan was upset over her reaction." Sam's voice was thoughtful.

"He's just a kid, Sam. Even the good ones don't have much idea of other people's viewpoints. But Nolan's like the rest—he'll grow up. And I think he'd make a good cadet. And a good soldier."

"What about Tom Blacksaddle?"

"Oh, he's another good kid. Being an Indian may give him a slight edge at getting into West Point or the Air Force Academy. His leadership credentials are nearly as good as Nolan's. He'd make a good officer, too. Good grades. Good athlete."

But Ramsey was frowning.

"Does he have some problem?" Sam's voice was mild.

"Not at school." Ramsey sighed. "His mother came by a couple of weeks ago—she's all concerned. Probably over nothing."

"He said she didn't want him to go to a service academy."

"Well, I understand her viewpoint. She and Ellison Blacksaddle started as antiwar protesters back in the sixties. So they're not real tickled with the idea of having a professional soldier in the family. Nowadays they've become our local environmental quality activists, and they're active in tribal affairs. They've worked overtime to make their kids proud of being Indians. Like Sonny and his braids, his war dancing."

Sam smiled. "It seems to be a wholesome hobby. And Sonny says he gets to meet every powwow princess in Oklahoma."

"Yeah, but Sonny had a heck of a time getting a law enforcement job because of those braids. He talked to me about it. But he wouldn't consider cutting them. Said they were a family tradition."

"Which Tom doesn't observe."

"Tom cut his hair about six months ago—about the time he began to date Starr."

"Starr said they aren't serious."

"Thank God! I'd have really had problems then! My mother's from the old school, you know."

Sam gave a short laugh. "Doesn't want her granddaughter fooling around with 'Injuns'?"

"Right. Then we had Tom's family, who wouldn't be happy with any girl he brought home who wasn't Kiowa. I was trying to stay neutral, but luckily the kids didn't get too interested. They seem to regard each other only as ideal lab partners."

Sam nodded, "Well, I'll talk to Tom and to Nolan after the football game, and I'll get out of your hair now, because I know you need to get ready for the game yourself."

"No problem, Sam. I want to help any way I can."

"Just two quick questions. Did you ever see or hear of this Damon Revels before he showed up in Holton last night?"

"Nope. I guess he was that stranger who was down at The Hangout. But I'd never seen him before."

"And the second question is, Where were you fifteen years ago?"

Ramsey's face hardened, and he gave a barking laugh. "Fifteen years ago! Why do you ask that?"

"Just humor me, Ramsey. I'm asking everybody. I keep expecting people to tell me they don't remember."

"Oh, I remember all right! I was plodding through So-so U—wasting my time, my mother says."

Southern Oklahoma State University—or So-so U in the local joke—is a small state college thirty miles from Holton. I'm a student there myself, taking a law enforcement class one day a week. Lots of Holton people go there, either to earn degrees or simply to pick up a few classes.

Ramsey was looking a bit embarrassed over his outburst. "Sorry," he said. "I didn't mean to bring out the family quarrel for public review. Going to SOSU was my youthful rebellion, you know."

"I went there two semesters myself," Sam said. "I transferred to OU when it came time to rebel."

"Well, my mother has never let me forget that I insisted on going there."

I was mystified. SOSU had seemed to be a good enough school to me. Why had Mrs. Engelman objected to it?

"It may not be Harvard—" I started.

Ramsey laughed bitterly. "From my mother's point of view it sure isn't! I know you're new around here,

Nicky, so you may not realize that the eastern idea of the importance of certain snob schools is not too prevalent in Oklahoma."

"Luckily," I said, "my mother was from the South and my father from the Midwest, so they never pushed for the name schools either. I went to the University of Michigan."

"Well, Michigan's a top-notch school," Ramsey said. "I don't know where my mother got the idea that there was no point in going to college if you didn't go Ivy League. Maybe because she went to a teacher's college herself. But my sister and I had that idea drilled into us from the first grade on. And she bulldozed Maryrose right into Vassar—where the poor kid threw her brains away. As I said, I rebelled. First I went to the Air Force, then I went to SOSU. And that's where I was fifteen years ago—a twenty-five-year-old senior with no more ambition than to be a small-town schoolman." He grimaced. "You can imagine what my mother thinks of that. I still have to put up with the snide remarks."

I didn't know what to reply to this outburst. Sam just nodded.

"So you didn't go to school with anybody named Damon Revels?"

Ramsey shook his head, then his eyes focused behind us.

"Oh, hi, Starr," he said. "Where'd you come from?"

"The gym, Uncle Ramsey."

Starr was standing in the doorway of her uncle's office. She wore blue pants and a white T-shirt with "Holton Heroes" across the chest in red script. She was holding a red Holton High band jacket over one shoulder. Her blond pageboy was smooth, and even in her uniform she looked as if she'd just stepped out of the Land's End catalog.

120

"Coach wants to see you before the team goes to dinner," she said.

"Back to work," Ramsey said. "Starr, you close up after Mr. and Mrs. Titus, please." We all said good-bye, and he took off down the corridor, his long legs striding along and his heavy body ready for anything.

Starr smiled at his retreating figure. "Uncle Ramsey's really worked hard since he came back to Holton as principal, you know. I think Grandmother feels that he doesn't get enough appreciation."

"A small-town principal has to take a lot of limelight with very little reward," Sam said. "I can imagine that it might not be the career a mother would choose for her son. But your grandmother always taught in Holton, didn't she? Until she started the day care center?"

"Yes, she started the center after she took early retirement from teaching. She raised my mom and Uncle Ramsey on a teacher's salary. And then she took me on. She had to put aside her own plans to see the world."

"Teachers can work anywhere," Sam said. "Why did she stay in Holton?"

"Well, both her husbands left her, you know. And her parents were old, and she had to take care of them. She says that by the time she could leave, it was just too late. Maybe that's why she hoped for better for her children. And for me."

Starr closed the office door and turned the handle to make sure the lock had caught. "So I guess she is a little disappointed that Uncle Ramsey wouldn't even try to go away to an important college."

"The way your mother did?"

Starr nodded. "Of course, Uncle Ramsey is quite intelligent—he could have gone someplace besides SOSU. Maybe not Harvard or Yale. But I guess my mother was really a good student."

"It must be a lot to live up to."

"My mother?"

"No. Your grandmother's expectations."

Starr smiled brightly. "Oh, no! I'm glad she expects me to do well. I don't want to stay around here all my life. I want to be successful—in research, maybe. Or be a doctor like my—" Her voice faltered, then went on. "That's the ticket out of Holton."

A slight sneer had crept into her voice, and she seemed to realize it, because she turned to Sam apologetically. "Not that Holton isn't a good place to be from."

Sam grinned. "Yeah. Far away from." They both laughed.

"I felt the same way for a long time," Sam said. "So I understand what you're saying. How about Nolan and Tom? Do they want to be far away from Holton?"

"Not as much as I do," Starr said.

"Where is Nolan? I tried to find him today, but he evidently skipped school," Sam said. "Is he down at the gym with the football team?"

"Yes, he's there. He wouldn't miss a game."

"Well, I won't interfere with the coach's game plans. It's not that urgent. But if you see Nolan, tell him I'd appreciate it if he'd talk to me after the game."

Starr looked dubious. "But I don't know if he'll be able to talk to you. His folks come to the games, and they expect him to go home with them right afterward."

"Well, I'll try."

"I'll tell him. But I don't know if he can."

Sam nodded.

"I mean—sometimes the coach wants to meet with the team. And Nolan's dad never wants him to be out late. He has to get up and do chores before school, you know."

Sam nodded again.

"I mean, his schedule's a real killer," Starr said. "Up before dawn to take care of his cattle, then working out before school, then classes all day, then football practice. And on Fridays, a game. He may just drop from exhaustion tonight. I don't know if you could get any sense out of him."

"Well, I'll give it a try," Sam said. "See you at the game."

We went out the front door and down the steps of the school.

"That was an odd reaction," I said.

"I'm beginning to wonder what Nolan's got to say. Some people don't seem to want him to talk to me."

"Well. He'll be at the game."

"Yep. Everybody in Catlin County ought to be at that game. And the major action will be in the stands, not on the field."

ELEVEN

....

HERO FIELD, WHERE THE HOLTON HIGH SCHOOL football games are played, is not exactly the Rose Bowl, but it draws a bigger crowd—proportionately.

Millions of people live within a thirty-mile radius of Pasadena, California. And maybe a hundred thousand of them go to the stadium for a big game. Between four and five thousand people live in Catlin County, and on any game night at least a tenth of them are in the stands at Hero Stadium. So it's easy to see which team has fans with the most loyalty.

Of course, as Sam's comment had hinted, the game is merely a sidelight at Hero Field. Even newcomers like me turn up at the game to see people, not football. The Hangout, the IGA (officially named "supermarket" even though it has only two checkout stands), the Co-Op, and the various churches are all major exchanges on the Holton news network, but the football games are the biggest communications centers in the county. When Sam's dad, Big Sam, got out of the hospital, the first place he went was the Heroes' opening game. He held court in a wheelchair and propped a pennant in his useless left hand. The doctor said the game did him more good than three weeks of physical therapy.

Hero Field is a rather grandiose name for two sets of aluminum bleachers facing each other across a field of grass that has as many brown patches as it has white lines. There's a concession stand under each set of bleachers, and the track where Sam does his running surrounds the field. There's even a "press box," an eight-by-eight room on stilts perched above the home team's bleachers. The press—personified by Leona Kephart's father—and the scorekeepers and the high school kid who operates the public address system climb up there on a ladder before the first kickoff.

But the playing field is exactly the same size as the one in the Rose Bowl, and the makeshift stands look great under the lights, with lots of Holton folks wearing red, white, and blue jackets with "Heroes" embroidered across the back. The players, both home and visitors, are arrayed in uniforms as wildly colorful as any big-time college teams, and the pep squad is as enthusiastic as the Dallas Cowboy Cheerleaders and just as sexy, in a wholesome way.

I'd been shooting some pictures at every game. I don't shoot a lot of color, since I don't develop it often enough to be expert, but I had been loading up my Minolta with color for the games. I loaded my favorite camera, the old Leica Flex, with black and white. Those pictures were for my portfolio—if I ever got them printed right.

I planned to donate any suitable shots to the high school yearbook, but I was really taking pictures just because the scene is so hokey and, well, all-American. I stand at attention and swallow hard every week when the Hero band screeches its way through "The Star-Spangled Banner," thinking of all the other American high schools taking the field across the nation at the same moment. I have to blink a lot when they play "Onward, Heroes!," the school fight song, sung to a tune that has an amazing resemblance to "On, Wisconsin!" And I didn't even go to school in Holton.

As soon as I saw the packed parking lot, I knew this week was going to be a little different. Sam was definitely right—the major action was going to be in the stands. The bleachers were packed tighter than usual, people were milling around the concession stands, and every Catlin County resident wanted a personal report on the murder from Sam, as the officer in charge.

He was the center of attention from the moment we arrived. As we stepped out of the sheriff's car, Jack and Nora Rich pulled in beside us. They're neighbors of Sam's parents, and Nora is the most enthusiastic cook I've ever known.

Nora rolled her window down and leaned out. "Sam! Young Sam! What's all this business about the murder? Is it true that Satanists are loose around here?"

She bounced her rotund shape out of the car, waving a colorful tin box and talking hard about two subjects at once. "Young Sam, people are all het up over this. Here, Nicky, stick these in your car. Is it true that this fellow was carved from end to end with crazy heathen symbols? I was baking cookies today, and I brought you and Sam a few." She stopped and stood with the tin box extended to me. "Just what is the world coming to?"

"I don't know," Sam answered. "I hope it's chocolate chips."

"Chocolate chips?" Nora looked at the box of cookies, then laughed heartily. "Young Sam, you are a caution! You'll have to settle for peanut butter. Now, tell me the truth about this murder."

I took the cookies, and Sam took the question. "We don't know just what's behind it, Nora. I don't want to say what killed the fellow until we get the autopsy report.

But it sounds as if the local rumor mill is improving on the facts."

"But the crazy symbols!"

"I don't want to overplay the importance of things until I know more facts, Nora."

By now Jack Rich had come around the car. "Have there been any animal mutilations, Sam?"

"None have been reported to our office, Jack."

Jack scratched his head. "Well, I heard that a calf was killed over by Sphinx Creek."

"I hadn't heard that, Jack." Sam reached in his shirt pocket and pulled out his notebook. "Tell me who to call, and I'll check it out."

"Oh, no! Oh, no! I don't want to be reporting something that might not be so. But I did move my herd into the near pasture." Jack opened the door Nora had slammed behind her and began to roll up the window. "Let's lock the car up tonight, honeybun."

Nora frowned. "Jack, did you take the keys out of the ignition this time?"

We left the Riches coping with the unfamiliar custom of locking their car and started for the gate. Sam was stopped at least a half dozen more times before we got there. After our season tickets had been punched, I left him with the citizens and took my camera down to the end of the field.

I'd planned to take photos of the flag raising ceremony, but I could barely get in position in time. People began to stop me and pump me about the case. Some of the comments were pretty unusual.

"Is it true that fellow's—well, that he'd been mutilated? Is it true they were stuffed in his mouth?"

"I heard that a ring of Satanists is planning to hold ceremonies on Mount Parker. I heard that they're coming clear from California. A busload of them stopped at the

Phillips station out by the turnpike. All dressed strange and talking a funny language."

"Sam's got to do something about these Satanists! You know they've been kidnapping blond-headed babies in Dallas shopping centers! Human sacrifices! We can't let that stuff get a foothold in Catlin County!"

A few comments did seem to have some relationship to fact.

"I heard that Satanists held a ceremony at Lattimore's Park. I heard they smoked something strange and sacrificed an animal. Is that true?" That question came from a member of the Maids and Matrons.

After the kickoff, I gave up trying to take pictures and joined Sam in the stands. He'd exhausted the subject with the people nearest, and for a few minutes we got to watch the game. Then the guy behind us went to get a Coke, and somebody new sat down. I recognized him as the kid who ran the gas pumps at the Co-Op.

"Hey, Young Sam. Is it true that strange lights were seen on Mount Parker?"

Sam hadn't lost his patience. "I hadn't heard the rumors about Mount Parker until tonight, J. B. Did you see them?"

"Naw. Billy Dale Simmons told me. He lives out that way."

"Well, I'll talk to Billy Dale tomorrow, then."

"Aw, Young Sam! Don't tell him I sicced you onto him. He'll be outdone with me."

And so it went, all through the first two quarters. The band was marching up and down the field at the half before anybody who seemed to have a fact approached Sam.

Strangely enough, it was Sam's dad.

My father-in-law, Big Sam Titus, had ranched in Catlin County for more than forty years. He was

born here, but his family lost their farm during the
Depression—an event Oklahomans who survived the Dust
Bowl still pronounce with a capital D. Big Sam served in
World War II, used the G.I. Bill to get a degree in agricul-
ture from Oklahoma State University, then came to Catlin
County to begin buying back the land his grandfather had
homesteaded in 1901. If he and Sam's mom, Marty, are
worth over a million today—a purely paper situation that
seems to have little relationship to money in the bank—
it's prosperity built on a foundation of hard work, sacrifice, and thrift.

The attack that had hospitalized Big Sam off and on
for three months, and had brought Sam and me to Catlin
County, had left Big Sam with little mental impairment.
His speech was slightly affected, and he still had only
limited use of his left side. But he could drag himself in
and out of a car or pickup, and Sam's mom drove him
around to look at cattle or to check on how much water
was in the ponds or how much grass in the pastures. She
also drove him to a rehab center for therapy and to see a
specialist in Oklahoma City. We hadn't expected them to
be at the game, because they'd been to see the specialist
that day. Four hours on the highway usually left Big Sam
saying he was "totally tuckered."

So I was surprised when Sam said, "There're the
folks." He got up and began making his way down the
bleachers, stepping over and between the gossipers and
football fans. I followed him.

Marty was walking beside Big Sam while Johnny
Garcia, who worked for the Titus Ranch full time, pushed
the wheelchair to the end of the bleachers. Marty can
manage the wheelchair most places, but the gravel walks
at Hero Field are too hard for her. She waved when she
saw us.

As he greeted them, Sam didn't touch either of his

parents, of course. He hugs his mom now and then, in the privacy of the family home, but the social kiss hasn't invaded Catlin County. And he and his dad have never so much as shaken hands in my sight. They love each other, but they declare that love in a code that includes such phrases as "You haven't been out to the house for a week, boy! Your mom's nervous as a mother cow who can't remember where she hid her calf," or "What do you mean, hauling yourself up those steps! You fall, and you'll roll back down and keep rolling until you hit that hospital again."

So Sam simply nodded as he joined his parents. "How was the trip?"

"Fine," Marty said. "The doctor's real pleased with your dad."

"Good."

Big Sam took a deep breath. "Your murder made state news on OETA," he said, mentioning the call letters for the Public Broadcasting System. Speech could be difficult for him, and he rushed to get the sounds out, then took another gulp of air. "What you doin' at the game? Thought you'd be out detectin'."

Sam grinned. "I am. I've heard more about the killing here than I have all day."

Big Sam made a noise that could only be called a snort, then gulped more air. "Any mutilations?"

Mysterious animal mutilations have been rumored to be associated with Satanism in some areas, so that's the most threatening aspect to cattlemen like Big Sam and Jack Rich.

"Jack Rich had heard a rumor about a calf," Sam said. "Over on Sphinx Creek. Did you hear anything?"

"Saw it. Harris place." Big Sam shook his head. "Calf already dead. Coyotes."

So Big Sam thought coyotes had gnawed the body of a calf that had died of natural causes. Sam nodded. Most animal mutilation rumors come down to natural causes, he says.

He sat down at the end of the bleacher and put his head close to Big Sam's. "Dad, if you wanted a rattle-snake, where would you look for one?"

Big Sam rolled his eyes at the thought of anyone wanting a rattlesnake.

"Come on," Sam said. "I'm serious. Is there a den anyplace?"

"Too warm."

"That's what I was afraid of."

Even I knew that rattlesnakes den up together in the winter. But we hadn't had any cold weather so far, so Big Sam apparently thought they wouldn't have taken to dens yet.

Big Sam gulped more air. "Any farm. Any rock."

Sam nodded. "I know. Somebody stumbles over one in the pasture."

"Hunters. Mount Parker."

Sam sat up straight. "Snake hunters?"

Big Sam nodded. "Waurika. Apache."

Sam gave a low whistle. "Now that is interesting. West side?"

"South." Big Sam rolled his eyes again. "Kids."

I was about to explode with curiosity, of course. Sam gave Marty the seat next to his dad, patting her shoulder and muttering that he'd try to get out to the house over the weekend.

"Johnny has everything under control," Marty said casually. "You work on your murder."

We went back to our seats. The crowd of the curious had cleared a bit, and I leaned close to Sam. "What was all that stuff your dad was telling you about rattlesnakes?"

"He said that snake hunters look for rattlers on the south side of Mount Parker."

I was still confused. "Why?"

"Because that's a good place to find them."

"I don't mean that! Why does anybody hunt snakes in the first place? What did he mean by 'Waurika' and 'Apache'? Is it some sort of Indian tribal custom?"

Sam laughed out loud and put his arm around my shoulder. "I keep forgetting you're still not quite Okie all the way through. Apache and Waurika are towns. Both of them sponsor rattlesnake roundups as community promotions. Big Sam meant that hunters go over to Mount Parker to gather snakes."

"Rattlesnake roundups? Why do they want to round up snakes?"

Sam shrugged. "No good reason I can see. Big Sam never encouraged us to kill snakes—unless they were right around the house where we might step on them unexpectedly and get hurt. He thinks they keep down mice. And you know he tries to keep a bullsnake in his barn."

"Yes, I remember." Sam and Johnny Garcia had laughed themselves silly when I met the bullsnake in the feed room and ran outdoors screaming. Marty had explained that Big Sam kept it there to keep rats and mice out of the grain. Ferdinand was, they all assured me, completely harmless to humans—unless he caused a new member of the family to have a heart attack.

Sam hugged me again. "I think the rattlesnake roundups are just something to draw tourists—though I've never understood why anybody thought being known as the home of champion rattlesnakes would give a town a good name. Sonny's parents led a protest of environmentalists at several of them one year. And the snake hunters are definitely a strange group."

"I'd think so."

"Well, some of them are just local farm boys out for

a lark, of course, but there are professionals who catch tons of snakes and take them from roundup to roundup trying for the prize money. And there was a case a few years ago—someplace up around Oklahoma City. A snake hunter turned his stock loose in a rent house. The landlord nearly died when he went by and found the guy had moved out and left about a hundred rattlers behind. Most of them had starved to death."

"That's horrible! Even a rattlesnake deserves better than that."

"I think that hunter was charged with cruelty to animals. If they ever caught him. But that information about Mount Parker's pretty interesting."

"Do you think snake hunters are mixed up in this murder?"

"I haven't seen any indication of that. But it is sort of odd."

"What is?"

"Well, if I was going to kill a snake, I'd chop its head off. But that one out at Lattimore's Park didn't seem to have a wound."

A cowboy-hatted figure had joined us. Sam gave my shoulder one more squeeze before he turned to speak to the new arrival.

"Hey, Joe," he said.

"Hey, Sam. What's this about Satanists taking over Catlin County?"

Joe, it turned out, was one of the band boosters. He'd been questioned by Sonny that afternoon, and he wanted to assure Sam personally that he hadn't seen a thing linked to the weird practices that were apparently going on over there at that oddball nondenominational church.

I tuned them out and thought about rattlesnake roundups. They sounded dreadful. Cruel and stupid. I sympathized with the Blacksaddles and their protest. No wonder Big Sam, who kept a bullsnake in his barn, had thought they were for "kids."

Joe the band booster was the first of a new wave of people who wanted to talk to Sam. These were people who'd been at the school or church the night before and who, like Joe, wanted to tell Sam that they hadn't seen a thing.

Strange how many people had been there and hadn't seen a thing. I was almost glad when Virginia Cramer showed up. At least I knew what she'd seen.

She joined us at the end of the half, just as the bands finished playing their medley from *Oklahoma!* We were standing up, all clapping rhythmically to the title tune, which naturally is the Sooner State's official song, when she popped up. Then the halftime show ended, and the band members went off, as they always did, for their third-quarter break. It was part of the ritual. The band played the first two quarters and the fourth quarter, but they had the third quarter free to socialize, roam the stadium, and stock up on soft drinks, popcorn, and hot dogs.

We sat down again, and Virginia settled her designer jeans and Heroes jacket beside me, then leaned across me to talk to Sam.

"Listen, Sam, I wanted to tell you something. I don't suppose you'll be in your office tomorrow morning?"

"I could be, Virginia."

"Well, it probably doesn't matter, but I'd like to set the record straight."

"Sure. There's one thing I forgot to ask you, too."

"What's that?"

"Where were you fifteen years ago?"

"Fifteen years ago? Lord, I don't know! Why do you need to know that?"

"I'm asking everybody." Sam always said that as if it were a reason, and so far nobody had challenged him.

Virginia didn't question it either. "Let's see. I was twenty-one. I guess I was a senior in college."

"Where'd you go?"

"SOSU."

Sam nodded, and the conversation more or less died. So I chimed in. "I guess you were a classmate of your principal, then."

Virginia's eyes widened. "Mr. Kelleher?" Then she began to talk very rapidly. "Was he there then? I really didn't know him in those days. I went to high school with his sister, Maryrose Engelman. We were real good friends, before she went back East and got mixed up with that bunch—" She broke off suddenly and leaned over me again. "Listen, Sam. I know everything's going to be confused about time schedules and such. Maybe I can set the time I left the Haunted House last night a little more firmly."

Sam raised his eyebrows slightly. "Well, so far everything checks out, Virginia. That truck of yours was over there until at least ten-thirty, and that jibes with what you said."

Virginia blinked and sat back. "Oh."

"You know Holton," I put in. "We all know where everybody else is at any given moment."

Virginia laughed nervously. "That's the truth." Then she stood up. "I see my husband looking this way. See you later."

I watched as she picked her way down the bleachers to the side of a tall, slim man. I'd never met Corey Cramer, and I was surprised by his appearance.

"He's fairly good looking," I said.

"Who?"

"Virginia's husband."

Sam gave his characteristic shrug. "I guess so. I'm afraid I just look at him as a DUI."

The teams ran out again then, and we actually watched the field for the third quarter and part of the fourth. The Holton Heroes were leading by a touchdown when a commotion at the foot of the stands caught my eye.

A young woman was waving her arms. I could see her lips move, but it was her agitated face that drew the eye. Then I realized her frightened gaze was aimed at Sam. She plunged into the stands and started toward us, shoving people and kicking aside paper cups full of Dr Pepper.

I grabbed Sam's arm. "Something's wrong!"

"So I see." He stood up.

"Sheriff! Sheriff!" the woman yelled. "Come quick! Come quick!"

"What's happened?"

"Murder! It's another murder!"

She almost lost her balance and swung her arms, teetering on the bleacher.

"It's Lucretia Engelman! She's dead!"

C   h   a   p   t   e   r

TWELVE

....

LUCRETIA ENGELMAN LOOKED AS IF SHE THOROUGHLY
disapproved of what had happened to her.

Mrs. Engelman had been taking care of eight babies
that night, all of them football fans' children. All had
apparently been asleep in their cribs during the killer's
activities. None of them had been disturbed, as far as we
could tell.

As soon as Sam had cleared the room of the tiny
witnesses, handing the children to their parents at the
door of the church, he motioned me and my camera into
the day care center. He closed the door to the hall firmly,
then motioned toward the lifeless hulk that had been
Lucretia Engelman.

"You sure you're up to this?" he asked me.

"I'm not wild about it, but it's better than a car
wreck. What do you want?"

"An overall shot of the scene first."

I switched on my strobe unit and got busy.

Mrs. Engelman was laid out—that's the only way to
describe it—in the center of the two-year-olds' playroom.
A small wooden baseball bat, sized for five-year-olds, had
been tossed into a corner. Sam said she had a bash on the
back of her head, just as Revels had had.

Unlike Revels, however, Lucretia Engelman was fully

clothed. A knife had been inserted squarely in the center of the red checked gingham tunic she wore as an apron.

The orange pentagram was there, but it had been drawn on the floor, not on her chest. She was lying on top of sections of it, and Sam said he believed she had been sitting at a children's table when she was struck down. There was blood all over that area, and a bloodstained plastic raincoat was tossed in the corner, with a splattered shower cap on top of it. The coat had belonged to Mrs. Engelman, and the cap had come from a supply used by the day care center cooks. A bloodstained book, a biography of King George VI of England, was lying on the table.

The killer had apparently drawn the pentagram after Mrs. Engelman was dead and had then moved the body into its center. The knife, Sam thought, was added after she was in place. Again, the knife appeared to have come from the church kitchen. The knife wound had not bled.

Mrs. Engelman's face wore an expression of disapproving surprise, as if she had witnessed a well-trained three-year-old wet his pants or as if a hitherto reliable parent had written her a hot check.

When I finished taking pictures, I left the day care room, following Sam to the other end of the church, where Tink and Lucretia Engelman's survivors, Ramsey Kelleher and Starr Engelman, were standing in a clump in the foyer.

"I think the medical examiner is going to tell us that death was instantaneous, Ramsey," Sam said. "I know this is trite, but I really don't think your mother knew what hit her."

Ramsey nodded. He pulled out a white handkerchief and wiped his right eye. "I'm sorry," he said. "It's just so hard to believe."

Starr's eyes were like saucers, but they were dry. Her

face was shiny and fresh scrubbed, and she looked pale. She didn't speak.

Kelleher hugged her with one arm. "Mother just opened up the center tonight as a sort of public service," he said. "She took only crib babies on nights like this. People can't get babysitters for football games, of course. And it was so handy to the game." He dabbed at his eye.

"You two go on home," Sam said. "I'll be busy here quite a while. I'll talk to you in the morning."

Kelleher nodded and wiped that eye again. "Come on, Starr. Looks like we're a team now. I'll stay over at the house tonight."

But before they could leave, there was a timid rap on the outside door. Virginia Cramer jumped inside. She shoved the door closed behind her and stood against it, her back yardstick-stiff. She definitely gave the impression that she was hiding.

All of us stared at her, but she looked directly and firmly at only one person. Then she held out her hands.

"Ramsey! I'm so sorry!"

In one stride Ramsey crossed to Virginia. He grabbed her by the upper arms. For a moment I thought he was going to shake her.

But that wasn't what he had in mind at all.

"Virginia!" he said. "You're here!"

He released his grip and slid his arms around her back. He pressed his cheek against her hair, then lowered his face to hers. He nuzzled her from ear to chin. He kissed her.

Virginia disappeared, except for her arms. They clutched at Ramsey's back, fingers kneading his spine.

It wasn't exactly the kind of sympathy I'd expected a bereaved principal to receive from a teacher.

A married teacher.

I stood there wondering if I was agile enough to kick

myself as a tribute to my stupidity. I'd been working with Virginia for weeks, and I'd noticed her uneasiness when Ramsey was around, uneasiness I now recognized as awareness. Ollie had even reported on how "rude" Virginia had been to Ramsey the night before, when they met at The Hangout. Why hadn't I guessed that they had a romance going?

We all knew her marriage had crashed, if not actually burned, but no one had ever hinted that a guy with a wrecker was about to haul the debris away.

Then Sam cleared his throat.

As I turned toward him, my gaze passed over Starr. She seemed to be hardly aware of what was happening.

Virginia tried to pull away from Ramsey, but he held her against his side. She gasped. "But—Ramsey! Starr! This isn't the time—"

"I don't care! We're not hiding anymore."

I could see Ramsey's chin work and his Adam's apple move up and down. "I just can't wait any longer," he said. His voice trembled. Then he looked at Starr.

Starr smiled sadly. "It's okay, Uncle Ramsey," she said. "I already knew."

Ramsey turned to Sam, still holding Virginia with one arm. "Look, Sam. I've gotten beyond caring about the Holton gossip."

Sam shook his head and held up his right hand. "Whoa! I tune into the news network, but I try not to broadcast on it. And I'm sure Tink knows the secrets of half the town. He and Nicky and I can keep our mouths shut."

Ramsey shook his head vigorously. "No! I don't care who you tell! I don't care what people think!"

"But, Ramsey!" Virginia's voice was plaintive. "You'll lose your job."

"I don't care! I'll dig ditches! But I can't stand for you to be living with that jerk any longer!"

"We don't live together!" The way Virginia stressed the word "live" clearly meant separate bedrooms. "I just don't want to involve you in a scandal."

"Scandal be damned." Ramsey stared angrily at the wall. "Life's too short to worry about what other people think, Virginia. If Mother's death shows me anything, it shows me that."

"All right." Virginia took a deep breath. "I'll move out tonight."

"Virginia!"

"I'll stay with my sister," Virginia said firmly.

Ramsey frowned and seemed ready to argue. But Sam stopped him with one of those "huhs" that he uses so expressively. "Why don't y'all go on home," he said. "Wherever your homes are."

Starr seemed less dazed than her uncle as they left. Tink was earnestly offering Virginia the guest room at the parsonage as he walked outside with them.

I was still standing there with my jaw flapping. I realized that I knew very little about the Engelman-Kelleher clan. "Kelleher's not married, too, is he?"

Sam shook his head. "He's been divorced quite a while. They never had any kids. But I guess he's got a kid now. I don't think Starr has any other family."

"The other night Starr said both her parents were dead. How old is she—seventeen? I guess she'll be off to Vassar or whatever eastern college she's got her heart set on before too long. I hope she and Virginia can get along for a year or so."

"I hope Ramsey's got some money saved. Virginia was right. He's going to lose his job—and so is she."

"Really?"

"You betcha. This is still a small town in the Bible Belt, Nicky."

Sam had asked members of the Sheriff's Reserve to

keep people away from the church, but they apparently weren't functioning very well, because someone else knocked at that moment.

Sonny had joined us, and he opened the door. "Sam didn't want anybody inside," he said.

"I'm the press! He can't keep me out!" It was Leona Kephart, with George Bullock close behind. They shoved past Sonny.

"They can come in the foyer," Sam said. He stood military style, with one arm bent at the elbow and held behind him. "What do you need, Mr. Bullock? Leona?"

"The story!" Leona said. "Two murders in one day! And both linked to Satanism! This would be big news in a real city, Sam! What's going on here?"

"I'm not sure yet, Leona. I'll certainly tell you as soon as I figure it out."

Leona straightened her scrawny body. "Listen, Sam. The public has a right to know!"

"I thought you said this afternoon that your deadline wasn't until Wednesday."

"Well—yes. But I've been hired as a stringer by KXXX in Dallas. They want daily updates."

"Oh?" Sam said quietly.

Leona nodded and looked at Bullock, apparently for approval. "I've got to cover the story anyway, and I can use the money."

Sam sighed. "I can understand that, Leona, though I can't feel too much responsibility for keeping some Dallas TV station informed. But I'll make sure I have a statement for the *Courier* by Tuesday afternoon. Right now we're waiting for the OSBI mobile lab, and I'd rather not have a lot of people tracking in and out until the technicians have collected their evidence."

Bullock had evidently held his tongue as long as he

could, because he stepped forward then. "Sheriff, I want to know what you're going to do about these Satanists!"

"The first thing I'm going to do, Mr. Bullock, is talk to Nolan Porter. He's dodged me all day, but I've sent a deputy over for him, and I'm talking to him tonight even if I have to yank him off the football field by his shoulder pads."

"Nolan! Nolan has nothing to do with this! He was scared spitless by the stuff he found! He's not the one you should be looking at!"

"Then who is? If you know anything else, if you know who I should be looking at, tell me."

"You should be looking at older people around here! People who lead these youngsters astray!"

"Bullock, you've been hinting at this since Thursday night. Just who do you have in mind? Who is this person you believe is leading Holton's youth down the path to perdition?"

"Oh, no, Sheriff! I won't be trapped into making statements you'd probably say were slanderous! If you can't see the evidence before your own eyes—"

"Bullock!" Sam was using his command voice again. "Two people have been murdered. If you know anything, I think you'd better share it."

Bullock stared at the floor.

Sam's voice didn't soften. "You obviously have no interest in helping find the murderer, Bullock, but I'd think you'd have some interest in your own safety."

"My safety!"

"Right. If the murderer thinks you know too much—"

"I don't know anything!"

Sam looked stolid. "I expect that's right, Bullock. I don't think you know diddly. But as long as you go around talking like you know it all, then you could be in danger."

"I don't have any facts, Sheriff, but I can tell which way the wind is blowing. I have an idea where you should look."

"Then share it with me." Sam still hadn't raised his voice, but I could see that the hand he held behind his back had turned into a fist.

Leona was staring at her pal. "George, you'd better tell him what you told me. About the goings-on at the high school."

"Leona! It's so hard to put your finger on."

"Tell him, George." Leona sounded impatient.

"Well—these Satanists may be high school kids, Sheriff."

"Satanists often are, Bullock."

"But I don't believe they're thinking up these things alone. Some adult is helping them."

"Who?"

"That's what I don't know, Sheriff!"

"Then we're not any further along."

"But there are indications—"

Leona's voice squeaked. "Suspicions."

"Who?" Sam wasn't making it easy for Bullock.

"Well—" Bullock raised his head, took a deep breath, and plunged in. "Well, you could look at English teachers who require students to read questionable books—books that encourage rebellion."

Well, I could figure that one out. Even a newcomer like me knew that Virginia Cramer taught all the junior and senior English classes at Holton High School. She'd probably assigned *The Catcher in the Rye.*

But Bullock was going on. "And you could look at church youth workers who have large collections of books on witchcraft, magic, and the occult! Including a Satanic Bible!"

Now that one stumped me. A church youth worker

with lots of books on witchcraft and the occult? A Satanic Bible in Holton? It didn't make a lot of sense. For one thing, I was fairly sure no church in Holton had a paid youth director, though at least half the fifteen or so churches had youth clubs of some sort.

Sam was frowning. "Who are you talking about, Bullock?"

"I'm not saying, Sheriff!"

"Well, then your suspicions are no good, Bullock. I can't possibly get search warrants and look over the personal libraries of every youth sponsor of every church in Catlin County."

Leona was looking uncomfortable, and I realized that she must know exactly what Bullock was talking about. Who could they mean? They were both members of the Community Church, and Katherine Dawkins was the sponsor of that church's youth group.

They couldn't mean Katherine owned a Satanic Bible. The idea was idiotic.

Of course, Tink and Katherine owned a lot of books. I pictured the interior of the parsonage, a remodeled bungalow in the center of Holton. Tink and Katherine had books in every room I'd been in. The living room had shelves on either side of the fireplace. The dining room was lined with shelves improvised from boards and bricks. The kitchen telephone sat on top of a rather beat-up bookcase, painted a shiny white. All these shelves were packed with books—hardbacks, paperbacks, textbooks, children's books, big flat books lying on their sides, and thick, squatty books standing up. I hadn't stopped to read all the titles.

I looked at Leona. She had a pained look on her face. She would probably have been at the parsonage for the famous circle meeting that caused the debate on whether or not Katherine could have written the devotional herself.

Leona glanced over her shoulder toward the door to the parking lot, the door Tink had just gone out.

Ah ha. I thought. She does mean Katherine.

She spoke then, and her voice was barely above a whisper. "Why would a church youth sponsor own books on that stuff?"

"Research?" Sam blinked again. "Curiosity? Gifts? From the way you're whispering, I deduce that you're talking about Katherine Dawkins."

Leona gasped, and Bullock had the grace to look embarrassed for a brief moment.

Then the coach cleared his throat pompously and patted his bald spot. "Well, someone is leading these kids into Satanism!" He made some effort to speak quietly, but his voice was a dull roar. "I certainly wouldn't want to believe my minister's wife is involved, but she surely does strange things with that youth group. And some of us would sure like to know why she's always busy but never leaves home. And what she keeps in that back bedroom. And what kind of strange stuff she grows in her garden. And how they could afford to pay cash for a car. And what she was doing at the church last night—and tonight!"

I had had enough. "Mr. Bullock! Katherine Dawkins is one of my best friends. She is among the most creative, witty, intelligent people I know. She is also just about the most kindhearted, down-to-earth friend I've ever had. And Katherine never has anything bad to say about anybody else! The idea of her being mixed up in Satanism is totally ludicrous."

Bullock glared at me. "I admire your loyalty, Mrs. Titus, but you must admit that your wonderful friend is largely responsible for one element of this whole Satanism business."

"What's that?"

"She freely admits that she suggested the Haunted House project to the Maids and Matrons."

"Yes, and it was a brilliant idea! It has the potential not only to give Holton's youth a wholesome activity for Halloween, but also to make a lot of money for community projects."

"That may be your viewpoint, Mrs. Titus."

"It's the correct viewpoint, Mr. Bullock! That Haunted House has more to do with Caspar the Friendly Ghost than with Satanism!"

"I certainly hope so," Bullock said. He spun on his heel, took a step forward, and swung open the door to the parking lot. He turned back to me and gave a gesture that was almost a shake of his fist. "I'd certainly hate to think that my minister's wife was involved with Satanism!" Then he plunged out the door and ran bodily into Nolan Porter.

Nolan jumped back. "Minister's wife! No minister's wife is involved! It's all my fault!"

"I wasn't talking to you," Bullock yelled. He pushed past Nolan and disappeared into the parking lot.

Big Sam would have said that Nolan's tail feathers were drooping. He looked dismayed and downhearted. But he took a deep breath and stepped inside the church.

"Sheriff Titus, I'm here to tell you the whole story. I've caused a lot of trouble, and I'm sorry. It's all my fault. But nobody else is involved."

THIRTEEN

....

I TOOK TEN DEEP BREATHS AND SETTLED MY TEMPER while Sam got the situation back under control. Within a few minutes he had bounced a shamefaced Leona Kephart out the door after her sweetie Bullock. He brought in Nolan and a bulky, dark-haired man introduced as Nolan's father. I was handed the tape recorder and told to tape the statement Nolan was insisting on making.

The kid faced Sam across the table in the church parlor. He looked absolutely miserable. He glanced at his dad, who nodded encouragingly.

"It was all a joke," Nolan said.

"I suspected as much," Sam answered. "How'd it start?"

Nolan folded his hands together, as if he were praying for forgiveness, and laid them on the table in front of him.

"Well, it was Mr. Bullock. He's such a jackass! He kept after us, you know—wanting the football players to tell him some dirt—you know, about stuff going on in school. We could tell that he wanted to get something on Mr. Kelleher."

"Kelleher?"

"Right! I think he must be after his job or something.

148

But we all like Mr. Kelleher. And nobody likes Mr. Bullock. So I decided to play a joke on him."

"What kind of joke?"

"Well, one day in class he took off on Satanism. It was a blight on America, it was ruining our youth, and all that crap. It was real annoying, when we were supposed to be reviewing for a test on the colonial period in American history. I'd had enough. I decided to do something about him. So after class I went up to him and asked him how you'd know if someone was involved in Satanism." Nolan looked at Sam. "I pretended to be real worried."

Nolan's dad spoke. "I just got all this out of him tonight, Sam."

Sam nodded. "I understand, Mr. Porter. Well, Nolan, I guess you got a good reaction from Bullock."

"Oh, yeah. He told me all about the stuff—pentagrams, animal sacrifices, crazy symbols, a fire, all that junk. I'd never heard of any of it, so I just followed his directions."

"You and your friends stage-dressed a scene out at Lattimore's Park."

Nolan looked up quickly "No, sir, Sheriff. Not me and my friends. I did it all by myself."

"Oh?" Sam tried giving Nolan his famous silent treatment, but the teenager ducked his head and plunged back into his story.

"The only problem was a cat. I didn't want to kill a cat. I don't even like to go hunting. But I got hold of a rattler, and that seemed to satisfy Bullock. I figured to let him stew over the weekend, then Monday I'd pass the word around school."

"How did Revels get mixed up in the deal?"

"You mean that guy you found dead this morning? He wasn't any part of it at all, Sheriff!"

"What do you mean?"

"We didn't have anything to do with any crazy ceremony! I never went near that shed! I didn't get a candle, and I sure didn't kill anybody!"

Nolan leaned forward. "Sheriff! That must have been real. Real! It must have been real Satanists!"

There was a long moment in which the soft whir of the tape recorder was the only sound. Nolan's sincerity was obvious. He was convinced that real Satanists had killed Damon Revels and Lucretia Engelman.

The boy's eyes were wide and frightened. On some superstitious level, I realized, he believed that his sham Satanism had unleashed the powers of darkness—that his practical joke on Bullock had been reflected in an actual outbreak of evil. A shiver tickled my shoulders, and I had to clench my teeth to keep them from chattering. Could he be right?

For a moment Satan himself seemed to loom over the beat-up oak dining table and threadbare couch in the parlor of the Holton Community Church.

Then Sam frowned and scratched his head. "Nolan, are you seriously suggesting that you happened to fake a Satanic ritual one day and that the next day real Satanists held a ceremony that included human sacrifice? In a town with a population of under twenty-five hundred?"

Nolan blinked, and I realized the kid was near tears. He rested his elbows on the table and held his head in his hands. "I just don't know what happened, Sheriff."

"Life's full of funny things, Nolan, but that one's a little too odd for me. I don't like coincidences."

"Like it or not, Sheriff, it looks like it happened."

Sam didn't answer for a minute, but it wasn't the silent treatment he uses so effectively. I realized that he was taking the facts Nolan had given him and adding them to his mental data bank.

In a minute he tried again. "Nolan, once I was seventeen, and I attended Holton High School. And I played my share of jokes on the teachers. And none of those jokes would have been any fun if I hadn't had someone to share them with. So it's hard for me to believe you did all that fake ritual stuff by yourself."

Nolan set his jaw. "Believe it or not, Sheriff, I did."

His jaw stayed set through the rest of Sam's questions. He had made the metal pentagons and pentagrams in a shed at the family farm, he claimed. He had caught the rattlesnake in the back pasture. Yes, by himself. He had not told anybody about his plan. He was going to spread it around school on Monday. And he certainly had not been near the church Thursday night or Friday night. He'd never been inside the Holton Community Church before in his life, he said, looking around as if it were populated by aliens.

After fifteen minutes, Sam gave a deep sigh, "Nolan, this situation scares the dickens out of me. If anybody besides you is in on that Satanism hoax—"

"But they weren't, Sheriff!"

"—if anybody was, Nolan, then that person might have told somebody else and that somebody else could be mixed up in these killings. You could be in danger. Your friends could be in danger."

"No way! That's impossible!"

Sam sat silently, staring at Nolan, but the kid had no more to say.

Finally Sam shrugged. "Okay, Nolan. I guess you can go home now. But I might ask you a favor sometime soon."

"Sure, Sheriff."

"My mother saw a big rattler out at the ranch—in the pasture right by the house. None of us is any good with snakes. Would you be willing to catch it for us? If it's as big as she thinks, we might give it to the Oklahoma City Zoo."

Nolan sat motionless, staring at Sam. The color slowly drained out of his face. He got as white as one of the gigantic, puffy clouds over the Wichita Mountains. Then he began to laugh.

He was still laughing when he and his dad went out the back door and climbed into a white Ford pickup. If the laughter had a slightly hysterical edge, who could blame him?

His father leaned out the truck's window. "Don't worry, Sam. He's not gettin' out of my sight," he said. He gunned the pickup's motor and drove away.

"What now?" I asked.

"I'll take you home," Sam said. "Then I'll come back and wait for the lab. And as soon as they get here, I'll track Bullock down again."

"Bullock? What for?"

"Like I said, I don't like coincidence. If Nolan's fake Satanism didn't inspire whatever happened to Revels, it could be the other way around."

"What do you mean?"

"I mean Bullock may have taken over his history class to shoot off his mouth about Satanism because he'd heard something—because he knew or suspected that something strange was already going on in Holton. Nolan's practical joke may have just confirmed something he already knew. He's not leveling with me yet."

We heard a noise behind us, and we turned to see Tink. He was coming out of the church foyer. I hadn't realized he'd been in the church at all, since he'd left with Ramsey Kelleher.

Sam had declared the church off limits until the lab men arrived, though he had allowed use of the foyer by grieving relatives and had taken Nolan into the parlor.

Those two areas were far away from the day care center, and he and Sonny hadn't seen any evidence that they were linked to the killing.

Tink was standing under a bright light, almost a spotlight, that hung over the entrance to the foyer. It cast deep shadows and harsh highlights over his face, turning it into a cubist design. His shoulders slumped, giving him a discouraged posture that showed me Tink's world was completely out of kilter.

"I thought you left with Ramsey and Starr," Sam said.

Tink shook his head. "No, Ramsey and Virginia didn't want me along, obviously, and Starr still seems numb. I'll talk to her tomorrow."

"You ought to go home," Sam said.

"No." The word was firm. "The church is my responsibility—the building as well as the people. I can't give in."

The three of us stood there silently, waiting. The football crowd had cleared out now, and I could see the half-dozen members of the Sheriff's Reserve, the ones who were keeping people away from the church, standing in a bunch at the edge of the highway. The night air was cool. Maybe winter really was coming sometime. I pulled my jacket around me, and I heard Tink's teeth click, just two quick chatters.

Then Tink made a sudden motion, a sweep of his hand that took in the church and the shed and the parking lot and the Haunted House. "What's going on here?" he said.

"That's what I'm trying to find out." Sam's voice was tight.

Tink went on as if Sam hadn't spoken. "The members of this church don't believe in the supernatural. Did you know that? I surveyed them when I first arrived in

Holton. I wanted to know what they thought—theologically." He lifted his face, but the harsh light left his eyes completely shadowed. "Besides, I used it in a class."

He paused and gulped. "The typical member of this church differentiates between the religious supernatural and the occult. They believe God exists and sometimes acts. Or they sort of believe it. Only a few of them would bet the farm on it. They don't believe the occult—ghosts, witches, Stephen King stuff—they don't believe all that exists at all.

"But the main thing I found out is that not ten percent of our members even expect an answer to prayer. They just see God as a benign spirit, and they see prayer as somehow putting themselves in tune with the universe—a good thing, but not much different from positive thinking. A lot of them don't fear Hell. They don't believe the Devil even exists!"

He turned toward us, and his voice became imploring. "How can a church so—so homogenized and spiritually namby-pamby—get involved with the occult?"

He gestured toward the Haunted House. "I had five anonymous calls this afternoon. Five! Wanting to know why we'd invited the powers of darkness into Holton by holding that Haunted House. This church is so ordinary! Why are these weird things happening to us?"

Sam laughed. His low, rumbling chuckle shocked me, and the jerk of Tink's head told me he also was shocked.

But in a moment Tink smiled. "I guess I am being overdramatic."

"Murder is as dramatic an event as we're likely to run into," Sam said, "and we've run into two today. If I laugh, it's not because the situation is funny, Tink. But you're right. Accusing this particular church of mixing in the occult is ridiculous. Laughable."

Sam wears a hat only to combat the elements, so his head was bare, and his sandy hair was shining under the light. He rubbed the back of his neck before he went on.

"In case you're taking another survey, you can put me in the column with the people who think belief in the occult is stupid. There may have been evil around here today, but it used human hands. And I believe we'll find it was inspired by human motives—not by any wish to serve a hellish master!" Sam looked directly at Tink. "And believe me, I intend to find out what happened. And what was behind it!"

He turned to me. "I'll get your camera bag, and then I'll take you home."

I started to follow him inside the church, but Tink put his hand on my arm.

"Thanks," he said. "Thanks for standing up for Katherine."

He went back into the church foyer so quickly I couldn't speak. But what could I say? If Tink had heard me defending Katherine, he had also heard Bullock's ridiculous charges against her.

Damn.

I went to the patrol car and got into the front seat, slamming the door viciously and imagining that Bullock's thumb was getting smashed in the process. No, his finger. All his fingers. His palm. Both palms. Smash. Pain. Agony. I pictured him with both arms in casts up to the elbows. Served the jerk right.

I was not in a Christian frame of mind.

Sam delivered me back to the sheriff's department, stopping in the office to check with Digby Doolin, the jailer and night dispatcher. Digby, who was someplace in his seventies, handled things most nights.

While Sam had been involved in killings all day, Catlin County life had continued as usual. Dig might have had Thursday night off because of lack of prisoners, but twenty-four hours later he was custodian for two common garden-variety drunks and an accused car thief.

Sam checked the deputies' reports and headed back to the church to wait for the OSBI mobile lab. I went upstairs, reminded myself that there was a deputy in the building—an elderly deputy true, but with access to weapons. Then I put on my nightgown. I covered it with a thick, terry-cloth robe, however. Somehow I didn't want to sit around in a sexy peignoir or even my short cotton robe. Mrs. Engelman's glare from beyond death had shaken me more than I wanted to admit.

What could have happened to her? Could a person as staid, prosaic, and authoritarian as Lucretia Engelman have been mixed up with Satanism? The idea was stupid.

Had she seen something? Something to do with Revels's death?

But she had apparently been one of the few people in Holton who hadn't been anywhere near the church Thursday night. She had no connection with the Haunted House. Sam said she hadn't even attended the band parents meeting at the high school, even though Starr was in the band.

Why would a woman who had merely spent the evening watching babies and television have been interrupted by a murderer?

Had the killer come into the church for some other reason? Had she surprised him?

No, that wouldn't work either. Sam thought she'd been sitting in a nursery school chair at a two-year-old-sized table, reading, when she was killed.

I dozed off sitting up in bed thinking about it. I dreamed that Lucretia Engelman was glaring disapprovingly at a PBS special on rattlesnakes and that one of the creatures was crawling out of the TV screen. Sam brushed my arm as he came to bed, and I jumped all over.

"Sorry," he said. "I didn't mean to wake you up."

His hair was wet, so I knew he'd had a shower, but I hadn't even heard him come in. I looked at the clock radio on the dresser. Its digital face read 3:32.

"Did you arrest anybody?"

"Not hardly." Sam propped his pillow against the headboard, sat down, and leaned back.

"Are you exhausted?"

"Pretty near." He closed his eyes. "We found traces of blood in the little girls' restroom. Somebody cleaned up in there."

"Hey! Any prints?"

"Bunches. Most of them four-year-old-sized. And none of the adult prints were in blood or anything. This guy's smart enough to wear some kind of gloves."

"Who isn't?"

"Yeah. That proves his IQ is fifty or above." Sam looked over at me. "I'm too keyed up to sleep. Do you mind if I read for a while?"

"Not if I can give you a backrub first."

Sam slid down in bed and rolled over on his stomach. "You don't have to ask twice."

The muscles in his shoulders were so tight they almost twanged. It took about a cup of hand lotion and a lot of action with palms and thumbs to make them relax, but they finally grew pliable, and Sam's breathing grew deep and regular. I thought he'd dropped off to sleep. Then he suddenly rolled over and pulled me down against him.

He kissed me; then he spoke. "It ought to be a law."

"What should?"

"That cops cannot be sworn in unless they come equipped with spouses who are willing to give backrubs in the middle of the night. It ought to be a requirement for everybody who enters every police academy."

He kissed me again. Thirty minutes later Sam really did fall asleep. I dropped off, too, but not deeply enough to keep that rattlesnake from crawling out of the TV set once more. When the clock radio said 6:06, I gave up and crept out of bed, being careful not to wake Sam.

Actually, I could have blown reveille; it wouldn't have disturbed him. Sam can stay up for long periods of time, but when he sleeps, he sleeps hard. He says he developed the knack growing up, when he was expected to help with chores as soon as he heard Big Sam leave for the barn. If he didn't hear him go, he didn't have to get up until somebody hollered at him.

I went into the living room and got my film together, ready to take to the high school to be developed. Then I didn't know what to do with myself. The daily paper, published in Lawton, arrived, and I read it. I didn't want to do anything noisy. So I decided to pretend it was a normal day and take my regular two-mile walk. Katherine and I usually skip Saturdays, so I didn't go by her house.

It was another lovely morning. The Holtonites kept telling me that southwest Oklahoma was due for a cold spell any day, but so far we were having clear, temperate days. I could tell it was fall, because the rising sun's rays were slanting at the autumn angle, but the overnight lows and daytime highs were about like July in Michigan, where I'd spent some time while I was growing up.

I walked briskly along my Holton exercise route—crunching the few leaves that had fallen and wondering why people often name kids April but rarely name them October, when October is such a terrific month—until I came to the church. The yellow crime scene tape was still strung around the parking lot. The deputies and lab folks were long gone.

The Haunted House was sitting stolidly at the end of the parking lot, not looking very scary in the mellow morning light, and I began to wonder how much space was available for the Cannibal Stew vignette. Katherine and I had been sidetracked before we could check out the space factor. I wasn't going to haul that garbage can rack over from the sheriff's office if it wouldn't fit into the cellar anyway.

The Haunted House was kept locked up, of course, since vandals exist even in Holton, U.S.A. I wondered if Virginia would open it up that morning, despite her personal crisis. Halloween was less than a week away, and I wouldn't be the only worker bee wanting in.

The thought had barely crossed my mind when I saw that the front door was slightly ajar, and I realized that Virginia must already be there. I couldn't see her usual parking spot.

I looked at my watch. Seven-sixteen. Virginia was early, especially for a Saturday. Maybe she was working there early so she could move out of her husband's house a little later. I trotted up the porch steps and pushed the door all the way open.

"Morning!" I called. "Virginia? It's Nicky!"

There was no answer. The Haunted House was very quiet. In fact, it was as silent as the grave. But maybe that wasn't a good analogy.

"Virginia!"

My voice rang hollowly. Then I heard a noise, a thump that came from the kitchen. Immediately I relaxed. Virginia was in the back, that was all. She very likely hadn't heard me.

I could hear her in the kitchen, where a walk-in pantry had been turned into a sort of storage area. As a matter of fact, that's where the tape measure should be. I'd go and borrow it. I started through the house. I heard Virginia's footsteps, and I wondered if she was near the back stairs.

Those back stairs were one feature that had made the old Preston place ideal for a Haunted House. The Prestons, Sam had told me, had been a pioneer Holton family, arriving at the 1901 opening. In fact, old "Yank" Preston (d. 1933) had been the wealthiest man in town at one time, a partner in the First Bank of Holton and owner of the Holton Cotton Gin, a major business back before the Dust Bowl pushed most Catlin County farmers out of cotton production and into wheat and cattle.

As his nickname indicated, "Yank" Preston had been from "up North," and he had built a home on the northern pattern. It had a basement, which is something of a rarity in southwest Oklahoma, and four spacious rooms on each of two floors. And it had a graceful set of front stairs, going up from an entry, and a narrow little set of back stairs, leading into the kitchen.

The Preston family had died out years earlier, and the old house had never been renovated or even kept up. It was definitely on the ramshackle side by the time the church acquired the property for its potential use for parking lot expansion. The church board had planned to tear the house down, but the Maids and Matrons Club prevailed on them to let us use it that year for the Haunted House.

It was ideal, since we could put all the nails we wanted in the walls and because we could send the customers up the front stairs and down the back, through the kitchen and into the basement, scaring them both upstairs and down and keeping them in line with a series of simple partitions. We didn't want our clients doubling back and getting two scares for the price of one.

Since all these partitions were already in place, I had to wind around to get to the kitchen.

The front parlor where the Prestons had once received guests, for example, was now the lair of the Spider Woman. Her webs stretched across the arched doorway and draped every corner. On the big night, a black-clad club member wearing a monstrous headdress would be reaching through the webs, trying to enmesh the teen-age customers. A Miss Muffet–like girl would already be wrapped up in the webs, screaming for help.

I noted that some real spiders had added a bit of trim as I walked by the room and went on toward the old back parlor, predecessor of today's family room. That room had become the Mummy's Lair, with a huge sarcophagus against the wall. At the proper moment, a giant figure trailing rotten bandages would emerge and snatch at the spectators while a recorded voice intoned an ancient curse.

Across from the back parlor was the dining room. On Halloween it would feature organ music and a weird musician who turned to show his misshapen face, Phantom of the Opera style. I stopped to look the organ over. Somebody had done wonders with a packing box and a bunch of mailing tubes donated by the Catlin County *Courier*.

I cut through the Phantom's scene and lifted a drapery that hid the door to the kitchen. As I did, I heard footsteps through the wall, and I realized that Virginia must be going up the back stairway. I went on into the kitchen, coming out through the small door that had once led to a broom closet.

The kitchen was now Dr. Frankenstein's Laboratory, complete with chains against the wall to hold the monster in place. Strange equipment—improvised from wires, springs, and old auto parts—hung here and there, and the kitchen shelves were now covered with a collection of odd bottles, beakers, and jars that Virginia had begged from all the members and borrowed from the Holton High science teacher. I vaguely remembered that some of the glassware had been in the shed when I first saw Revels's body. I was glad Sam had been able to let Virginia remove it.

A table would keep the spectators out of the laboratory scene and would guide them to the back stairs. I put my head into the door that led to the second floor.

"Virginia! It's Nicky! I need your tape measure!"

Virginia didn't answer, but I could hear footsteps.

"Virginia!" I looked up the stairs, toward the open door that came out on the second floor. The narrow, enclosed stairwell was dim and shadowy.

"Virginia! Yoohoo!"

I ran up the stairs.

I had nearly reached the top, and had put my hand out to touch the doorframe, when the door slammed in my face.

It almost caught my hand and smashed my nose as it cut off the light.

I stood there in the sudden blackness, listening to footsteps running down the hall behind the door.

And it finally occurred to me that the other person in the Haunted House wasn't Virginia Cramer.

FOURTEEN

....

I RAN BACK DOWN THOSE STAIRS LIKE A BRANDED CALF heading for its mama.

I don't think I bawled the way a calf does, but I was plenty noisy. The dim light at the bottom of the staircase was all I had to go for, and I pounded down those wooden steps. Talk about thundering sneakers.

I burst out into Frankenstein's lab and ran to the back door. I yanked the door open and slammed it back against the wall. A glassed-in porch was on the other side, a porch with a door to the backyard. I crossed the porch in one jump and grabbed the handle of that door, my escape hatch.

The damn thing was locked.

The door had a window in it, and for a moment I beat my fist on it helplessly. The glass rattled, and I real-ized that breaking the pane out with my bare hands was not likely to improve my situation. The door would still be locked, and I'd probably need stitches.

Was I trapped?

I stopped and whirled around, ready to face the unknown intruder. I stood there, my back against the door, panting. Listening.

And I heard nothing. The house was silent again.

Then, a long way away, upstairs, I heard sliding noise, wood against wood.

If the intruder was upstairs, the way out the front of the house was clear.

I ran back through the downstairs. Through Frankenstein's lab, past the Phantom's organ, the Mummy's Lair, and the Spider Woman's Web. I threw open the front door, ran across the porch, and jumped over the steps. I landed in the gravel parking lot running toward downtown, back to Sam and my own warm spot on top of the jail.

When I dared to look back, there was no one after me.

I didn't run the whole half mile to the sheriff's office. I walked the last few blocks. I would have stopped and called Sam, but the one store on the way was closed. I passed one of Holton's two outdoor pay phones, but I didn't have any money. The streets behind me continued to be almost bare, and with no one following me, I didn't have quite enough nerve to stop at a house along the way and ask to use the phone.

I was still shaky and panting when I unlocked the new lock on the back door to the sheriff's department building and trotted up the stairs to our apartment, but I had begun to wonder if I should wake Sam up.

After all, the intruder wasn't necessarily the killer of Damon Revels and/or Lucretia Engelman. It could have been a kid, just in for a sneak preview of the Haunted House. It could even have been another member of Maids and Matrons. I might have scared her more than she scared me.

No, that wasn't possible. Not only had I yelled out my name, but anybody more scared than I had been would have been nothing but a damp and quivering heap in the upstairs hall.

But what was I going to tell Sam had happened?

Somebody slammed a door in my face?

164

Baldly stated, it sounded as if I'd overreacted. Sam had been asleep only three hours; should I get him up to tell him about an episode that might have nothing to do with the case that had kept him out most of the night?

As I opened the door to the apartment, I could hear the radio. Sam was already up. One problem solved. I went into the bedroom. Sam was taking clean underwear out of his drawer. I leaned against the doorframe and gulped. He looked at me. He can usually read my mind.

"What's wrong?" he asked.

I tried to joke. "I went over to the Haunted House, and a spook scared me!" Then my aplomb failed, and I had to blink several times, real fast.

"Hey," Sam said. "Hey! No spook's going to get away with that!" Then he put his arms around me, and I began to feel a lot better.

Especially because he didn't make any remarks about the intelligence of a person who casually strolls into a deserted house next door to the place two murders have been committed.

After thirty minutes, most of it spent holding each other while we stood in the shower, Sam said he'd go over to the Haunted House and figure out what had been going on. He'd sent a deputy over there before getting into the shower, of course.

He picked up the clean underwear he'd dropped on the floor and put it on, then pulled a pair of khakis and a tan sheriff's department shirt out of the closet. "As soon as you're dressed, call Virginia Cramer and tell her to come on over to that Haunted House. I expect your intruder is long gone, but she can tell us if something's missing or damaged."

I was a lot calmer by the time Virginia and I got to the Haunted House. We pulled up one behind the other, my old red Volkswagen behind her old white Ford pickup. Sam and Sonny Blacksaddle were standing on the porch. Sonny held two paper evidence bags.

"What did you find?" I asked.

"More worms," Sam said. "Probably nothing."

Sonny opened one of the bags, and I saw that it held little boxes like the ones Sam had used for the curlicues of mud he had taken from the church closet.

"The front door was forced," Sam said. "And your intruder got out over the roof of that screened-in porch."

"That's impossible!" Virginia sounded adamant.

"Why?"

"The only way to get out on that roof is through that funny little window in the bathroom."

Sam nodded.

"But we couldn't get that window open," Virginia said.

I remembered then. That window had been held shut by maybe a dozen coats of paint. Even on the hottest days of September—and the amenities of the Haunted House did not include air conditioning—no member of the Maids and Matrons had been able to open that window.

"Well, it's open now," Sam said.

The four of us walked through the entire Haunted House, turning on all the lights and checking in all the corners. And that window was all we could find that had been disturbed.

Nothing was damaged or missing. The intruder had apparently broken in and scared me spitless just so he could force open a previously jammed window, climb out onto a porch roof, jump off, and slip away into the woods along the creek that ran behind the house. The tracks on the bank of the stream could not be identified, Sonny said, and my "spook" had apparently run up the creek through the water. Sonny was going to wade the creek for a mile or so, but he thought it unlikely that he'd be able to find any proof of who had been in the Haunted House.

"I guess it was just some kid," I said.

But Sam looked serious. "Even if it was a kid, I'd like to know what he was up to. Kids don't do things for no reason. It may be a reason adults don't readily fathom, but they have a reason."

"Amen," Virginia said. "If you want a teacher's opinion."

So the only clue was the window. Sonny dusted it for fingerprints, but he found only smudges. "Probably Maids and Matrons," he told Sam.

He and Sam closed the window, which was over a claw-footed bathtub, then tried to open it. Even now it was stiff, and Sam had to shove hard to push it open.

He looked at me and raised his eyebrows. "I'm happy you didn't tangle with this guy, Nicky. If he opened this window, he stars at upper-body strength."

"An athlete?"

Sam shrugged. "Or a ditch digger, a wheat shoveler, a calf roper. Maybe a roughneck or a roustabout."

"A roughneck or roustabout?"

"Yeah. Oil field workers. Or maybe he's just naturally strong."

After forty-five minutes of poking around, we all decided to get on with our Saturday. Developing my film was first on my list. Virginia volunteered to let me into the high school in half an hour, after she'd collected the keys from Ramsey.

"If I can find him," she said. "I think he stayed with Starr last night, but his van was gone when I drove past Mrs. Engelman's house."

Sonny sighed as she drove away. "I'll wade that creek now," he said. "But even if we find tracks, what's it going to prove?"

"Well, they might match the worms," Sam said.

I had really grown curious about those "worms," those squiggles of mud Sam kept collecting as evidence.

"Why are you so interested in those bits of mud?" I asked.

"They came out of tennis shoe soles." Sam answered.

"So? Everybody wears tennis shoes." I held up my own foot and pointed.

Sam knelt beside me and held my ankle. "Yeah, but your soles are wavy." He pointed to the pattern in the rubber. "These worms we've picked up in the church and here—and there were a couple in the storage shed, but you can keep quiet about that—well, they zigzag."

"Zigzag?"

"Right."

"Then you can identify the murderer's shoes!"

Sonny laughed. "Not hardly."

Sam was grinning, too. "That's going too far, Nicky. I was noticing shoes at the football game last night, and a whole bunch of people had on shoes with soles that zigzag. It might give us a hint, that's all." He turned to Sonny. "Which reminds me. We haven't checked out those traces out back."

Sonny frowned and stared at the ground before he led the way around the house.

The traces Sam had brought up had been left by the intruder as he jumped from the porch roof and ran for the creek. He had skidded across mud as he landed, leaving tracks that were indecipherable—at least to me. Then he had raced across about fifty feet of mowed field to reach the trees along the creek bank. Again, vegetation had hidden his tracks.

But Sam and Sonny ignored the creek bank and looked at the mowed area. And after they pointed it out, I could see the mud the intruder had left on the field.

Sonny squatted down and looked at the smears. "I'd guess he's under six feet," he said.

I felt my eyes widen. I was actually seeing an Indian tracker in action!

"Of course, that's an extremely unscientific guess," Sonny said. "I ran across the mud over in the parking lot, then I measured my stride, and this guy's stride was about three inches shorter than mine, and I'm right at six feet."

He looked at Sam and grinned. "On the other hand, he could have short legs and a long body."

Sam nodded. "Or he could have been using a shorter than usual step because he was trying not to slip on this grass."

"Right." Sonny stood up. "It doesn't really mean a darn thing. Well, I'm off to go wading."

He pointed his right forefinger up, then toward Sam, then straight out to the side at shoulder level. "*Ha-get-tie-gah*," he said. "Or, as you round-eyes put it, 'That's cool.'" He grinned and left.

I felt a bit let down. Oh, well. Sonny was a nice guy, even if he did depend more on science than on Indian lore. I was almost laughing at myself as he went off down the creek, trying to find out where the intruder left the stream.

I looked up to see Sam eyeing me seriously. "Let's retrace the episode from this morning," he said. "You say the front door was standing open?"

We went back to the front porch, and I showed him about how many inches the door had been open.

"I went in and called out to Virginia."

"How come you went on in, if you didn't get an answer?"

"I heard a noise. It was back in the kitchen. I thought Virginia was there and couldn't hear me."

"I see." Sam motioned to me. "What did you do then?"

I demonstrated, retracing my footsteps past the Spider Woman and Mummy's Lair scenes and cutting through the Phantom of the Opera scene to lift the drapery that had been used to hide the kitchen door.

Sam stopped and examined the way the drapery was hung. "That's interesting. I wouldn't have guessed there was a door behind there," he said. "Is that the only way to get through to the kitchen?"

"You could go up the front stairs and down the back stairs, I guess."

He nodded. "So you went through here to the kitchen?"

"Right. As I came through the Mummy's room, I heard footsteps on the back stairs, and I thought Virginia was going on up."

Sam went into the kitchen and looked around. "So the intruder was in here when you came in the front door. He didn't go back upstairs until you began walking through the hall, headed for the door from the dining room to the kitchen."

"Right."

"And that door from the dining room to the kitchen is pretty well hidden."

I could see Sam's brain churning, adding data to his mental computer. "So the guy came in the front door, walked through the hall, then up the front stairs."

"How do you know that?"

"We don't. It's just a guess from where we found the mud. Then he went down the back stairs into the kitchen."

"More mud?"

"Nope. A witness. You. You heard him in there."

"Oh."

Suddenly Sam put his arms around me. "My God! I'm glad you're all right. You had the guy trapped!"

"Trapped?"

"Right. He'd come in the front door, and the back door was locked. He might not have known about the door from the dining room to the kitchen. He might have thought you'd have to go upstairs and down to get into the kitchen."

"You mean, he might have gone upstairs to intercept me, not to avoid me?"

Sam shook his head and released his embrace. "Darned if I know. But I wonder what he was doing in the kitchen."

We looked around the room. It had been effectively turned into Frankenstein's lab. The chains and manacles were bolted into the wall at the left. Curls of wire led from the ceiling to a helmet, supposedly for the monster. Esoteric lab equipment was scattered over a table in the center of the room.

"This committee is coming along pretty well," I said. "All they have to do is push that table over here to make a sort of hallway, and they'll be through. Of course, this is Virginia's own room."

"This is what she was working on Thursday night, isn't it?"

"Right. She said she was glueing down the glass stuff for that shelf." I pointed to a line of strangely shaped bottles and jars mounted on the wall over the old kitchen sink. "That was out in the shed. I'm surprised you let her take it away."

"The lab guys went over every inch of it first." Sam walked over to the window and looked at the shelf. "It didn't have as much as a fingerprint—except for Virginia's."

Then his head became immobile, and his eyes pinpointed a spot on the shelf. He suddenly looked as alert as a bird dog on the point.

"What is it?" I asked.

Sam brought a chair from the corner, placed it in front of the sink, and stood on it. He looked down into the glass jars glued to the shelf.

Then he beckoned to me. "Stand up here, but don't touch anything," he said.

When I looked down onto the shelf, I could see a flat object in the bottom of a wide-mouthed jar. It was bright orange and looked as if it were made of nylon. It was maybe four inches square and one inch thick.

"What is it?" I asked again.

"It's a billfold. A man's billfold."

"Orange?"

"I guess you can buy anything in California."

"California?" How do you know it came from California?"

"Because I saw a Californian carrying it."

"Who?"

"When we picked Revels up on the road Thursday, I asked him for ID," Sam said. "Unless my memory is failing me completely, that's the billfold he pulled his driver's license out of."

Sam lifted the billfold out of the jar with a pair of tongs he brought from a kit in the car. He checked it over himself, taking the contents out with tweezers, before he placed it in an evidence bag while I watched.

There was nothing unusual in the billfold, and nothing obvious was missing—except money. The only identification was the driver's license and a card with a Social Security number. Another card gave a schedule for a plasma center. Revels had evidently been selling his blood.

"If the lab men checked that whole shelf over before

you let Virginia take it out of the shed, how did they miss that billfold?" I asked.

"They didn't."

"Then how did it get there?"

Sam blinked. "I expect your intruder put it in there."

"Oh! Then the guy didn't break in to take something. He broke in to hide something!"

"Maybe." Sam straightened his glasses. "It makes you wonder."

"What about?"

"That pentagram in Revels's bedroll."

At that point he retreated into one of his deep thinking fits, and I gave up on him. I was due to meet Virginia at the school anyway.

Her old white Ford pickup was already in front of the school, and she climbed down from the driver's seat as I parked the red Volkswagen beside her.

"The janitor doesn't come in until noon on Saturday," she said. "Luckily Ramsey was still at his house. He said Starr was sleeping soundly about four, and he was pacing nervously, so he went on home for a while. I think he finally got some rest."

She waited on the steps to the red brick building while I pulled my bag of film and photographic paper out of the Volkswagen.

"You won't be nervous in here alone, will you?" Virginia asked. "I always think a big empty building is sort of spooky."

"What else can happen today?"

"Well, there's that." Virginia fumbled with the lock. "So far it seems that all the excitement's been across the street."

She threw the door open, and the two of us stared into the hall.

Total devastation.

173

"My God," Virginia breathed.

The hall had been completely wrecked. Papers, paint, furniture, and office equipment were tossed in the middle of the floor as if a tornado had hit.

I turned and ran back across the highway, yelling for Sam. When I came back into the building, Virginia was still standing there, apparently stunned.

"My God," she murmured again.

The hall was a disaster area, and a look through the big glass window at the right revealed that the office itself had also been demolished.

Filing cabinets had been yanked open, papers and manila folders were strewn everywhere, lamps had been thrown onto the floor, typewriters were tossed around the room like dice on a Monopoly board.

And it was colorful. Blue paint streaked the window that separated the office from the hall. A red design coiled across the glass in the trophy case in the hall. Yellow covered the top of a desk.

But what really drew the eye was the orange—two giant orange pentagrams.

One covered the entire floor of the hall, stretching from trophy case to office with its single, lower point at the outside door. The other was painted across the entire back wall of the office, clearly visible from the front door.

Sam sent Virginia and me outside, and I used the radio in his car to call Nadine and instruct her to find Ramsey Kelleher and send him over.

When I finished the call, I saw that Virgina was weeping.

"Why do you have to call Ramsey?" She pulled a tissue out of the pocket of her jeans and wiped her eyes. "His mother was just murdered last night."

"I know. But he's the principal. He's got to know about this, even if he tells someone else to take care of it."

"I guess so." Virginia gulped and sobbed at the same time. She stood there weeping until a white van came flying up the highway. She pointed at the van as it skidded into the high school's gravel parking lot, but she didn't seem to be able to speak.

The van pulled up beside us, and Ramsey Kelleher jumped out.

"Virginia!" he yelled. "Are you all right?"

Virginia nodded and pointed at the school.

But Ramsey didn't look at the red brick building. He strode up to her and put his arms around her.

"When they said you'd discovered the high school vandalized, it scared me to death!"

"It's awful, Ramsey."

The principal agreed with the assessment after he'd seen the wreckage. But he told Sam he had no idea who could have done the damage. No, there'd been no unusual activity among the high school students. No, he hadn't suspended anyone or punished anyone who didn't seem fairly good humored about it. He had no idea who could have wrecked the school office so thoroughly.

Sam said he'd check a few things in the office for fingerprints, and Ramsey, Sam, and I walked outside with Virginia, who was assuring Ramsey she did not want him to help her move to her sister's house.

"No!" she said. "If Corey keeps acting this tacky way, he's going to cause trouble. I'd rather you stayed away from him."

Then she looked back at me and blinked rapidly. "Sorry. I never thought I'd be mixed up in a sordid situation like this one."

I did feel sorry for her, but I didn't know what to say, so I nodded.

Ramsey reached over and took her hand. "Corey's being a pain," he said. "He's barely been home for months—spent days and nights at Parker's Point. Now that Virginia's finally left, he acts as if he's shocked. He pitched a fit and said she wasn't going to get any of his money."

"Money? I thought—" I broke off. I hated to admit I'd listened to the Holton gossip about the Cramers' financial situation.

Virginia stared at the floor. "I don't know what he's talking about. He's been in bad financial shape ever since that restaurant opened."

"Virginia's supported him for the past five years," Ramsey said angrily. "She'll be lucky if she doesn't have to pay him, instead of getting money! I think he's nuts!"

Virginia yanked her hand away. "Let's drop it! Sam, I've got to tell you the truth now."

"What about?"

"About Thursday night."

I threw my mind back into Thursday night's mode. That was the night Damon Revels had been killed in the church's shed. What was Virginia talking about?

"You remember that I said I was at the Haunted House until ten-thirty?"

Sam nodded.

"Well, that wasn't exactly true. Actually, I left around nine. I drove over to Ramsey's."

Ramsey squeezed her hand.

Sam left his face expressionless. "Y'all were together?"

They both nodded.

"I didn't see anything while I was at the Haunted House," Virginia said. "I really don't know a thing about the murder. I just wanted to set the record straight about when I left."

Sam allowed his stone brow to frown as she drove off, and he continued frowning as Ramsey went back into the school.

"What's wrong?" I asked.

"Things always get complicated."

"How?"

"Alibis. If Virginia left the Haunted House around nine, how did Katherine manage to see her truck at the church at ten-thirty?"

He turned to me, still frowning. "Nicky, maybe you could go ask her."

FifTEEN

....

I WAS AMAZED. I HAD TRIED TO BE A SUPPORTIVE WIFE to Sam. I took his pictures. I joined Maids and Matrons because I thought it would help him if I got acquainted around his hometown. I belonged to the Sheriff's Reserve, and I had even enrolled in a beginning law enforcement class—just so I could understand his work better.

But he had never wanted me to question anyone.

The idea scared me. "Is that legal?" I asked.

Sam nodded. "Sure. It's just unofficial. That's why I want you to do it. Frankly, it might embarrass Katherine and me both if I had to ask her if she lied to cover up for Virginia Cramer."

"Oh."

"Tell her that Virginia and Ramsey have come clean about seeing each other. I'm going down to the office. If she's willing to change her story, she can come by and do it with no sweat. Your visit will be strictly informal."

So I drove over to the parsonage, chewing my nails, and found Katherine sitting on her back step, watching her little boy, John Peter, climb on his jungle gym. She held a sketch pad in her lap.

After she had furnished me with a glass of iced tea, she held the pad up and showed me what she'd been drawing. "What do you think?"

The word "Katherine" centered the design on the sketch pad, with "Tink" and "John Peter" curving below it. A border of open books had been drawn down the left and right edges. Plants and flowers grew from the bottom margin. A heart had been roughly sketched in toward the top, but the drawing had not been completed.

"What is it?" I asked.

"It's an idea I had for a youth group program. Virginia Cramer showed me something like it that she did back in 4-H. You take your name, then you use the other important elements of your life—family, friends, hobbies, work—to make a design. It ought to be a vehicle to talk about understanding ourselves."

I looked at the design. "Interesting. I see Tink, John Peter, your garden, and your books. What's going in up there with the heart in the corner?"

"Oh, I was just fooling around." Katherine flushed slightly and laid the pad on the porch, facedown. "I guess it keeps me from thinking about all this trouble at the church. And at the Haunted House. Tink said Mr. Bullock told Sam I was at the church last night. Does Sam want me to give him another statement?"

"Oh, yes, even if you didn't see anything. But the real excitement is Virginia and Ramsey Kelleher. Did Tink tell you?"

Katherine shook her head, and her eyes grew wide as I described the scene in the church in which Ramsey and Virginia had revealed their status as lovers.

"Anyway, they're still standing around holding hands in public this morning," I said. "So I guess it's okay to tell people. Or did you already know?"

"No!" Katherine leaned back against the porch rail and laughed. "A big romance going on right under my nose! And I didn't even see it! That sure says a lot about my work."

Her comment puzzled me. "Your work?"

"Yeah. I mean—" Katherine picked up her own iced tea and took three deep gulps—"I mean, it says something about my observation of human nature. There's a lot lacking in it, I fear."

"Well, I'd thought maybe you'd known." Now I had to get down to asking her if she'd lied to Sam, and I began to get nervous.

"Tink kept that to himself, even last night, and I had no idea. Not that I would have said anything, if I had known." She looked at me. "And don't let my guffaw give you the impression that I approve. We may have become pretty liberal Christians, but Tink and I do draw the line at condoning adultery—even if I can hardly blame Virginia for wanting out of a rotten marriage. But she ought to drop one husband before she takes after another one."

"Well—" I didn't know how to go on.

Katherine leaned toward me. "But Nicky, I wouldn't have said or done anything. Unless they had asked my opinion. Do you think I'm being too judgmental?"

"Oh, no! I agree about Virginia and Ramsey—at least in theory. But—well, it's Virginia's alibi. I'm supposed to ask you about it."

"Alibi? Does Virginia need an alibi?"

"No, I don't mean that. I mean that she's changed her story on when she left the Haunted House Thursday night. Now she says she left at nine. She and Ramsey say they were together—well, I don't know how long. But from nine-fifteen on."

"So?"

"But you said you didn't leave the church until ten-thirty."

Katherine's eyes widened. "Oh! Her truck!"

"Yeah. You said it was still there when you left, and

now she says it was gone by nine o'clock. You weren't just backing up her story, were you?"

"Oh, no!"

"Could you be mistaken about the time?"

"Well, I got there about nine-thirty, and it took me about an hour to fool with my copying."

It crossed my mind that that was a long time to be slaving over the copier. "Did the machine act up?" I asked.

"No. For once it behaved. But Nicky, I'm sure I was there until well after ten o'clock."

"Are you sure Virginia's truck was there? Could you have just thought you had seen it because you were expecting to see it?"

"I don't believe so. No, I'm sure I saw it. I remember thinking that I hoped Virginia didn't get stuck because of the rain. So that must have been Thursday, because that's the only night it rained."

"And you weren't just backing up her story to help keep her secret, to avoid telling about her affair with Ramsey?"

Katherine stared at me solemnly. She slowly shook her head. "Uh-uh. No, Nicky. I wouldn't have gone out of my way to tell everybody about the big romance, but I wouldn't have helped Virginia cover up." She traced a miniature X on her chest. "Cross my heart and hope to die. That truck was there when I left."

Her answer puzzled me as I drove back to the sheriff's office. If Katherine was telling the truth, and I saw no reason for her to lie, Virginia had not left the Haunted House at nine o'clock. But why would Virginia lie?

Could she have had something to do with Revels's death? Of course, we didn't yet know exactly when he died. The pathologist might have preliminary results today, but it would be at least a week before his report was complete. And then it might not show the exact time of death.

It was too confusing for me. I hoped Sam had more ideas.

And Sam did seem to be full of ideas. When I came in the door of the sheriff's department, he was talking on the phone.

"Yes, sir!" he said. "That's exactly the kind of information I wanted. You've been a big help."

He hung up, waved at me, and went over to the radio before I could say anything. He got Sonny on the air.

"Sonny, find Bullock and bring him over here for questioning. You don't have to be too polite."

Then he turned toward me. His grin was happy. "What did you find out?"

"I'm afraid it's not very good," I said. But the negative information I passed on didn't make Sam's grin fade.

"I thought that might be the case," he said.

He turned to Nadine. "Okay. Proceed."

"All righty." Nadine nodded.

I was feeling left out. "What's going on?"

But before Sam could answer, the back door swung open. Sonny and George Bullock came through the back hall.

Bullock was huffy. "Just what's going on here!"

"We need a new statement from you," Sam said. "Sonny, take Mr. Bullock into the interrogation room."

That told me Sam was hauling out the big guns. He did a lot of "interrogating" in his office, in sessions the interrogatees usually thought were merely casual conversation. Even on Thursday night, when I'd run the tape recorder for an official statement from Bullock, he'd quizzed the man while we all sat in the outer office. If he was taking Bullock into that miserable little closet on the second floor, he was planning to use every psychological weapon he had—including a Miranda warning—against Bullock.

Did this mean Sam thought Bullock was the killer? Why would Bullock call attention to Satanism if he were mixed up in it himself? It hardly seemed credible. But at that point nothing else seemed credible, either.

I was madly curious, but Sam and Sonny didn't need my help, so I went upstairs and grabbed a sandwich, then split for the high school photo lab. It was two hours before I came back, loaded with prints.

Sam and Sonny were sitting in Sam's office with the tape recorder on the desk between them. They were laughing.

I tossed the photos on Sam's desk. "Where's Bullock? Did he demand a lawyer?"

"Uh-uh. He didn't think he needed a lawyer to deal with a couple of rural cops."

"Did you lock him up?"

Sam reached for the prints. "Nope. But we scared him into next week."

"You're a couple of bullies."

He grinned and flexed a muscle in his upper arm. "We had a little help from the Dallas police."

"Bullock has a record?"

"Not exactly. Just a few things he'd rather not have get around Holton."

"Hey! Come on! Tell me!"

Sam folded his hands sanctimoniously on his chest. "We promised we wouldn't tell a soul. And in exchange—" He raised his eyebrows—"in exchange, he spilled his guts."

Sonny chuckled. "I don't think Mr. Bullock's feeling quite so superior to us Catlin County hicks right now."

"Did he know anything?" I asked.

"He thought he did." Sam reached for the tape recorder and punched the fast forward button. "I'll play the key part for you."

He listened to the whir, checked the numbers that showed how far the tape had advanced, and punched again. Bullock's voice rasped out of the speaker of the pocket-sized tape recorder. "Well, I wouldn't call it eavesdropping, Sheriff."

"What would you call hiding behind a bank of lockers and listening to the football players while they get dressed?"

"I just happened to be there, Sheriff. Looking for a key I had lost. But the point is, I heard something."

"What?"

"They were talking about the Satanic initiation."

"Just what did they say?"

"They said that the Satanic initiation would be that night."

"What night?"

"A week ago Thursday."

I could hear a rustling I realized must be calendar pages, and Sam's voice named a date.

"Right," Bullock said. "I can remember exactly what the one boy said. 'I'll pick you up for the Satanic initiation at seven. And after it's over, let's go out to Mount Parker.' That was it, Sheriff. That was exactly what he said."

At that Sam punched the stop button, and he and Sonny laughed so hard they nearly fell off their chairs.

"What's so funny?" I asked.

"He thought they said 'Satanic' initiation! He thought it was some sort of pagan rite." Sam gasped.

"I don't get it. What did Bullock hear? If the football players weren't talking about a Satanic rite of some sort, what were they talking about?"

Sam pointed at Sonny. "Ask this guy. He's a 'Satanic' alumnus."

Sonny toned his guffaws down to a chuckle. "The Native American club at Holton High is called the Satanta Club, Nicky. Satanta was a famous Kiowa chief." He thumped his chest. "One of our people."

"He may have given General Sherman the devil," Sam said, "but he had nothing to do with Satanism."

"And we checked with the high school," Sonny went on. "The Satanta Club did have initiation for new members a week ago Thursday."

I sat down and laughed, too. "That Bullock is a total jackass! But you'd think he would have heard of the club, since he's a teacher at the high school."

"Ramsey Kelleher says one of Bullock's problems has been that he's completely impervious to anything but athletics. And the club does have an unusual name. He would have been expecting the 'Native American Union' or some such term."

I shook my head. "Except for comic relief, then, Bullock was a washout? He didn't tell you anything that helped?"

Sam sat forward. "His evidence is like Virginia's and Katherine's. It's negative evidence. But anything that eliminates the wrong answers brings us closer to the right one."

He turned his head and looked at Sonny. "And I did wonder why the football players were going out to Mount Parker."

My gaze followed Sam's, and I saw that Sonny's face had lost its grin. He dropped his head and stared at his boots for a long minute.

Then I began to wonder about Mount Parker, too. Mount Parker was a local scenic drive and the location of

Corey Cramer's failed restaurant, Parker's Point. A year ago he had apparently been bragging that it would make him rich, that people would drive from all over Oklahoma and north Texas to eat dinner and look at the spectacular view. It hadn't worked out that way. The location was simply too remote and the food not good enough. The restaurant had turned into a beer joint that served nothing more edible than potato chips. Why would kids go out to Mount Parker?

Well, I could see why a football player might take his girl out there. It was probably well supplied with good parking spots. But why would he take a fellow football player? The local athletes' oddities didn't seem to lean in that direction.

Sonny raised his head. "Yeah. I've had my doubts about Mount Parker." He stood up. "And I'm well aware that my brother is one of only four Indians on the football team. It's time that kid answered a few questions. Sam, do you need me to do anything more on this killing? Or can I work on that this afternoon?"

"That's probably a good idea. But don't go out to Parker's Point alone."

Sonny nodded and, still frowning, left the office.

"Why don't you want Sonny to go up to Parker's Point alone?" I asked. "There's nothing out there but a beer joint, is there?"

"I hope not." Sam stood up. "I'm going out to the ranch. Want to come?"

"Sure. But what are you going for?"

"Oh, check on the new feeder cattle. Look at the water level in the Kiowa Creek pond. Find that washtub you wanted to borrow. Think a few minutes without being interrupted by the telephone."

"Sure you want me along?"

He came around the desk and put his arms around me. "Yeah. I'm sure."

We stood nose to nose for a few moments. "Sure enjoyed my shower this morning," he said.

Then he led the way out into the main office. "Nadine, I'll be back to the church by four," he said.

Nadine put her hand over the telephone receiver. "That when you and Reverend Dawkins have called that press conference?"

"Shur 'nuff." Sam's talking more and more like an Okie these days. We went out the back door and got into the patrol car.

It was a gorgeous day. The leaves on these southwestern trees hadn't really begun to turn yet, though a few cottonwoods and pecans were crowned with narrow bands of gold. The pastures were brown, tinged with green, and low sumac plants banked the fences with a rusty red. Next June's wheat crop had been planted in September for use as pasture during the winter, and the young plants were now covering the fields with a brilliant green that seemed garish compared to the rest of the soft autumn colors.

Sam reached over and turned on the commercial radio station, tuning in University of Oklahoma football. Even Oklahomans who didn't go to college at OU follow the Sooners, I'd discovered, and Sam was an OU alumnus, so he watched the team's fortunes closely. We'd managed to get hold of tickets for a game in November.

He listened until he heard the score. Nebraska was ahead by a touchdown.

"Damn!" Sam snapped off the radio. "I hope Big Sam didn't hear that."

Sam's dad had gone to Oklahoma's other large state university, Oklahoma State, and football afternoons get testy around the Titus Ranch.

I wasn't interested in football, but I knew Sam wanted to think about something besides the murders for a few minutes—to clear his mind. So I looked at the scenery and didn't talk. When we stopped at the ranch house, Marty and Big Sam weren't home. Sam loaded the galvanized washtub into the backseat.

He continued his silence as we drove back toward Holton. He didn't even talk much when we stopped at the pasture where he and Johnny Garcia had put the young steers, the feeder cattle Sam had bought to put on wheat pasture in six weeks or so. He stopped the car, got out, and stood by the barbed wire fence. I stood on the front bumper of the patrol car, and we both silently counted cattle.

In a few minutes Sam looked at me. "Thirty-two," he said.

"I only got thirty-one."

"Did you count two over in the back corner?"

I looked again. "Oh. Yeah. I see them now that they've moved. And all thirty-two are up and grazing."

Reassured that the steers had made their move to the Titus Ranch in good shape, we got back in the patrol car, and Sam drove to the blacktop that led toward Holton. He was still quiet.

I kept quiet, too, but my mind kept trudging over and over the strange events of the past thirty-six hours. My curiosity finally burst out my mouth. "Why did you say—" Then I shut up. Sam was trying to take a break from law enforcement.

"Sorry," I said.

"It's okay. What do you have on your mind?"

"You don't want to talk about the case."

"Go ahead. Questions might help."

I considered a minute. "I hate to be the specter at the feast, Sam, but I don't see that you're any further ahead at all. We still don't know who Revels came to see in Holton in the first place. We don't know if he met the person he'd come to find or if he tangled with some total stranger. And I don't understand this Satanism business at all. Revels apparently had some link with devil worship— judging by the pentagram in his bed roll and maybe that crazy sampler—but now it turns out that Bullock was wrong about there being Satanists in Holton. That whole business came from his mixup over the Indian club and Nolan's joke. And we don't know what Mrs. Engelman had to do with anything."

"No, but we do know a few things, Nicky. We know that the killer very likely had a key to the church and was familiar with the building. Familiar enough to find the candle and that other stuff in the closet, and to go in the kitchen to get that cap he used to keep blood off his hair when Mrs. Engelman was killed. We know Revels could have been killed any time after nine o'clock, if that's when Virginia left the Haunted House."

"If. If that's when she left. Katherine still thinks she was there until ten-thirty."

Sam nodded, but my interruption didn't seem to disturb him. "Right, but I think I've got that figured out. I agree that we don't know for sure why anybody would want to kill Mrs. Engelman, but we do know almost exactly when they did it. And we know somebody broke into the Haunted House. Somebody wrecked the school office. And somebody pulled Nadine's purse out of her desk."

"Huh? What do those things have to do with the murders? I mean, they painted pentagrams over the high school office, but Nolan claimed to be the one who was setting up the fake Satanism evidence. I can't believe he wrecked the school office. But if he didn't, who did? And what does that have to do with the intruder in the

Haunted House and that weird business with Nadine's purse?"

"Darned if I know. But I sure do hate coincidences."

Sam drove on. He'd made several remarks I didn't understand, but before I could ask about them, we reached the Pecan Grove church, the spot where we had first seen Damon Revels two days earlier. I was surprised when Sam slowed and turned in at the gate.

"Why are you stopping here?" I asked.

Sam pointed ahead. "Mom and Dad are down there."

I got out and opened the gate, then closed it after Sam drove through.

The Pecan Grove church really does sit on one of the most beautiful spots on the Titus Ranch. As I understand it, the church site had been deeded to a pioneer congregation by Sam's great-grandfather, with the property to revert to the original owner if it ceased to be used as a place of worship. When the Pecan Grove Methodists merged into the Holton Community Church, the Tituses got the property back. Sam and Marty had made it clear that they did not want to discuss their contribution to the new church's building fund, but I had an idea it had been substantial. The church had probably come out better financially than it would have if the old building had been sold. After all, who wants an old church except another congregation?

But the Pecan Grove church is a beautiful old building. I love its soft red brick and its whimsical steeple. It sits in a broad, grassy lot lined with crape myrtles, which were now showing their bronzy fall leaves. The land behind the church slopes down to a creek that's filled with giant pecan trees. The trees and the view of the Wichita Mountains make the setting ideal.

Southwest Oklahoma's mountains are short, maybe, but their contrast with the surrounding plains gives them a certain drama. The giant boulders that cover their slopes, and the sheer cliffs that top them off, are also pretty impressive.

I could see the tailgate of Big Sam's blue pickup sticking out from behind the church. Sam drove through what had once been a gravel parking lot and parked the patrol car beside the truck.

Big Sam was sitting in a webbed aluminum chair in the shade of the pecan tree nearest the church. Marty stood beside him. She held a sketch pad.

"Hi!" Big Sam called. "Thought you'd be busy detectin'."

"Reporters are coming in at four. Clear from Oklahoma City and Dallas. I wanted to get my head straight before I face the heat."

"You'll be facin' it, too." Big Sam shook his head. "Even OETA made this case sound pretty peculiar last night."

I knew that Big Sam never missed the state news on the OETA, the Oklahoma Public Broadcasting station. We all knew not to call or try to talk to him between six-thirty and seven o'clock any weeknight.

My Sam grinned. "Let's talk about something else. How'd I do on those feeder cattle?"

"Well, they look pretty good, boy. We may make a rancher out of you yet."

Sam pretended to mop sweat from his forehead. Actually, he knows a lot about ranching. He was raised on the Titus Ranch, after all, and went through 4-H and Future Farmers. He even did a year as a college ag major before he changed to political science and law enforcement. I get a bit annoyed with Big Sam when he treats Sam like a kid, when he seems to ignore the fact that Sam may be sacrificing his military career out of family loyalty.

But Sam would probably be embarrassed if his father said anything about it. So I stay out of it.

Sam and Big Sam started talking cattle, and I joined Marty. "May I look?" I asked.

"Oh, sure. It's just studies. I'm thinking of trying an acrylic in a couple of weeks, after the foliage gets colorful enough to inspire me. I'm just sketching trees today."

I was amazed. Every painting I had seen by Marty so far had been a sunset—an abstract sunset. "You're going to paint trees?"

"I think so.

"Not sunsets?"

"The sunsets started out as color experiments, and the whole thing got out of hand. I may try something more representational next. I think it's time for something new." She cut her eyes in my direction. "What have you been working on lately?"

"Camerawise?"

She nodded.

I hated to tell her I had hardly worked on my photography in a month, so I shrugged. "Oh, just stuff for Sam. I had an idea, but—well, it would be mainly for Christmas presents."

We talked about our work for a few minutes. Marty's an outstanding painter, and I have a diploma that says "bachelor of fine arts," a scrap of paper that's supposed to certify my credentials as a photographer. Only I hadn't taken any artistic photos lately. It was frustrating to take them when I didn't have access to my own darkroom, a place where I could leave my chemicals set up, where I could spend a whole day working if I felt like it.

I'd thought of taking a series of the Titus Ranch. Even if I didn't show any of them, they would make a nice present for Big Sam. But I couldn't seem to get started on the project. I thought of the enlarger crated in the corner of the bedroom.

Then Sam was standing beside me. "Guess we'd better go on back pretty quick, Nicky." He looked at Marty's sketch pad and raised his eyebrows. "What's this? Trees? You're going to paint a setting sun behind them, right?"

Marty laughed. "Maybe. Listen, Sam, I've been meaning to talk to you. Nicky's got to have a darkroom."

"Oh!" I interrupted. I nagged enough. I didn't want Sam's mother pressuring him about that. "We'll get around to it, Marty."

She ignored me. "How about that room off the barn? You could run a water line from the tank in there. And Nicky could get into the room from the west side. She wouldn't have to go through the barnyard."

I stood silently, picturing the room she meant. It wouldn't be fancy, but it might work, especially with an outside entrance. There are no horses, pigs, or chickens on the Titus Ranch, and cattle weren't usually put in the barn unless they were sick or expected to have difficult deliveries or something. If I could have a darkroom, I'd be happy to share it with a pregnant cow now and then.

But Sam was frowning. "I don't think so, Mom. There's no heat."

"You'd have to get a space heater."

He still frowned. "Pipes might freeze. I'm not too crazy about that idea. We'll come up with something else."

"When?" Marty's voice was stern.

"Pretty quick." Sam gestured toward her sketch, and I realized he was trying to change the subject. "What's that up in the corner."

"Oh, it's the cliff. I'm trying to decide whether or not to put it in. I've done it both ways. With the cliff and without." She lifted up the top sheet and showed the drawing underneath.

"Which one do you like? Shall I leave it out? Or put it in?"

She flipped the sheet back and forth. "In? Out?"

Sam stared at her wooden faced. Then a slow grin spread over his face, like the moon coming out from behind a tree.

"Put it in! Put it in! And take it out!" He swept his mother up in a monster hug. "A sheriff's best friend is his mother! That's the answer!"

He dropped Marty and grabbed my hand. "Come on, Nicky! I got to get back to work!"

Sixteen

WE MADE ONE STOP ON THE WAY BACK TO THE PRESS
conference—the high school.

Sam hurried in the door, and I followed him, eager to
see what had happened to the mess the vandal had made.
A gang of teachers and students was cleaning up, and they
seemed to be having a good time doing it. Starr was one of
three girls who were painting the back wall of the office.

When he saw Starr, Sam motioned her into Ramsey's
office. "Starr, tell me which of the high school kids were
in The Hangout Thursday night when you and Nolan
dropped by there."

Starr looked surprised. "How'd you know about that?"

"Part of the job. I had to trace Revels's movements."

"Oh." Starr paused. Then she began to list names.

Sam wrote them down. "Thanks," he said.

Starr kept looking at him. "That's all I needed,
Starr," Sam said. "Thanks."

She looked over her shoulder, frowning, as she went
back to her paint brush. I followed her out.

"Looks like you girls drew a messy job," I said.
"Starr, are you sure you should be here?"

"Oh, it's okay!" Starr said. "Uncle Ramsey said I
could stay out at his house, but I thought it would be
better to keep busy. I picked out something for Grand-

mother to wear, and that's all we can do until—after the—" She stopped in mid-sentence.

I nodded, mentally adding the word "autopsy." Starr's grandmother had raised her. Lucretia Engelman's murder must have been an awful shock to the girl. I patted her shoulder and turned away.

The office was full of people. Two husky boys were helping the custodian take up the damaged tile in the hall. An older woman in glasses was sorting through boxes of papers and file folders, assisted by two girls. Two more boys were cleaning spray paint off the window that overlooked the front hall. Nolan wasn't in the crowd.

Sam came out of Ramsey's office then, and we headed over to the church, where Sam and Tink had decided to hold their press conference. The parking lot already held several cars and a half dozen panel trucks, most of them with television station logos on the sides.

Tink was standing at the door to the church. His face looked pinched. "I'm glad to see you, Sam," he said. He jerked his head toward the sanctuary. "The crowd's getting a bit restless."

"I'm afraid they're going to be disappointed in me," Sam answered. "I don't intend to speculate."

I followed them into the sanctuary—which is a fancy name for a very ordinary, unadorned auditorium with plain oak pews and a few windows of multicolored stained glass in abstract, nonreligious designs. The pulpit and the altar table, which always made me wonder if they had been a closeout special in the church supply catalog, had been pushed against the back wall, and Sam and Tink merely stood at the front to talk to the press.

I saw Katherine's ponytail at the right edge of the room, four rows from the front, so I joined her.

Even for a bizarre case like this one, a press conference in Holton has little in common with the scenes we all see on television—the national press corps waving note-books and yelling "Mr. President!" Around fifteen or twenty reporters, photographers, and TV camera crew members were in the sanctuary. They had all set up their equipment before Sam and Tink came in.

Katherine and I thought our husbands handled them-selves very well—considering that neither of them was used to dealing with more press representatives than the Catlin County *Courier* in the person of Leona Kephart or the area reporter for the Lawton paper, the only daily newspaper delivered in Holton. Leona had to take her own pictures, but the Lawton reporter had brought along a photographer.

Most of the reporters were polite, too. Leona turned out to be the only pain in the neck.

Sam gave a very matter-of-fact description of the two killings. He didn't downplay the Satanism angle, but his flat, dryland Okie accent came on strong, and his unemo-tional delivery made the whole thing seem dull as dirt. To hear Sam talk, you'd think Satanists were sacrificing each other in every church in America. He didn't actually say "No big deal," but he acted totally calm about the case.

Tink was a bit more upset, of course, but he joined Sam in saying that there was no possible link between the church, the Haunted House, and Satanism.

"I think they picked on the church's shed because it was easy to break into, and the church was unlocked last night because the nursery was open," Sam told the report-ers. He let his mouth twitch into a brief grin. "Security's not a big thing in Holton. We haven't figured out the connection between Mrs. Engelman and Revels's deaths, but she may have surprised someone who was—well, linked to the first killing."

That's when Leona Kephart spoke up. "But the evi-dence points to Satanism, doesn't it?"

"Maybe."

"Maybe?" Her voice was sharp. "Candles, pentagrams—do you know anything at all about Satanism, Sam?"

"Not really." Sam shrugged. "That's why I called somebody who does."

The reporters murmured, and a pretty blonde from an Oklahoma City television station spoke. "Who is that? Who did you consult?"

Sam gave the name of a Chicago police officer. "He seems to know as much as anybody about such cases," he said.

"What did he say?" Leona asked.

"He said we had some of the elements of Satanism," Sam replied.

"Some! What do you mean 'some' elements?"

Sam sighed. "Leona, I've not sure whether or not we've got Satanists in Holton, but I am sure we've got a killer. I'd like to know a few things he doesn't know I know. So I'm going to keep a bit of my information back."

Leona stood up. "It seems to me, Sam, that you're keeping a lot of the information back! And I'd like to know why that is!"

Sam's voice remained mild. "I'm not going to show my entire hand to a killer, Leona."

"You're not protecting anyone?" Leona's voice had grown shrill, and all the other reporters were staring at her. "You're not covering up for some of the so-called leaders of this community? For your friends? For people who can help you get reelected?"

"No." Sam's voice was very quiet, a sure sign that he was furious. "No, Leona. I'm not covering up for anybody. Not for a friend. Not for a community leader. And as for my election plans—I was appointed to fill out an unexpired term, as you know, and I'm very far from deciding to run for the office. But it doesn't strike me that letting killers go loose would enhance my chances at winning an election."

He turned away from her, but Leona kept on.

"But have you looked into the angle of Satan worship? Isn't it true that a Holton church worker has a large collection of books on Satanism?"

I didn't hear Sam's reply because Katherine had grabbed my arm. Her eyes and mouth were as round as her face.

"Books on Satanism!" She gasped the words out in a strangled whisper. "Where'd she get that?"

I leaned my head toward her and whispered back. "Oh, she and Bullock brought it up last night." I didn't want to tell Katherine that she was the church worker who'd been accused.

"Oh, golly!" Katherine sat back in the pew and shook her head. She looked down at her lap, then up at Tink, then over at me. She gulped; then she stood up.

"When this is over, tell Tink and Sam I need to talk to them. I'll wait in Tink's office," she whispered. Then she slipped out of the pew and went down the aisle and out of the sanctuary.

I stared at her. Had she started crying? I almost got up and went down the hall after her. What could be wrong? Did she and Tink really own books on Satanism?

I reminded myself that the whole thing was ridiculous. Katherine was too levelheaded to be interested in Satanism.

It was another ten minutes before the press was through with Sam. Then the TV crews had to tape their reports, of course, with well-coiffed reporters standing in front of the colored window to pontificate. It was hard to see any relationship between what Sam and Tink had said and what they were recording. Most of them seemed to have written their reports before they arrived.

Tink said he had to wait until they had left, so Sam and I went on down to Tink's office to meet Katherine. Her round face showed signs of tears, but they were dry by the time we arrived.

"I want to know what Mr. Bullock had to say last night," she said. "I have a feeling that this is the reason Tink's been so upset all day."

Sam looked troubled, but he went ahead and told her, assuring her that he and I didn't believe she was mixed up with Satanism.

"Poor Tink!" Katherine fluffed her bangs and brushed them to one side. "No wonder he's been so morose." Then she lifted her chin and smiled at Sam. "I guess it's time for me to tell the truth, the whole truth. Tink's been after me to come clean about why I've been hanging around the church at night."

Sam sat down beside Tink's desk. "Well, Katherine, even after Bullock threw his little hissy fit, it hadn't occurred to me to doubt your story."

"Oh, my story was true, Sam."

"Then there's no problem. I'll be getting statements from people who were at the church Friday night, but unless you saw something connected to Mrs. Engelman's death, I hardly think you need to do this before Monday."

"I'd just like to set the record straight. I guess it's time to reveal my guilty secret."

I stood up. "Maybe you'd rather talk to Sam alone—"

Katherine reached out and took my hand. "Oh, don't be silly, Nicky! It's not that guilty. The truth that I've been trying to keep from Tink's parishioners is—well, I write."

Sam frowned. "You write? You write what?"

"Books. Novels. I even sell what I write—or most of it."

"Well—that doesn't sound too 'guilty,' Katherine. What kind of books do you write?"

"That's the guilty part. I write romances. Stupid,

trivial, escapist romance novels for women looking for a few hours away from their troubles."

I stared at her, feeling my jaw drop. There were lots of would-be writers among the arty crowd I'd run with when I lived in New York. These people were longing to sell novels—any type of novels. They worked hard and connived and politicked to "make a sale." And Katherine was writing—and selling—fiction. Why did she call this a guilty secret?

"But that's wonderful!" I said. "You write novels that actually sell? You should be proud! There's nothing wrong with light fiction! We all read it. What's wrong with that?"

Katherine wrinkled her nose. "Well, besides being stupid, trivial, and escapist, some of my books are also sexy."

Sam and I looked at her a long moment, then I began to laugh.

Sam grinned. "You mean, you've kept this a secret because the old biddies in the church might object?"

"Well, them and—my father, I guess."

"Your father? Didn't Nicky tell me you're a preacher's daughter?"

"Yes. See, he's a real fundamentalist. He already thinks Tink and I are bound for Hell because Tink doesn't agree with his theology any more than I do."

She leaned forward and clasped her hands. "You know, Sam, by the time I was eighteen I'd entirely given up any belief in God. The stuff my father kept telling me I had to believe was just ludicrous. I didn't believe it, though I showed up for church twice every Sunday to avoid arguments. When I went away to college, I stopped going to church entirely. The last thing I thought I'd wind up being was a minister's wife, though I guess ministers' wives don't have to pass any particular theological test.

"But when I was twenty, I was somewhere between

an atheist and an agnostic. When you're brought up the way I was—well, you can't help feeling guilty when you quit believing what you were raised on."

She smiled. "Then I met Tink, and my opinions changed."

Sam grinned. "I gather he had quite a bit to do with the new Katherine."

Katherine's face grew rosier. "I know Tink wouldn't be a dream of love for just anybody, but for me—well, we were in a philosophy class together our senior year. We both had to work on a group report, and I guess I became his first convert. Finally somebody explained Christianity to me in a way that made it seem logical and reflected the real world—not some never-never land. He showed me that I didn't have to park my brain outside the church."

"Then Tink doesn't have any problem with your novels?"

"Oh, no! They're not immoral, you know. They'd just shock some of the people in the church—and my father."

I couldn't keep quiet any longer. "How'd you get into this kind of writing, Katherine?"

"Well, I got pregnant on my honeymoon. Johnny was a real accident. I'd been teaching, and Tink was just starting seminary. We needed my salary, but I had some problems. The doctor told me I had to quit work and be prepared to take lots of bed rest. A friend brought me a bunch of romances to while away the time." She laughed. "Like most people, once I'd read a few I began to think I could write one. So I did."

"And it sold?"

"Well, I had to do a lot of rewriting. I didn't get much money for the first one, but last year I wrote three, so it adds up. I make about what I would teaching. And I can stay home with Johnny."

Sam grinned. "I'll have to read one of your books, Katherine. But what does all this have to do with recent events at the church?"

"That's why I was up there—last night and the night before. I'm trying to get *Love's Last Lament* off to New York."

"You said you were using the copier."

"Right. I photocopy my manuscripts before I send them off to my publisher. I pay the church, of course. But that's why I was there so long."

"Both nights?"

"Well, I was there only about twenty minutes last night. My manuscript's due in New York Monday. I copied it Thursday night, then looked it over Friday, and I had to redo several pages."

"How are you going to get it to New York by Monday?"

"I took it over to the Lawton post office early this morning and sent it overnight mail. I usually take my manuscripts over there. That's been part of my secrecy campaign."

"Yeah, standing in the Holton post office line—everybody would read the address on the package."

"Right."

"When were you at the church Friday?"

"I didn't really check the time, but I waited until after the kickoff of the Heroes game, until the football traffic was past its worst. I could hear the band—oh, Holton must have made a touchdown around the time I arrived. I heard a big yell, and then the band played the fight song."

Sam nodded. "The first touchdown was around ten minutes into the first quarter. Did you see Lucretia Engelman?"

"Yes, I popped my head into the crib nursery and said hi. She was rocking the Jordans' little boy and watching television—PBS, of course. She sneered at all the other networks."

"Did she have anything to say?"

"No. Just scowled."

"Scowled?"

"Yes, but that wasn't unusual, Sam. She wasn't the most pleasant person to deal with."

I couldn't resist saying something then. "That's always fascinated me, Katherine. The few times I met Mrs. Engelman, she was rather short-tempered. Yet her clients—well, Brenda swears by her, and Billy and Lee Anna seem to love to go to the day care center. You take Johnny there. How did she get away with that brusque act?"

"Partly because she had the only licensed day care center in Holton, I'm sure, Nicky. But it's a really good center. Her nursery school classes are excellent—they encourage learning without pushing the children. And she didn't usually work directly with children herself, you know."

"Oh?" Sam's voice was calm. "Then it was unusual for her to be in the nursery herself?"

"Oh, yes. She hired people who are good with kids, then trained them to use the type of discipline and teaching she liked. She made the lesson plans and did all the dealing with parents, but she didn't usually get down on the floor with the kids or fix the lunches."

"Then someone who was looking for her wouldn't have expected to find her at the church Friday night?"

"No. I was quite surprised to see her. She said that the regular person got sick. That's another thing she was real good about—if a teacher was sick, she wasn't allowed to hang around and infect the kids. But Mrs. Engelman didn't usually fill in herself."

And that was apparently all Katherine had seen at

the church. Mrs. Engelman's presence had been unexpected, and she had been the only adult in the church. The outer door was open, for the convenience of parents dropping off children. Katherine had stayed about twenty minutes.

She shook her head when Sam asked if she had gone back into the nursery as she left.

"I wish I had. Maybe I could have stopped—"

Sam cut her off grimly. "Or maybe you would have been victim number three."

Katherine's eyes widened. "Then you think that more crimes—more murders—could be committed?"

"I think we'd better assume it's a possibility. I'd just as soon everybody stayed away from the church at night until we get this figured out."

Katherine frowned. "I wasn't nervous after that guy was killed in the shed—I mean, no one knew anything about him. I guess we all just assumed he was mixed up in something crooked, and that he brought his death on himself some way. But Mrs. Engelman—this is different."

Sam nodded. "Yep. She was a Holton person. This press conference isn't going to be the last reaction over this—especially the Satanism angle."

Katherine gasped. "Oh, I didn't tell you! And that was the main reason I wanted to talk to you."

"Tell me what?"

"The books. The books on Satanism. *The Satanic Bible*. Those are mine. Not Tink's."

"Yours?"

"Yes. I used Satanism in one of my romances. The heroine was persecuted by devil worshipers. I had to read up on the occult. And believe me, it's a hard subject to research."

"Why?"

"Because books on Satanism fall into two types—pro and con. Either they're trying to convert the reader to Satanism, or they're trying to reveal it as a threat. Hardly anything involving objective research has been done on the subject, or at least I couldn't find anything. I finally had the most luck in the paperback true crime section. And I picked up a copy of *The Satanic Bible* in a second-hand store."

"Where do you keep those books?"

"In the dining room. I didn't think of them as any more exotic than books on—well, Paris. One of my heroines took a trip there, and I bought several guidebooks."

"Did any visitor to your house show any special interest in those books?"

"No. Not really. I guess Leona Kephart must have looked the shelf over the day I was hostess for the women's group and then reported back to Mr. Bullock. I wasn't aware of it at the time." Katherine stopped talking and bit her lip. "I can hardly blame her for thinking they were odd books to be found in a minister's library, I guess."

I wasn't as charitable as Katherine. "She's a nosy bitch," I said. "The books you and Tink own, and the reasons you own them, are none of her business!"

Katherine laughed, but the laugh had a slight tremble to it. "Thanks for being on my side, Nicky. Tink's been against this all along—hiding my writing, I mean. He says he's proud—"

There was a rap at the door of the office, and she stopped talking.

It was Sonny. He pushed Tom into the room ahead of him, and he smiled grimly.

"I think I solved our other big case," Sonny said.

Tink passed in the hall, and Katherine went out the door, calling his name. Sam reached over and closed the door behind her, then looked at Sonny and Tom, frowning. "I can't believe Tom is mixed up in anything like that," he said.

Sonny shook his head. "Naw, he's just got a case of terminal dumbness."

Tom glared at his older brother. "Sonny! You creep! I would have told you if I'd known it mattered. Get off my back!"

"Okay, you two," Sam said. "Drop the sibling rivalry and tell me what's going on."

"Tell him," Sonny said.

Tom looked all around Tink's cluttered office. "Okay! Okay! So I've been catching rattlers for a guy over at Okeene."

Sam thought about that a minute before he spoke. "Well, that's not illegal, Tom."

"Try telling my mom that!"

I remembered then. Tom and Sonny's mother and dad were environmental activists. They'd even led demonstrations against snake hunts. Yes, Tom could be in serious trouble at home if he had been earning money in a way that they didn't consider environmentally sound.

"That's only one reason he's been hanging around out at Mount Parker," Sonny said. "Go on! Tell him the rest!"

"Sonny, you used to buy beer when you were in high school! Quit making such a big deal out of a couple of six-packs!"

Sam nodded. "So Corey Cramer's the current tavern owner who's supplying the underage crowd. Well, now we know. But I thought something worse was going on out there."

"That's what Tom was too dumb to catch on to," Sonny said. "Go on, Tom! Tell about what happened last weekend."

"You quit callin' me dumb, Sonny!"

Sonny took a deep breath, but Sam made a calming

gesture. "Evidently Sonny thinks what happened was important, Tom. Tell me about it."

"Well, I was up on the hill behind the restaurant, with my snake gear, gettin' a line on dens for next spring, and I began to smell something funny."

"Funny?" Sam tensed. "Funny how?"

"Awful! It was the worst stink I ever ran into. It was terrible! Like a rotten hospital."

Sonny looked triumphant, and he and Sam exchanged significant looks. "Very interesting," Sam said.

"Then I heard this slipping and sliding and cussing, and Mr. Cramer came tumbling down the hill. He'd lost his footing, and he slid quite a ways. He landed right at my feet."

Tom's fingers did a ski jump in the air. He looked at Sam, and Sam nodded encouragingly. "So I asked him if he was hurt, and he gave me a look that was meaner than any rattler I ever caught, and he said no. Then he said what the hell was I doin' up there on his property."

Tom shrugged and waved his hands again. "So I held up my gunnysack—I had three big rattlers in it—and said I was catchin' snakes." He frowned. "You know, for a minute there I thought he was going to punch me, but the rattlers sort of made him jump back. But he said for me not to hang around up there anymore."

"He'd made me mad, so I yelled at him. 'Don't worry! I'm not comin' back up here as long as the whole place stinks.' And he gave me another one of those rattle-snake looks and went on down the hill."

Sonny waved his clinched fist in the air. "Dumb! Talk about dumb!"

Tom turned toward him angrily. "Sonny!"

But Sam laid a hand on the teenager's arm. "Tom, I think Sonny's upset because you've had a very narrow escape."

"A narrow escape?"

"Yup. That smell was probably ether from a drug lab we've been looking for. Those guys are no good to fool around with."

"You mean he might have—done something to shut me up?"

"I mean that sack full of rattlers may have saved your life. Corey doesn't have any drug record. He's probably renting some building out there to the cranksters."

Tom looked blank. "Cranksters?"

Sonny spoke angrily. "The drug cookers, stupid. Crank is amphetamines. Cranksters are gangsters who mess around with crank, dummy."

Tom turned to Sonny. "Well, you big jerk, I'd think you'd be happy to find out I didn't know that!"

Sam made another soothing gesture as the two of them glared, but I gasped. "Oh! That's where Corey Cramer must be getting his money."

Sam and Sonny both looked at me strangely. I repeated Ramsey's tale about Corey threatening to fight Virginia over finances.

"So maybe he does have some money," I said.

"Yeah," said Sam. "Maybe. But maybe Virginia better not count on a big settlement." He turned to Sonny. "Did you call the drug enforcement guys?"

Before Sonny could answer, another knock sounded at the door to the office. Sam opened it. A bulky, dark-haired man wearing a billed cap stood in the opening.

"Hi, Sam," he said. "Is Nolan around here?"

SEVENTEEN

I REALIZED THAT THE MAN WAS NOLAN PORTER'S father.

"No, I haven't seen him," Sam said. "Why did you think he'd be here?"

Mr. Porter took off his cap. "Well, that phone call—" He stopped talking and scratched his head.

"What phone call?" Sam got to his feet.

"We-ell." Porter drew the word into two syllables. "I don't know, really. The wife said somebody called for Nolan, and he said he had to go check something out—and to help with the investigation. So she let him leave the house."

"Just a minute." Sam reached for the church phone and punched seven numbers. "Nadine? Has Nolan Porter showed up there? No? Has he called?" He listened. "Okay. Get all the deputies on the radio and tell them to come to the Community Church parking lot. Nolan's missing." He hung up.

Mr. Porter was looking dismayed, but he tried to smile. "Aw, come on, Sam. I can't believe anything's happened to the boy."

Sam put his hand on Mr. Porter's shoulder and led him toward the door. "You're probably right. He's probably just gone for a Coke at The Hangout, but I don't want to take any chances." He turned back to me. "Nicky, you call Holton PD. Let's get the city police in on this, too."

He went outside, leaving me with a knot of fear in my stomach. Did Sam think something had happened to Nolan? Or did he think Nolan was likely to do something to hurt someone else?

I called the police, then followed Sam and Nolan's dad outside. The two of them were talking, with Mr. Porter seeming to be trying to assure Sam that Nolan's disappearance was not ominous. Sam held up a hand, like a traffic cop stopping a line of football fans, and halted the flow of Porter's talk.

He turned toward me. "Nicky, run over to the high school and tell those kids not to go anywhere until I can talk to them, okay?"

I looked at the school, and I saw that the cleanup crew was leaving. Kids in jeans and sneakers were jumping down the steps toward the cars in the parking lot, with the teachers and maintenance men right behind them. Ramsey Kelleher stood in the doorway, shooing the last ones out. Katherine was beside him.

Sam's radio crackled, and he reached inside the patrol car. "Tell that bunch at the high school I'll be over there as quick as I can be," he told me.

I trotted across the highway—as usual there was no traffic coming—and waved my arms. The adults were ready to go home, and the delay didn't please them. But the kids had been having fun and didn't seem to mind waiting. I didn't explain why Sam wanted to talk to them.

The two girls who had been painting with Starr and the two who had helped the secretary sort the files were standing in a group, giggling. Starr was standing apart, looking like a catalog model. She was still her serene self, but she seemed to personify one of Big Sam's expressions—"downright downhearted."

I felt sorry for her. "I guess you're exhausted, Starr," I said. "You've had a busy and emotionally wearing day."

She gave me a sad smile and turned the bluer than blue eyes in my direction. "I guess I haven't really taken in what happened to Grandmother."

"I understand, believe me. I remember that when my mother died, I could hardly believe it, even though she'd been terribly ill for months. And when something happens so suddenly—"

Starr gulped, and I wondered if I'd done the wrong thing in talking to her. But she gave me another shy smile. "I'll always remember what I owe her," she said. "She not only gave me a home when I needed one, she gave me a wider view of the world. She gave me confidence and ambition."

"That's quite a heritage."

Starr raised her chin. "It's one I'm proud of. Believe me, I'm going to hang on to it. I will—" She stopped and repeated the words firmly. "I will—I will get admitted to Vassar. I will do well there. I will go on to medical school. I will. Nothing will stop me."

The force of her speech took me by surprise. Such firm ambition is rare in a seventeen-year-old kid. When I was a senior in high school, all I was interested in was the photography club and a date to the senior prom. Of course, I hadn't aimed at a high-paying profession either. I'd just wanted to do something artistic.

I guess my surprise showed, because Starr looked at me and dropped her eyes.

"It's what Grandmother would have wanted me to do," she muttered.

"Of course it is." I touched her arm. I decided to wait to tell her she had to dream her own dreams, not fulfill her grandmother's ambitions for her. This didn't seem to be the right time for that subject.

Starr kept looking at the ground. "Of course, in a way this may help me," she said. "Grandmother's estate won't amount to much. The day care center won't be worth anything without her to run it. We can sell her house, but I'll have to split that with Uncle Ramsey. If I can be declared independent financially, it'll be easier to get scholarships."

I didn't know just how to react to that, so I looked away from her. She was certainly being practical.

Luckily, Sam pulled the patrol car into the parking lot at that point. The first person he spoke to was me. "I put the washtub by the church's back door," he said. "We'll have to get it into the Haunted House later. Do you mind getting a ride home with Tink and Katherine?"

"Don't worry about me," I said. "I walk to and from that church every morning. And I can surely carry a washtub across a parking lot."

He nodded and turned to the assembled students and school personnel. "Have any of y'all seen Nolan Porter?"

He continued talking, explaining that Nolan was missing and that it was important to find him. Behind his back I saw a blue Ford pickup pull out of the church parking lot. It turned right, and I saw that the driver was Mr. Porter. Then the church's interior lights went out, and Tink and Katherine came out of the building and headed for Tink's Chevy. I was about to miss my ride. I decided that I didn't care. I'd just walk home. It was nearly sundown, but I could make the ten-minute walk to our apartment before dark. I watched as Tink and Katherine drove away.

I waited until Sam had finished with the group at the school. No one admitted knowing anything about Nolan's whereabouts, and they were all becoming impatient to be off. Starr stamped her feet and paced up and down until Sam said they could leave. Then she led the way out of the parking lot, driving a gray Oldsmobile that must have been her grandmother's.

I gave Sam a wave as he drove away, leaving me standing on the school's steps along with Virginia and Ramsey.

"I guess you two are about ready to call it a day, too," I said.

Ramsey shook his head. "I've got to finish checking those files Sam asked me to look at."

"I'm heading out to my sister's," Virginia said.

"So long." I started down the steps, then stopped. That tub. I could see it sitting beside the back door of the church. "Oh, rats!"

"What's wrong?" Virginia asked.

"Oh, I forgot that washtub. It needs to go inside the Haunted House. I was going to borrow the key from Tink, and I've let him get away."

Virginia opened her purse. "Here. Use this." She held up a key ring and took a key off it. "This opens the new lock and the dead bolt on the front door. We had to replace it after the intruder messed the old one up."

"Thanks. I'll sling the washtub inside and bring the key right back."

But Virginia was already climbing into her white truck. "Never mind. I have a key to the back door. You can give it to me tomorrow. Or Monday." She started the motor. "My life is so confusing right now that I don't really give a pee-diddly damn about that Haunted House."

She drove on off without a word. Not even a good-bye for the man she was supposedly in love with.

I sneaked a glance at Ramsey, and he caught me.

"Things aren't going well?" I asked.

"Corey's not being a gracious loser," he said. He turned toward the door of the school. "Well, I've got one more file to check. Then I'll call the sheriff's office."

I didn't know what he was talking about, but I assured him Sam would be pleased. I went across the highway to the church, hefted the tub, and carried it on over to the Haunted House. Virginia's key opened the new lock readily, and I went in. I was nervous enough that I locked the door behind me—key-operated dead bolt and all.

The setting sun was shining in the living room windows, so I didn't fumble for the light switch. I carried the tub past the Mummy's Lair and the Spider Woman's Web, then maneuvered it through the hidden door from the Phantom of the Opera scene into Dr. Frankenstein's Laboratory, humming to fill the silence. I didn't linger with my tub; despite the bright sunshine and the calm atmosphere, the Haunted House did seem ominous. The Maids and Matrons had tried hard to make the place spooky, and at that moment I was convinced that we'd succeeded.

The basement stairs were dark, and I switched on a light—just a bare bulb, but comforting—as I carried the washtub down. I put the thing in the middle of the floor and looked around.

The basement was classically gloomy. It had no furnishings except for some built-in shelves, not even the furnace that would have been a fixture of a northern basement. Central heating had been unknown in Oklahoma when this house was built, I'd been told. There were gas connections for space heaters in every room upstairs.

The abandoned cardboard pillars Katherine and I had been working on for Dracula's Tomb stood here and there, along with some dead branches. The room was a mess. We'd have our hands full turning it into a tropical island for our cannibals.

As I looked it over, I realized I never had measured the area to see how things were going to fit in. I paced it off, estimating the size, but I still couldn't understand just what Katherine had had in mind. I thought she was overestimating the floor space.

"Heck fire!" I said aloud, copying one of my father-in-law's pet expressions. "I'll just find the measuring tape and see who's right."

My voice bounced off the walls with a hollow echo, so I reassured myself out loud. "There's nothing to worry about, and I'll never have a better opportunity."

I trotted up to the first floor, into Dr. Frankenstein's Laboratory, laid the house key on a table there, and checked the storage closet. The box of odds and ends—pencils, chalk, straight pins, safety pins, thumb tacks, and electrical tape—was in its usual place. But the box did not hold the metal carpenter's tape I had expected to find.

Being in the empty Haunted House was still making me nervous, I guess, because I spoke aloud again. "Maybe that tape is upstairs in the dressing room cupboard."

I took the narrow back stairwell fast, trying to outrun the memory of how that door at the top had slammed in my face only that morning. But the door remained open this time, and when I bounded out upstairs, the hall was empty. I started toward the dressing room, which was next to the bathroom and the upstairs storage cupboard. The western sun was still beating in, lighting the upstairs, but the cheery light didn't keep me from checking behind every door as I walked along.

There were to be three scary vignettes upstairs. The first was the Ghost Room. Right now it looked as if sheets had been hung out to dry there, but lights and scary sounds would transform it on Halloween.

Next door was the Voodoo Priest's Altar. Thanks to Virginia's efficient nagging, it was all set up, looking weird, with the dolls all properly stabbed full of pins and the fake dead chicken sprinkled with fake blood.

The house was peaceful. And I was completely alone, just me and the setting sun. I went on down the hall.

I checked the final room, my favorite, the Witch's Parlor. It really was clever, a travesty of a homey scene. The fake fireplace looked sweet, until you noticed what was roasting on the spit. The earthen teapot on the mantel was shaped like a skull. On close examination, the knitting lying in the rocking chair turned out to be a sweater with three arms. The rocking chair itself appeared to be electrified. The room was a bit sick, but it was witty, the only part of the Haunted House with a sense of humor. A lot of the jokes had been stolen from Charles Addams cartoons.

The sunlight didn't shine on this corner of the house, and in spite of the room's wit, I always found it the scariest of all. The juxtaposition of the wholesome and the horrible appealed in a bizarre kind of way to my imagination. I shivered as I looked in the door.

But I looked. It was too lonesome in that house not to check every room as I went by it. So I forced myself to look at the Witch's Parlor dispassionately. I looked at the sampler in the rustic frame that hung over the fake fireplace and even checked out the print of black cats on the chair cushion.

Then I looked at the sampler again. It was the same design that Katherine had been drawing on her sketch pad that morning.

That was odd.

I walked over to the sampler and looked at it more closely, and I saw that the resemblance was only in the overall design. Katherine's drawing had been based around her own name, of course. This one was based on "Virginia."

Then I remembered. Katherine had told me she got the idea for the youth group project from Virginia

Cramer, who had "done something like it back in 4-H." Virginia's 4-H project had taken the form of a sampler, and Katherine was using the same idea as a drawing. She probably thought drawings would appeal to the boys in the senior high Sunday school class more than embroidery would.

I looked the sampler over, wondering what clues it gave to Virginia's adolescent identity. Like Katherine's design, Virginia's contained books, a forerunner of her career as an English teacher. Instead of Katherine's flowers, the young Virginia had used kittens and tomato plants. And in one corner was a scale. Virginia, I decided, must be a Libra.

The whole thing seemed terribly familiar. Sure, I told myself. It reminds you of Katherine's design. Nope, myself answered. It's something else, something different.

I actually shrugged and turned away before I remembered. And then, rather than a light coming on above my head, the light went out. The setting sun slid behind a corner of the roof, and I found myself standing in the door to the Witch's Parlor in near-darkness.

And I remembered. Virginia's sampler reminded me of the one that had been folded up in Damon Revels's Bible.

I whirled around and grabbed the sampler off the wall. I ran with it into the hall, where the sunlight still streamed. Yes! They were almost the same.

My heart began to pound. "Sam!" I gasped aloud. I could hardly wait to tell him that I had discovered a clue—maybe a major clue—to the link between Damon Revels and Holton, America.

If Virginia had made the sampler as a 4-H project, probably a lot of Holton women of her age had done the same thing. Maybe Sam would be able to find the identity of the person who had made Revels's sampler, the scrap of cloth that Revels had prized highly enough to keep folded in his Bible.

I abandoned the hunt for the tape measure and started for the front stairs, on my way to the sheriff's office to share my find. I was on the top step when the truck pulled in.

I saw it go past the front windows. It was Virginia's battered white Ford truck, heading to her regular parking place. She had evidently decided she did give a pee-diddly damn about the Haunted House, and she'd come back to do some errand.

I didn't want to see her, but for a moment I didn't know why not.

It was something about that sampler. I was still carrying it in my hand, and I didn't want to explain that it might be evidence in a murder case. I stood there at the top of the stairs, one foot poised to step down, and I decided I was going to try to sneak out while Virginia was going around to the back door.

But the key to the front door—including its key-operated dead bolt—was still lying on a table in the kitchen. Could I get it and still dodge Virginia?

I whirled and crossed the hall to the back stairs. I carefully closed the door to the upstairs hall behind me, and I crept down the dark, narrow stairway, placing my feet as quietly as possible and listening for Virginia's key in the lock.

So far, so good. I had reached the bottom step, and I reached out and put my hand on the door to the old kitchen, now Dr. Frankenstein's Laboratory.

Then, almost in my ear, there came a loud "Bang!" Wood thudded against wood.

A second later I realized that I hadn't really wet my pants. I had just thought I had. And my heart was still beating, too.

Then I identified the sound. The back door had flown open and slammed against the wall.

I exhaled slowly. Virginia had been faster than I'd expected, and she had come in the back door. I'd been caught. I was being stupid. I'd just go out into the kitchen, hold the sampler casually while I said hi, then walk on home. I inhaled.

Then a voice spoke, and I froze.

"I don't get it," the voice said. "Why won't you let me tell the sheriff that you killed the snake for me? And why don't you want anybody to know you helped me make those metal gadgets we left out at the park?"

It was a male voice, a young male voice. I had found Nolan Porter.

EIGHTEEN

....

I COULDN'T MOVE.

Surprise and curiosity turned me into part of the house. I stood there in the dark stairwell with my hand on the door handle, absolutely powerless to reveal my presence or in any way intervene in the conversation going on in Dr. Frankenstein's Laboratory.

Nolan was still talking. "I don't get it. The sheriff's not mad. He thinks Bullock is a real jerk, just the way we do. So why don't you want me to tell him about the snake?"

I heard a restless movement; then Nolan's voice went on. "For that matter, why did you want me to meet you here? How'd you get a key to this place?"

"I snitched it from the minister's key ring. I just wanted a private place to talk to you."

It was a deep voice, but definitely feminine. And young. With each word pronounced distinctly and with only a slight Okie accent.

It was Starr.

Starr? Only twenty minutes earlier I had heard Sam ask Starr and her friends if they knew where Nolan was. She had joined the others in denying any such knowledge. Yet if she had asked Nolan to meet her, she had already called him and set up the date before Sam quizzed the kids.

Why had she lied?

"Well, what did you want to talk about, Starr?"

"About that snake, Nolan. Please don't tell the sheriff I was mixed up in that Satanism business."

Of course. Starr was the expert on snakes. Thursday night, when she had come to our apartment with Nolan and Tom Blacksaddle, Nolan had told us proudly that Starr and Tom had won a big science fair prize with their display of mounted prairie animals, a group that would definitely include rattlesnakes. But Tom had said he had been the collector and had given Starr the credit for mounting the specimens. Did that mean he caught them alive, and she killed them?

No wonder Nolan had nearly fainted when Sam asked him to catch a rattlesnake. He was probably as scared of them as I am.

"Look, Starr," Nolan was saying, "I don't want to tell on you, but the sheriff didn't believe my story. He's figured out that I couldn't catch a snake live and kill it with chloroform. I'd be lucky to kill one with a hoe. He's going to ask me again. I'm going to ask Tom to tell about his part in the joke. You'd better do the same thing."

"Why does the sheriff have to know I was in on it? Why does it matter?"

I understood Starr's question. Just why had Sam been so interested in Nolan's evidence? If the kids were involved in fake Satanism, then what did that have to do with Revels's death?

The question almost answered itself, and I stifled a gasp of surprise. Sam must believe that the person who killed Revels had faked the Satanic evidence at the scene of his death. But that meant that the murderer had known about the fake Satanism before Revels was killed—as early as Thursday night.

And Bullock swore he hadn't told anyone except Tink

before he talked to Sam. He had talked to the Holton police chief, but Chief Evans had been on his way out of town. It was unlikely that the chief had talked to anybody.

Nolan swore he hadn't told anyone, because he wanted to hit Bullock with ridicule on Monday. But now it appeared that Starr and Tom had been in on the joke all along.

So on Thursday night only five people had known about the Satanic rumor—Tink, Bullock, Starr, Nolan, and Tom Blacksaddle. Well, seven people, if you counted Sam and me. Eight if you counted Nadine. Nine if you counted Katherine, who had been told by Tink.

I didn't think Sam, Nadine, Tink, Katherine, or I had blabbed, but Bullock or any of the three kids could have told someone else.

But it seemed obvious that the motive for Revels's death had not been Satanism, but the connection Revels had with someone from Holton, someone he had known fifteen years earlier—when he had been mixed up in the drug culture.

That let the kids out. After all, fifteen years earlier Starr, Nolan, and Tom had been worried about diaper rash, not drugs.

Did that mean that Bullock was connected with the crime in some way?

Starr repeated her question. "Why does it matter?"

I heard Nolan move again before he answered. "It doesn't matter, really! We just need to set the record straight. Like I said, the sheriff's not mad. He just wants to know—so he can prove that we weren't involved in this murder!"

I eavesdropped, hugging the framed sampler against my chest.

"Listen, Nolan, I'm not going to argue," Starr said. "I'm not going to let a dumb stunt like this keep me out of Vassar. I'm going there, and I'm going to make it. I'm not going to turn out like my mother!"

Starr's mother? What could Starr mean by an implication that her mother had not turned out well? Starr's mother had been the brainiest person ever to come out of Holton High School, that was pretty well established. Ramsey, her brother, said it was so, and Virginia, who had been her classmate, agreed.

Virginia. Her classmate. I thought about her. Virginia, who had made the sampler I was clutching. Virginia, who had done the embroidery as a 4-H project. Virginia, who had told me she knew Starr's mother in high school, in 4-H Club.

I closed my eyes. If the sampler was a 4-H project, then Starr's mother had probably made a similar one. Maybe one like the needlework tucked into Revels's Bible.

Frantically, I tried to remember what the needlework from Revels's Bible had looked like. It hadn't been designed around a name, I remembered that. The central symbol had been a pentagram.

A pentagram, which is nothing in the world except an upside-down star.

Or maybe a starr? But how could it be linked to Maryrose Engelman's daughter? A design of columns, flowers, and dainty little bulls.

The memory of the babyish bulls answered the question. The sampler had been made for a baby. Instead of the baby's name, Maryrose Engelman had used a symbol for the child's name—a star. And I was willing to believe that Starr's astrological sign must be Taurus—the sign of the bull, the cute little baby bull.

And the star was surrounded by a design that included flowers. Roses, of course. Like the one that was part of Starr's mother's name, Maryrose.

But what could a young girl like Starr have had to

do with a drifter like Damon Revels? And how had Revels gotten hold of the sampler?

More than my muscles were becoming wooden. My innards had turned to balsa—soft, pulpy balsa.

I could hear Nolan pace up and down on the worn linoleum of Dr. Frankenstein's lab. "I don't know why you won't tell, Starr! This was just a joke! Nobody's going to be mad—except Bullock, and he doesn't count."

"I won't let it link me to a crime."

"A crime? You mean the murder? I know you didn't have anything to do with that. Besides, you were with Tom. You can back each other up. And I know when you brought back my truck."

The truck. Nolan's beat-up white Ford pickup. The one I had mistaken for Virginia's only minutes earlier.

Oh, Lordy.

Now I saw that Virginia hadn't lied about leaving the Haunted House at nine o'clock Thursday night. The truck Katherine had seen at the Haunted House at ten-thirty wasn't Virginia's. It had been Nolan's truck, which he had lent to Starr Thursday night so she could take Tom home. And I saw that Sam had already realized this. He hadn't been surprised when Katherine had claimed to see the truck an hour after Virginia said she'd left the Haunted House. In fact, I'd heard him tell Nadine to "go ahead." He must have wanted her to check with Motor Vehicle Registrations, to find out who else in Catlin County owned a white Ford pickup. He'd realized there were two white trucks.

Nolan spoke again. "After all, with your grandmother gone, Starr, you and Tom won't have to sneak around any more."

That was the nudge I needed to propel my wooden muscles into action. I pushed open the door to Dr. Frankenstein's lab.

The scene was much as I had guessed from eaves-dropping. Nolan was pacing nervously and had just reached a point near the window. Starr was standing closer to the door, with her back to me. She had picked up one of the heavy crocks that were among the props for Dr. Frankenstein and was holding it behind her, fondling its neck. Her back was as taut as a coiled spring.

And the hands that held the crock were encased in plastic gloves—cheap, throwaway plastic gloves like those worn by food handlers, by people who—like Starr—pre-pared food for day care centers.

Before I could do more than look at the scene, Starr spoke.

"Nolan! There's someone outside!"

"So what?" Nolan said. But he turned, pulled the curtain aside, and looked out the window.

In a movement so fast I could hardly believe it, Starr uncoiled, lifted the heavy crock high above her head and leaped across the room toward Nolan's unprotected back.

I barely had time to scream.

"Nolan!"

Nolan turned, but it was too late. The crock con-nected with his forehead and smashed into pieces. Blood spurted, and he dropped like a stone.

Starr stood over his body. She clenched her fists and gave a sob. Then, slowly, almost deliberately, she turned toward me.

"You!" she growled. "You're not keeping me out of Vassar!"

I was to be her next victim.

She charged toward me, and I jumped back into the stairwell and slammed the door in her face.

Then I raced back up to the second floor. I'd have to go up, then down the front steps to make the front door. If she followed me, I'd have a good chance.

When I reached the top of the steps, I slammed the door to the stairway and stood against it listening.

Had she followed me? Or had she been quick enough to realize she could get between me and the front door by cutting through the Phantom of the Opera's room?

There was no sound on the stairway behind me. And now I realized something else. I couldn't get out the front door. I had relocked the dead bolt and left the key on the table in the kitchen.

The back door. Maybe Starr had left it unlocked. If I could get back into the kitchen, maybe I could get outside that way. At least I could get hold of the key. If Starr hadn't found it first.

I tiptoed across the hall and looked down the front stairs. The upstairs was nearly dark now, and the light switch was at the top of the stairs. I fingered it, but decided that darkness might be more of an ally than light. I peered down the stairway. Was Starr lurking at the bottom? Or was she coming up the back stairs, behind me? Did she have me trapped? Was there no way I could get to the kitchen?

I looked at the door to the back stairs. It moved.

That decided me. I slid into the Voodoo room, leaned around the door, and threw the sampler down the hall, toward the bathroom at the end. It landed on the floor and slid, banging into the bathroom door.

I jumped back against the wall and listened until Starr's footsteps went by the Voodoo room and I heard the bathroom door open. Then I moved silently out of my hiding place and down the front stairs, running on tiptoe. I reached the bottom and ran across the hall, into the Mummy's Lair. I slid behind the sarcophagus and dropped to my knees, panting.

Had she heard me?

No sound. The house was silent. I barely breathed.

I was all too aware that I was five feet, three inches tall, weighed less than 120 pounds, and walked two miles every day for exercise. Starr was at least five feet, nine inches tall, and weighed more like 145. And as a high school athlete she lifted weights and ran laps under the guidance of a professional coach. She'd been strong enough to open that jammed window. The comparison made it easy for me to stay still.

But I was looking around. There was a window behind me. It was covered with plasterboard and painted with mock Egyptian hieroglyphics. I'd have to get into the Phantom of the Opera Loft to reach a window that would open or to get to the back door. Was there a place to hide there?

The building was silent. Damn old "Yank" Preston. Why'd he have to build such a sturdy house?

Then a noise sounded. Starr was in the upstairs hall. Maybe she thought I was still on the second story. I could hear her walk down the hall, pausing. She must be looking in each room. I held my breath until I heard a noise at the end of the hall, down where I had thrown the sampler.

This was my chance.

I jumped to my feet and scampered into the Phantom of the Opera room. I was a bit surprised to find the curtain pushed back, not hiding the door into the lab. I crept through the cubbyhole that had once been a broom closet and opened the door. The coast seemed to be clear. I had only to grab the key from the table, to ensure that Starr didn't get it, and head for the back porch. Then I'd be outside and on my way for help.

Quietly now. I didn't want Starr to know I'd escaped. I stepped carefully into the dark kitchen.

I was just even with the door to the back stairs when it swung open, and Starr stepped out.

In books, the good guy and the bad guy usually have one of these face-to-face confrontations. Usually the bad guy takes the opportunity to explain just what had driven him to crime, to justify his evil actions.

Starr didn't do that. Even in the dim light, I could see that she looked wild-eyed and determined. "You're not getting away!" she yelled. Then she rushed at me.

I screamed. Loudly. Noise was my only chance, and I made plenty. I shoved Dr. Frankenstein's fake lab table over. It crashed. I shrieked. She grabbed my arm. I yelled. She got a handful of hair. I roared. She threw a bearhug on me. I screeched. She got her hands around my neck. I scratched at her face.

She was cutting off my air supply, and I began to see bright lights shooting around the room. Was I losing consciousness?

Suddenly I was flung across the room. I rolled and whanged against the overturned lab table. I took a deep breath and yelled again.

Then I heard Sam's voice. I don't remember yet just what he said, but I knew he was coming, and I scrambled around the lab table to wait for him, still yelling.

The shooting lights, I realized now, were not a hallucination. They were shining through the kitchen windows. They were car lights.

Starr huddled against the wall, holding up her hands to shield her eyes from the brightness. Then she bolted for the door into the Phantom's room.

She swung it open, then jumped back. We were both screaming.

A hideous, bloody monster stood in the doorway. It lifted its hands, threatening Starr.

She turned and ran. She ran toward the back porch. But Sam spoke again, and the sound seemed to stop her.

She turned back and yanked open the doorway in between. The doorway she must have thought led to the back stairs. She rushed through the door.

There was a loud scream, then a tremendous knocking and thumping.

Then silence.

I was alone with the hideous, bloody figure that had frightened Starr.

It leaned against the wall and rubbed its arm clumsily over its forehead.

"What happened?"

The monstrous figure had Nolan's voice.

I stood up and walked to its side. "We'll get you a doctor, Nolan. You'll be okay."

"But what happened?" he repeated.

"Starr must have thought she was running upstairs," I answered, "but she opened the wrong doorway. She's fallen down the basement steps."

Sam and Sonny were in the house by then, and they turned on the light in Frankenstein's lab, then followed my motion down the basement stairs.

Sonny came back up immediately. "I'll call the doc and get the first aid kit from the car," he said. "But it's not gonna do any good. She's a goner."

NINETEEN

I STOOD ON THE FRONT PORCH, HOLDING SAM'S HAND and waiting for the ambulance that would take Starr away.

Dr. Thomas, Holton's only doctor, had declared her dead, then taken Nolan to the Holton hospital to be stitched up and watched overnight. Nolan didn't seem to be seriously hurt, the doctor said. I was comforted by the idea that my first scream had spoiled Starr's aim and might have saved Nolan's life and reason.

But my own reason was about to go. My head was spinning. Starr had apparently killed Revels, then her own grandmother. Why?

"Sam, just what was Revels's connection with the Engelman family?" I asked. "Why did Starr kill him? What did he have to do with her?"

Sam dropped my hand and dug through the papers fastened to his clipboard. He pulled out a photostat and handed it to me. I held it up to the porch light and read it.

It was a birth certificate. It certified that an infant girl named Mary Starrette Engelman had been born to Maryrose Engelman on a Monday in May. She had weighed eight pounds, six ounces, and her eyes had been treated routinely.

In the space for "father" was the name "Damon Starrett Revels."

I gasped. "Revels was her father?"

"That's what it says."

"But that's more confusing than ever! Starr apparently hadn't seen him since she was five—"

"Yeah. That's the year he was sent to prison. And Starr's mother died of a drug overdose."

"A drug overdose?"

My voice had risen in surprise, so I was embarrassed when Ramsey Kelleher came out of the house.

But Ramsey was perfectly calm. "Yes," he said, "my sister died of a drug overdose."

"Ramsey, I'm so sorry," I said. "About Starr. About everything."

Ramsey walked across the porch and sat on the rail. "Sorry about Starr? I don't know whether I should be sorry about her or for her, Nicky."

"Both, I guess," Sam said.

Ramsey nodded. "It was the ultimate irony of my mother's life, of course. She pushed my sister so hard, shoved her into Vassar. And what happened? She got mixed up with some guy, quit school, and lived with him. My mother went up there to 'straighten her out.' She'd never tell me what happened, but she quit bragging about how wonderful Maryrose was."

He sighed deeply. "I guess Maryrose and her boyfriend were heavily into drugs and were living in some sort of hippie commune. She must have laughed at Mother. Then five years later we heard that she was dead of a drug overdose and the boyfriend—they were still together—was bound for prison. At least he had the decency to call Mother and ask her if she'd take Starr."

"You and your mother did your best for Starr, Ramsey."

"No! Mother made all the same mistakes she'd made with Maryrose and I—I stayed away. I could only cope with Mother by avoiding her. I moved away—just came back two years ago. I left poor Starr to be given the same set of false standards that had destroyed her mother."

"You shouldn't be so hard on yourself."

"Why not? I was forbidden to tell Starr the truth, while Mother built a whole life of lies for the child. She gave her this stupid myth about her brilliant mother, cruelly cut down in her prime in an accident. About her socially prominent father, the promising young doctor. About the way she could follow in their footsteps and go to an elite eastern college—as if that were Valhalla!"

He held his head in his hands a moment, then looked up at Sam.

"I want you to believe me. I never knew the name of Starr's father. And I'm sure Starr didn't either. Mother always said his name sounded 'too foreign' for southwest Oklahoma. Of course, Engelman was Starr's legal name, since her parents never married. But I had no idea who her father was until we found that birth certificate in Mother's desk."

Sam was nodding as I turned to him.

"You dug this out?" I said. "Why did you suspect that Revels was connected with Starr?"

"I didn't," Sam answered. "I became convinced that some high school kid was involved because of the mud on the floor of the church and the shed."

"Those things you called 'worms'?"

"Right. The tennis shoes Starr, Nolan, and Tom wore left similar ones in the sheriff's office Thursday night."

"But all the high school kids are wearing that same kind of shoe."

"Right. They're the latest fad, so that didn't link

Starr to the scene, any more than any other kid. But the break-in at the high school, coming on top of the intruder at the Haunted House, made things a little clearer—once I'd gotten a clue from Mom."

"You mean the 'putting things in and taking things out' remark?"

"Yeah. It made me realize that the intruder had put something in—Revels's billfold—at the Haunted House. And I suspected the intruder had put something in—the pentagram necklace in Revels's bedroll—at the sheriff's office. But the killer had gotten into the church and taken something out—the candles and knife and lipstick. That made me wonder if something had been either put in or taken out at the high school, with the vandalism as a cover-up."

I was completely confused. "And had it?"

Ramsey answered. "Yes, Nicky. Starr's birth certificate was missing, although we should have had a photostat of it. Since she'd entered school for the first time at Holton—starting with kindergarten—we should have had a copy of that birth certificate."

"How'd you know to check her file?"

Sam answered. "I didn't have Ramsey check only her file. He checked the files of all the kids I had identified as being in The Hangout Thursday night at the same time Revels was there. Neither Ramsey nor I expected Starr's file to be the one with the anomaly."

He stopped talking as Ramsey stood up.

"I should have guessed that there was an extremely loose screw somewhere in Starr's personality," Ramsey said. "No one could have been as 'good' as she was. There was never a sign of normal teenage rebellion, except for her romance with Tom Blacksaddle, and she kept that pretty low key. Mother kept her completely repressed. And the other kids didn't really like her."

He turned to Sam. "Did you say you found a necklace with a pentagram in Revels's bedroll?"

"It had been a star necklace originally. The loop for the chain had been pried off and resoldered upside down."

"Well, I gave Starr a cheap little necklace with a star on it last year at Christmas. And there's a soldering iron in Mother's garage. I noticed it was out on the workbench."

Sam nodded.

"But how did you guys know Starr was at the Haunted House?" I asked.

"We didn't," Sam answered. "After Ramsey found that Starr's birth certificate was missing, he went over to his mother's house and found another copy. And Sonny still had Tom in the office putting the fear of God into him by threatening to tell his mother about the snake hunting. So we asked Tom if he'd heard from Nolan, and he had. He said Starr had asked both of them to meet her. Sonny had grabbed Tom before he could leave, but Tom assumed Nolan had kept the date. So we started looking for Nolan's truck. And where—in a town the size of Holton—could you hide a white Ford truck? The Haunted House was the obvious answer, because we'd all gotten used to seeing Virginia's truck here."

I nodded. "When they pulled in, I thought it was Virginia."

"Right. Virginia had hung out over here so much that none of us thought anything about it when a truck that looked like hers was parked outside. So I came over, just to check."

I shivered and took his hand again.

"But I still don't understand why Starr would kill Revels. Just because he was her father? And why would she kill her grandmother?"

"Revels must have been an awful shock to Starr," Ramsey said.

"A shock?"

"Yes. I was in The Hangout that night. I remember. He was loud and strange. He giggled a lot. He definitely didn't act normal."

"That's true. But that's no reason to kill him."

"Not for you or me, maybe," Ramsey said. "But remember that Mother had stuffed Starr full of this story about her brilliant, intelligent, sophisticated father-the-doctor."

"How did she even know who Revels was?"

Sam stirred and spoke. "I think it was partly coincidence, Nicky. You remember that Revels had slung his bedroll in the back hall at the sheriff's department?"

"Yes, we all commented on it as—" I broke off.

"Yeah. We all commented on the unusual bedroll, and I told Starr, Nolan, and Tom that it belonged to a weird hitchhiker we'd picked up. I may have even mentioned his name, but I'm willing to bet that Starr remembered that bedroll."

I nodded. "But would Revels have had that bedroll fifteen years ago?"

"He'd spent a lot of those years in prison, Nicky. The bedroll would have been in storage someplace. That bright star on the end would have stayed in a child's mind. And I'm willing to bet that Revels called ahead to see if Starr was still in Holton. I'll bet she'd talked to him before he came.

"Anyway, somehow Starr figured out who he was. She must have approached him when he left The Hangout."

"After she borrowed Nolan's truck and dropped Tom at home."

Sam nodded. "Yeah, Tom confirms that she took him straight home, but Nolan was left standing around The Hangout for more than an hour.

"Starr must have waited for Revels. They probably talked, and she figured out that she was right. He actually was her father."

"Christ!" Ramsey said. "What a shock to Starr!"

"Especially when Revels made it clear that he wanted to stick around and establish a father-daughter relationship," Sam said.

"How do you know that?"

"From what that minister in California told us, Nicky. Revels had gotten religion, and he was trying to make up for his past misdeeds."

I thought about that before I spoke. "So here was Starr, absolutely bent on getting into an elite eastern college, and her long-lost father shows up. And he's not a brilliant doctor from a socially prominent family. He's a half-crazy ex-druggie. And broke. A hitchhiker."

Ramsey took out a handkerchief and blew his nose. "She probably thought he'd keep her from getting into Vassar."

"Actually, I don't think he'd have had any effect," Sam said quietly. "But Starr could have believed he would have. Of course, we're just speculating."

We all thought that over. But I was still confused.

"But what about Mrs. Engelman?"

Ramsey gave a barking laugh. "Christ!" he said again. Then he stood up. "The ambulance is here." He went back into the house and Sam followed him.

Sam and I didn't have another chance to talk until long after midnight, when Sam finally got up to our apartment. I was still confused, and I demanded answers before he could even take off his uniform.

"Did Starr really kill her own grandmother?"

"I think so, Nicky. She probably knew something, and Starr acted to shut her up."

"But Mrs. Engelman was ignoring the whole thing! She bawled out Bullock for making it into a big deal, and she refused to join in the speculation."

"But she watched television."

"She sneered at television! She wouldn't allow the children to watch anything but 'Sesame Street.' Oh!" I stopped and gasped. "Katherine said she was watching OETA when she went up to the church Friday night."

"Right. And what comes on OETA at six-thirty every weeknight?"

"Your dad's favorite show. 'Oklahoma Report.' And the news about Revels's murder was on there."

Sam nodded. "Right. Big Sam mentioned it at the football game. It was the first time Revels's name had been publicly announced."

Lucretia Engelman had obviously known the name of her daughter's lover, had even met him. I contemplated the effect hearing that name would have had on her.

"Lordy! That must have been a thunderbolt to her," I said.

"I'm guessing," Sam said, "but I'll bet that Starr went across to the church during the third quarter of the game, when the band gets their break. The news of Revels's identity would have been fresh in Mrs. Engelman's mind. I'm sure she would have said something—even if she didn't suspect Starr of any link with Revels's death."

"It could have been the first time that Starr realized her grandmother knew who Damon Revels was."

"Right. At the least, Mrs. Engelman must have told her they must tell the authorities that they were the people Revels had come to Holton to see. But Starr couldn't afford to do that."

I sat on the edge of the bed. "It's too horrible to think about! A young girl! Killing her own father and grandmother!"

"And trying to kill her two best friends."

"Two?" I gasped. "Nolan, of course—but you mean Tom—"

"Tom knew too much. He'd have been out of her way by midnight."

"Horrible!"

Sam sat beside me. He stared at the floor a long moment. Then he spoke. "Horrible is the right word, Nicky. If I stay in law enforcement for fifty more years, I don't think I'll run into a more horrible case than this one."

"It's just impossible to understand."

"Ramsey may be right; Mrs. Engelman may have filled the girl with such tales of wonderful parents that she couldn't cope with the truth about her father and with the lies from her grandmother. Maybe she just snapped."

He stood up and unbuttoned his shirt. "Or maybe there's another answer," he said. "Maybe she was just evil."

He looked terribly forlorn. I stood up and put my arms around him. We held each other.

Then Sam kissed my forehead. "I know it's late," he said, "but let's get up and go to church in the morning. I need a few hymns. Maybe Tink can make sense of this. I can't."

TWENTY

THE CHURCH PARKING LOT WAS ONLY A QUARTER filled when we arrived the next morning.

"What's wrong?" I asked. "You don't suppose this Satanism business is keeping the congregation home?"

Sam laughed. "Nope. Look at the time."

I checked my watch. "Ten-thirty-five. Church starts in ten minutes."

"Nope. Sunday school starts in ten minutes. We forgot daylight savings time. It ended at two A.M. The week we finally got around to coming to church, we got here an hour early."

We both laughed.

"Well, how about a cup of coffee in the church kitchen?" I asked. "Or do you want to go home and read the paper?"

But Sam was checking his watch again. "I've got another stop to suggest. A place I've been meaning to take you."

He swung the car around and silently drove toward the Titus Ranch. When he reached the old Titus Pecan Grove, where we had first run into Revels, he stopped. I got out and opened the gate, and he pulled the patrol car in, parked it beside the church building, then turned off the motor. We got out of the car.

We stood looking at the building. It was as pretty as ever, its old brick a deep rose in the fall light. Johnny Garcia had mowed recently. The grass was smooth, and the leaves of the crape myrtles were turning a rich purple. Gold rimmed the tops of the pecan trees. We walked to the back of the building.

"The trim needs a coat of paint," Sam said.

The paint was peeling around the beautiful arched window and under the eaves. "It's not too bad," I said. "But Big Sam said he can't find a buyer. Maybe he thinks there's not much point in painting."

"Maybe not," Sam said. Then he reached in his pocket. "I've got the key."

He led the way back to the entry and opened the door. I went through a little hall lined with coat hooks and entered the old sanctuary. The pews had been sold, so it was a bare room of perhaps fifty by thirty-five feet, with a ceiling that followed the roof line up until it was around twenty-five feet high at the center. Everything smelled musty, but the morning sunlight flooded the room, and it looked pleasant and homey.

I walked to the front of the church, where the altar had once stood, and looked out the neo-Gothic window. It framed a spectacular view of the Wichita Mountains.

"I still love that view!" I said. "More inspirational than any stained glass."

Sam opened a door beside the altar platform, and I followed him into a small room behind the sanctuary, a room that once must have been the minister's office. He gestured toward another door. "They added a restroom back here, so there is plumbing. It's not in very good shape, but Big Sam says the septic system's plenty adequate."

"If you say so." I was beginning to wonder what we were doing there.

"You could put a darkroom any place you wanted it in here."

I stared at him. A darkroom? In an abandoned church? What in the world was he talking about?

"The building would have to have all new plumbing anyway," he said.

I gulped. "A darkroom? New plumbing? Sam, what are you talking about?"

He ducked his head and rubbed a hand over the wall. "Well, if you don't like the idea—"

"What idea?"

"The idea of remodeling the Pecan Grove Church into a house. For us."

"Oh!"

I looked around the office, then ran back out into the sanctuary. "Oh!" I stared out the giant window at the view, then looked at the proportions of the big room.

Sam was standing in the office door, looking worried. "It's just a suggestion, Nicky. Well, I thought that the ceiling might be high enough for a sleeping loft back here. Big Sam says he can't get anybody else interested in buying it, and he'll sell it to us for a dollar. We'd have to get a sizable mortgage for the remodeling. And we might do a lot of work and get stuck with an unsalable house if I go back to the army. Of course, we'd have it as a permanent address. If you don't think it would work—"

I ran back to him and threw my arms around his neck. "Sam, I love you! It's a wonderful idea. You're a genius!"

Ten minutes later we had it sketched out in the dust. The altar area, with its dramatic window, would become a dining alcove. The old office would become a new entry hall, and the old storage room would be a kitchen. We'd keep the high-pitched ceiling through the center section, and that would become a living room.

"You've heard of cathedral ceilings?" I said. "We'll have a country church ceiling!"

We'd build a sleeping loft across the back half of the sanctuary, with the front open so that we could wake up in the morning to a view of the mountains. The little bell tower would become a cosy upstairs sitting room. And the bathroom and closets would go across the end.

We could put a smaller bedroom underneath the loft. We'd build a downstairs bathroom and a utility room there, too.

And a darkroom.

Sam said he would get a contractor on the job the next week.

"If he can get the plumbing and the outside painting done before bad weather really sets in," he said, "the rest will be inside work. Johnny Garcia and I can do a lot of it."

"I can paint! I can run a sander!" I hugged Sam again.

"Sure you can," he said. "But that's not what I want you to do."

I kissed him. "Just what do you have in mind?" I kissed him again.

"Well," he said in a moment, "you can keep this kind of stuff up as a hobby. But I really want to see you in that darkroom." He gave me a pat. "Full time. You've been laying off, fooling around with the Sheriff's Reserve and the Maids and Matrons, and spoiling me, long enough. We'll get a point-and-shoot camera for the sheriff's department. Sonny and the other deputies can operate it for ordinary cases. As soon as we get that darkroom set up, you get back to your real work."

I ducked my head into his chest and swallowed hard for a few minutes. Then I looked up. "Do you think Big Sam would like some black-and-whites of the Titus Ranch? As a Christmas present?"

"He'd be tickled to death." He kissed my forehead, then both my eyes. "I love you, Nicky," he said. "And now we're about to be late to church."

This time the Holton Community Church's parking lot was packed. Apparently every member had come, hoping to hear the latest gossip.

And the very latest was that Leona Kephart had been on the phone that morning with the superintendent of schools, trying to get George Bullock fired.

It seemed George had punched her in the jaw the night before. When she called an old Dallas friend for sympathy, she found out his ex-wife at one time had put him under a peace bond, telling Texas authorities he'd beaten her.

Bullock had lost his Holton patron.

Sam didn't act surprised, and I recalled his phone conversation with the Dallas police, a call that had given him the leverage to make Bullock "spill his guts."

Tink gave a forceful sermon, but I had trouble concentrating on it. I was trying to make sense of all the events of the past two days.

Three people dead and another injured. The community, school, and church split by gossip and rumor and bad feelings. Had it all happened merely because people wanted to be things they weren't?

Katherine had wanted to be the perfect minister's wife and had hidden her true identity as a romance writer.

George Bullock had wanted to be Holton's high school principal, and instead of competing for the job on merit, had poked, pried, and started rumors trying to discredit Ramsey Kelleher.

Virginia had wanted Ramsey, but had pretended to be a loyal wife to Corey.

Lucretia Engelman had wanted to live her own

dreams through her granddaughter and had lied to Starr to attain that goal.

And Starr had wanted the dream her grandmother planted and had killed her two closest relatives when they threatened that vision.

I shivered, and Sam took my hand.

Had I been lying, too? Had I been telling myself I was being a loyal wife to Sam by involving myself in the Maids and Matrons and the Sheriff's Reserve—when I had really been selling out my own dream? Had it been easier for me to do that than to risk failure as I tried to photograph new subjects, to move on to new ideas? Had the lack of a darkroom merely been an excuse for me to stop taking pictures?

Tink was summing up. "On Thursday I was upset by a rumor of devil worship in Holton. That tale of Satanic rituals and rites, we now discover, was untrue. But the devil worship rumor was true! The devil was worshiped in Holton this week!

"He was worshiped not with eerie ritual, but with malice, innuendo, uncharitable acts, and actual violence. Each of us took part in this worship. Each of us must atone for our actions."

The crowd was subdued at the after-church coffee hour, but a group of the Maids and Matrons did gather around Virginia.

"We'll have to have a meeting," she said, "but I'm going to suggest that we go on with the Haunted House. We'll eliminate the basement room completely. We'll just use the first and second floors. Nicky, maybe you and Katherine could work on the Spider Woman's Web and the refreshment stand, since you'll be losing your own room."

"Sure, Virginia."

She smiled. "If you can get the hang of the refreshment stand, maybe you could be chairman for it at the county basketball tournament. That's in January. It's the Maids and Matrons' other big fund-raiser."

I shook my head. "Sorry. I'd better not take it on. I'm going to be working full time by then."

9 781451 613209